So you think you know fairy tales? Guess again.

Candy Houses

Greta didn't get her happy ending her first time around. And now that she's a Grimm—special kind of guardian angel and official ass-kicker in the paranormal world—romance is hard to find. Besides, there's only ever been one man who made her heart race, and the fact that he did scared her right out of his arms. Now Rip is back. And just in time too, because Greta needs his help.

On a mission he knows is going to test all of his strengths and skills, the last person Rip expected to see is the one woman who broke his heart. Working together seems to be their only hope. But, when faced with a danger neither of them anticipated, the question is, how will they face the danger to their hearts—assuming they survive, of course.

Warning: Dark, sexy, a little bit scary—this fairy tale is only for grownups and is best saved for bedtime.

Her Happy-Ever-After has been a long time coming...

No Prince Charming

Elle spent years trying to get over her so-called Prince Charming, and she's finally getting the hang of it. A Grimm—a guardian angel with unique gifts—she spends her nights trolling for demons and kicking ass, and lately, her days have been spent with her on-and-off-again lover, Ren, a fellow Grimm. But fate has other plans in store for Elle, plans that include Michael, the prince from her youth who broke her heart.

"What do you choose...live for her? Or would you rather die?" That was the choice Michael was given all those years ago. Although he knew she'd never forgive him, when Michael was given the chance to become a Grimm, he took it. Still, he isn't so sure Elle needs him in her life. With a lover at her side and a mission before her, Elle looks like she's doing just fine without him.

But the not-so-charming prince isn't going to back off that easily...not if there's a chance she might need him again. He'd do anything to save her. Kill for her, live for her, die for her...

Warning: This dark, twisted version of Cinderella involves demons, deceit, desire, and debauchery between a princess and two sexy guardian angels, both determined to win the fair Cinderella.

Look for these titles by
Shiloh Walker

Now Available:

The First Book of

Grimm

Shiloh Walker

A SAMHAIN PUBLISHING, LTD. publication.

Samhain Publishing, Ltd.
577 Mulberry Street, Suite 1520
Macon, GA 31201
www.samhainpublishing.com

The First Book of Grimm
Print ISBN: 978-1-60504-915-1
Candy Houses Copyright © 2010 by Shiloh Walker
No Prince Charming Copyright © 2010 by Shiloh Walker

Editing by Heidi Moore
Cover by Kanaxa

Candy Houses, ISBN 978-1-60504-801-7
First Samhain Publishing, Ltd. electronic publication: October 2009
No Prince Charming, ISBN 978-1-60504-886-4
First Samhain Publishing, Ltd. electronic publication: January 2010
First Samhain Publishing, Ltd. print publication: October 2010

Contents

Candy Houses

Dedication

For my editor, Heidi, who liked how I bastardized fairy tales...and for letting me keep my weird title.

And for my family. Always for my family. I thank God for you. Every day.

A Time for All Things

"Is this a trick?"

His question went unanswered. Frustrated, he pinched the bridge of his nose and wished for the millionth time that being immortal meant he didn't suffer such mortal maladies as *headaches*.

"May I beg to know why?"

This time he was answered. Not in words. The knowledge was just *there*.

It was time.

There was a time for everything under heaven and this was *their* time.

"I can handle the problem. I do not need to send Rip out." But even as he made the offer, the response echoed through him.

This is how it was meant to be.

"I don't entirely understand why it has to be so complicated. Why not just... Fine. Fine. Let's make it complicated."

Everything was complicated, really. And at the same time, it was abysmally simple.

In moments, he was alone in his thoughts—or as alone as he could ever expect to be. Reaching up, he closed his hand around the medallion that hung on a silver chain around his neck.

Chapter One

You may have heard of me. My name is Greta. It's short for Gretel.

As in...*Hansel and Gretel.*

Yes, as in Hansel, Gretel, breadcrumbs, wicked witches, gingerbread houses with sugar candy for the windows...except there weren't any breadcrumbs.

I never did get what you'd call a happy ending and the house wasn't made out of gingerbread, either. The wicked witch who lived in the house wasn't really all that wicked. Wasn't really even a witch, for that matter. She was unusual, definitely, but not a witch.

Hans was real, though. And if you want to talk *wicked*, we could talk about him. I was seven when he first started molesting me. They didn't call it *molesting*, though. Not then. And *he* wasn't the one doing anything wrong.

I was.

I was making up stories. I had a devil inside me. I was trying to cause trouble.

My stepmother came up with all sorts of reasons why *I* was the bad one. Me, when it was her son doing that to me. It didn't start until after my father died. Hans knew better. My father would have believed me, and he would have killed the sorry little shit.

I'm getting off topic, though. That story is already done, already over with. It was another life ago, and I mean that literally. That life ended when I was twenty—it ended the night I died.

The night I made my choice.

I don't want to go into detail about that night, though. It

was painful. I don't remember much of anything beyond the pain. But in order to receive the power of the Grimm, a human has to die. For a few minutes, at least. When we wake up it's like we'd gone to sleep and, while we slept, somebody played around with our bodies—we're stronger, we're faster, we're nearly indestructible...and we see demons. It's not anything you can be prepared for. Trust me, I know. Mary had warned me when she told me what she was...what *I* could be. She prepared me as best as she could, but some things you just have to experience.

So are you confused yet? I guess I could explain.

Like a lot of fairy tales, this one happened a long time ago...

A poor woodcutter lived with his wife and his daughter on the edge of a large forest...

The girl was called Gretel. The woodcutter did not have much food around the house, and they were poor.

But they were happy.

Then his wife fell ill and, as she lay on deathbed, she asked a favor of her beloved husband. "Do not mourn me for long. Find yourself a new wife, a woman who will love you and my daughter. Be happy."

After the loss of his beloved wife, the woodcutter fought the despair that threatened to overwhelm him. He couldn't lie down beside his wife and quietly grieve himself to death, no matter how much he wished, for his precious daughter Gretel needed him.

The summer after his wife's passing, he met a woman with a son just a few years older than his Gretel. The lady was lovely with a winsome smile, long blonde hair and laughing blue eyes. Her son, Hans, shared her smile, her blonde hair and her laughing blue eyes. Thinking it would do both him and his daughter good to have laughter in the house again, he courted her.

Their wedding was a quiet, simple affair. After all, they were poor.

For a time, he was happy. For a time.

But then he realized sweet Gretel wasn't as happy as he would have hoped. She remained somber eyed and unsmiling, and when he returned home each night from a hard day's work in the forest, she clung to him as though something had filled her with fear. She slept poorly and only when he remained at her side until she drifted away.

She was unhappy. He loved his precious Gretel. How could he possibly hope for happiness when she was so miserable? He had made her mother a promise—he'd see to Gretel's happiness. It was a promise he meant to keep, but he couldn't do so until he knew what had saddened her so.

Tragedy fell before he ever learned what grieved her so. One day while he was out chopping wood, there was a horrific accident.

Now Gretel was left to the not-so-kind mercies of her stepmother and her stepbrother. While her father had lived, Hans had been content with petty cruelties and her new stepmother had sat by and watched. But no true harm had been brought upon her.

After her father's death her sad life turned into a nightmare. Two nights after her father was buried, she awoke to find Hans standing by her little bed under the stairs. She cried and pleaded, but her cries and pleas went unanswered.

A great famine fell across the land.

By day, Gretel worked like a servant girl, hired out by her stepmother for pennies. If not for the kindness of some of those strangers, Gretel might have starved, for although Hans and her stepmother always had a bit to eat, there was nothing to be found for her.

By night, she cringed and cowered in her bed, fearing the times when Hans would creep into her room.

Every night she prayed.

Every morning she prayed.

"Dear Father in Heaven, I pray you would send one of your angels to save me."

"Dear Father in Heaven, I pray you would send one of your angels to feed me."

"Dear Father in Heaven, I pray you would send one of your angels to make Hans stop hurting me."

It seemed that her prayers would go unanswered. Then came the day when her stepmother told her that she wouldn't be going into town to clean homes, scrub floors or fetch water. Instead, she was to go deeper into the woods. An old woman who lived in the deep woods had need of her and had offered to pay handsomely.

Hans would escort her.

"But when will I return, stepmother?" She was unhappy in the home, but it had been her father's home. It had been the only home she'd ever known.

"I pray you do not return, Gretel. Ungrateful, lying wretch of a child. Now leave me."

With tears in her eyes, Gretel left, following along after Hans. For a time, she dared not take her eyes from him, terrified he would touch her again. But he did not. They walked all through the morning and then stopped so Hans could eat. His mother had sent along with him a small lunch, bread and meat and an apple. There was nothing for Gretel and Hans did not share, but Gretel was used to being hungry and she sat quietly while he ate.

After he finished eating, they once more started to walk. Gretel's small legs ached and her feet were sore and raw by the time they reached a small clearing in the woods. In that clearing sat a lovely house with windows that glittered under the sunshine that filtered through the leaves overhead. There was a small barn with chickens and a gurgling creek ran through the yard. Gretel's throat was painfully dry, but she did not dare pause for a drink. Still, she walked too slowly and Hans reached out, grabbing her arm and hauling her along with him as he headed for the door.

It opened before they reached it and in the doorway there stood a woman with kind eyes and a kind smile on her face. "Hello, Gretel."

She said nothing to Hans.

Gretel blinked and stared at the lovely lady. She wasn't old, not at all. Her black hair had not even a strand of white and her face was smooth and unlined.

"My stepmother told me that I was to go work for an old woman," she said without thinking. "You are not old."

"Appearances are deceiving," the lady replied. Stepping aside, she gestured to them. "Come inside."

Inside the house was the wonderful aroma of cooking meat, stewed vegetables and warm bread. Gretel's empty stomach rumbled and the lady sighed as she passed by. Stroking a hand down Gretel's hair, she asked, "Child, how long has it been since you had a good meal?"

Hans spoke up before Gretel could reply. "Just this past lunchtime. Mother packed both of us a wonderful lunch."

The lady turned her head and studied Hans. It was the first time she had looked upon him, and as she did so, she frowned. "You are a dishonest boy, Hans. Dishonest and cruel. You ate at lunchtime while your stepsister sat and watched. You shared nothing with her. "

Hans went pale, then red. "That is an ugly lie."

"If anybody should understand ugliness and lies, it would be you, would it not?" She held out a hand for Gretel and said, "Come, young one. Let's get you cleaned up and fed."

But Hans did not let go of Gretel's arm. "You're to give me the money first. You told my mother you would pay for Gretel."

"Indeed." She slipped a hand inside her skirt and drew out her hand, offering Hans the silver coins she held. "There is your money. Take it."

He grabbed it and stuffed it in his pocket. With a sly smile, he continued to hold tight to Gretel's arm. "It is a long walk back home and I'm terribly hungry myself."

The lady lifted a black brow and then gestured to a basket on the table. "You will find yourself a meal inside there. Take it and go. Do not return here, Hans. Never again."

Hans left, leaving Gretel alone with the strange lady. With fear knotting her belly and her body weak from hunger, Gretel followed along behind her new mistress. They entered the kitchen and Gretel asked, "Should I get to work now...?"

What did she call this lady? Gretel did not know.

"My name is Mary. You may call me Mary and I will call you Gretel. And no, you shouldn't get to work." She swept her skirts aside and settled on the bench by the table. "Let me see your hands."

"My hands?"

Mary nodded. "Yes, Gretel. Your hands."

Gretel held out her hands, cracked and thin. They were rough from hours spent cleaning and chapped from hours spent washing dishes and doing laundry.

"Oh, dear one. You've the hands of a scullery maid."

"I am not afraid of hard work," Gretel mumbled, looking away. She felt ashamed, standing there in her threadbare dress, with her thin legs and calloused hands.

Mary wore a fine gown, finer than any Gretel had ever seen. It was a lovely shade of blue. Her long black hair was worn swept away from her face and her cheeks glowed with health. Her hands were soft. There was a chain around her neck and from it there was something shiny, round and silver as the coins she'd given to Hans.

"I'm pleased to hear it, Gretel. You will work hard here. But there is a difference between hard work and slaving away." Then she squeezed Gretel's hands gently and said, "That is something we may discuss later. For now, let's get you fed and cleaned up."

For the first time since her father died, Gretel sat a table and ate her fill.

For the first time since her father died, Gretel went to bed and didn't fear the dark.

For the first time since her father died, Gretel didn't weep herself to sleep.

Yeah, yeah, I know.

It's not exactly the version you're familiar with.

But what's more believable? That Gretel was an unhappy, orphaned girl, or that Hansel and Gretel skipped merrily through the woods, leaving a trail of breadcrumbs as they walked in hopes that it would lead them back home?

Come on. Even back then children weren't idiots. Throwing bread on the ground usually results in something trying to *eat* the bread.

Hans might have been stupid enough to try a trick like that, but I certainly wasn't. Besides, if my parents had been deliberately trying to get rid of me, there's no way I would have kept trying to find my way back.

The Brothers Grimm never asked me, though. It was the popular version that got recorded for the ages, not the real one.

The real one involved things even uglier than a woman sending her children off to starve in the woods. I guess the real one had a happy enough ending, though, now that I think about it. Hans died, my stepmother left me alone, and I didn't have to live my life in fear.

Yes, Hans died. That's probably what led to the story ending up in a Grimm fairy tale.

It wasn't long after his death that my stepmother went a teensy bit crazy. Okay. A *lot* crazy. People would hear her rambling, like the madwoman she was. Back then, people didn't really *get* insanity, if you know what I mean. They thought she was possessed, or that she was a witch, communing with the devil and demons and that was what led to her ruin.

Maybe that's where the idea of a witch came from. It certainly didn't have anything to do with Mary.

Mary had been...different.

She saved me. When she took me in, bought my "services" from my stepmother for a few pieces of silver, she saved my life.

But it came with a price. Nothing is free in this world. Not now. Not then.

Not ever, I'd guess.

So you want to know the price? Well, think of Buffy. Yes, as in *Buffy the Vampire Slayer*. Think of her, more or less. I say more or less because I'm both *more* and *less*. Less because I don't come with the super strength. I'm a little stronger than the typical person, but I can't send a man flying through the air when I punch him.

That's okay, because I *can* knock a man to the ground and that's perfectly sufficient. I also don't come with visions or prophecies. Much to my disgust, there's probably no Angel or Spike in my future, either. I'm not petite. I'm not blonde. I'm not beautiful.

I'm just me.

So definitely *less* on some front.

But more on others...because...well, there's *more*. Nobody looking at me would ever realize just how much lies below the surface. They'd never believe the things I've seen, the things I've done. The lives I've taken. The lives I've saved.

I don't have super strength, but—well... I guess you could say, I'm hard to kill. And man, oh man, have people tried.

Old age won't kill me, because I don't age.

Injuries won't do it, because my body has been blessed

with the ability to heal from even the most mortal of wounds, a bit like the vamps from Buffy in that aspect. If you cut out my heart or take off my head, I'll die. Maybe drop me inside a vat of acid, but that sounds really painful.

Kind of gross too. Actually, it all sounds kind of gross. It's even worse in reality. I've had to cut out hearts, and I've had to take heads. Never had to resort to acid...

Sorry. My thoughts to tend wander and often they get really morbid when I'm bored. And right now, I'm really, really bored.

I've been bored ever since I stepped foot inside Ann Arbor, Michigan, a week ago. This is a college town and it's Friday night. There should be *something* going on.

Plenty of parties. I can feel them, the rush of energy, the laughter, the jealousy and anger.

But nothing I can act on.

Nobody who needs me.

It really sucks, because my entire life is centered on being needed.

Chapter Two

You must be joking.

Rip stood across the street in the shadows, watching as the brunette made her way down the sidewalk, staring into the bars and restaurants, like she was searching for somebody.

She was.

That what their kind did. They searched for those who needed them. That's why the Circle existed, after all. Under normal circumstances, he wouldn't mind seeing pretty little Greta. Under normal circumstances, he wouldn't mind teasing her and seeing if he could get those blue eyes to blaze fire at him. Under normal circumstances, he wouldn't mind trying to figure out how to convince her to get naked with him again.

It was a task he'd been working for close to a hundred years, ever since that first—and last—time.

She ignored him, though. All too easily. If he didn't know women as well as he did, he might have even believed that feigned disinterest. She was good at hiding it, but she wasn't as oblivious of him as she liked to pretend. On the odd occasion their paths crossed, he would see the heat in her eyes. Heat...hunger...and need. A need that just might match his own.

It was a hope that kept him going through many a night and yes, under normal circumstances he'd be more than happy to see her sauntering down a city street, taking in everything with those big blue eyes. More than happy to approach her and see what it would take to get those blue eyes to focus him.

But right now he wasn't functioning under normal circumstances.

He was on a hunt and he wasn't about to get distracted,

not even by the very distractible Greta. Even though he'd much rather be distracted by Greta.

As he stared at her, brooding, she stopped on the sidewalk and cocked her head to the side. Her eyes narrowed and he saw the change come over her, watched as she went from bored to predatory. Watched as she became aware. He saw the intent interest flare in her eyes and knew without a doubt she'd caught scent of something.

"Shit, don't let it be *my* something," he muttered, reaching back and grabbing the band that held his hair secured at his nape. He shoved a hand through his hair and then gathered it back into a queue. He wasn't sharing this quarry, not with anybody. Not even Greta. He couldn't.

Hell.

This was even worse than being distracted by Greta.

If she picked up on his hunt, she would want to get involved, and she'd do just that. She'd get involved, and in a very big way, simply by placing herself at his side. Definitely not what he wanted to see happen. She was a pit bull. Once she got a hold of something, she didn't let go.

Not ever.

Not until the job was done.

Of course, if he didn't keep his attention where it belonged, he was going to become a job, of sorts, himself, when his associates had to track down his killer. He felt the warning ripple down his spine and jerked aside just in time to evade the downward stroke a wicked-sharp Kel-Tech knife. It wasn't big enough to take his head off unless somebody was either very patient, very fast or very strong. The demon-possessed man in front of him looked to be very, very strong, even without aid of the demon that had settled inside his body. His body was no longer his own, though. It belonged to the demon. He was nothing more than a host—basically just a vehicle for the monster inside.

The demon was called a *paraisei*—sounds a lot like parasite and that's exactly what this kind of demon was. A parasite. It picked out a victim, set up housekeeping and whittled away at the victim's will until the human was no longer strong enough to fight. Once they reached that point, there was no saving the victim. They were trapped until the victim was either killed or the body gave out.

With the *paraisei*, it didn't take long for one of those endings to come about. They were vicious and a lot of them ended up going on murderous rampages, the kind that often ended up in death.

Since the demon didn't need food to live, those *paraisei*-infected humans who didn't meet a bloody, brutal end had the pleasure of dying of thirst and starvation.

Usually, the demon vacated its host right before death. The only way to kill one of the monsters was to kill the host before the demon left it. To Rip's eyes, the face was still human. Barely. It had probably only been a few days since the *paraisei* had taken complete control.

The typical person looking at the demon-possessed wouldn't see anything but the insanity lurking inside his eyes.

The demon wasn't insane.

It was actually very sane—functioning exactly as his kind did. Feeding on the misery of others, taking them over. It was too late for this one—the demon was in control and the only way Rip would set this poor bastard free was if he killed the *paraisei* inside.

"Aren't you due a nap, Grimm?"

Rip was startled. Not at the raspy, obviously inhuman voice that came from the man's throat, but by the words. The *paraisei* knew him. He pushed the surprise aside. It was something he'd worry about later.

He was curious, though. The *paraisei* *knew* him. Not many in the world did—within the Circle, among the demons, anywhere.

Curling his lips in a smile, he said, "Don't worry...dealing with you is going to leave me so bored, I may just sleep for a week. When I'm done."

Keeping the knife in sight, he circled around, moving away from the mouth of the alley. He wanted this done as quietly as possible, and preferably without drawing anybody's attention.

Namely, Greta's. If she knew there was prey to be found in Ann Arbor, she wouldn't be leaving any time soon and he'd work a lot better if he didn't have to worry about her pretty little neck.

He gave the *paraisei* a taunting grin. "That's a nice looking blade. Hope you don't mind if I decide to use it for a while."

It chuckled. "Do you truly think you can take it from this

body so easy?"

"Yes." Rip launched himself forward, tucking his body and rolling. He came up in a crouch and immediately spun on one foot, catching the host just above the knee. The sickening crunch of bone seemed horrifically loud.

The victim could still feel pain—the demon couldn't and the demon's will was stronger. Although Rip could see the man's face contorting with pain, the only sound was a furious growl.

Coming to his feet, Rip kicked again, this time aiming for the face. The *paraisei* snarled and tried to get his host to scramble away, but the leg with the busted knee couldn't support any weight. *Stupid things—they never do get the idea just because they don't feel pain doesn't mean they can't be injured.*

That mistake would prove costly. Rip evaded the hand clawing for his ankle. The thing was trying to slice and dice with the knife, and crawl away at the same time.

Rip caught the host's wrist and at the same time, took out the elbow in much the same fashion he'd used to take out the knee.

After that, getting the knife away was child's play. Rip flipped the host over onto his belly and caught the one good hand, shoving it high between the shoulder blades. "Let's chat, then *you* get to take the nap. Although you won't be waking up anytime soon. Not in twenty minutes. Not in twenty years..."

"Go fuck yourself, Grimm."

I heard something off to my left. A struggle. The skin along the back of my neck tingled. There was a faint scent in the air, one I recognized. My heart skipped a few beats. I didn't go investigate, though. As much as I wanted to, there was something else out there.

Pulling at me.

Drawing me.

I felt like a fish with a hook in my mouth, dragging me along.

Normally, I'll admit, I'd have followed the sounds of the struggle first. I'm so insanely nosy. I can't recall if there's a fairy tale out there about how curiosity killed the cat, but if there isn't, I could probably be the basis for *that* one too.

But there was something...something else.

In all my years—and whoa, we're talking a lot of years—I couldn't recall feeling something tugging at me like *this*. Ahead of me, there were a group of noisy college kids laughing and talking a mile a minute. Their voices were an annoyance just then, intruding and interfering with whatever it was I needed to be doing.

I cut through an alley—a good plan. I managed to avoid the college crew and get a little closer too.

Closer to what, though? I just didn't know.

A few miles later, I found myself in a rundown, mostly abandoned park on the outskirts of town. There was a shelter off to my right, covered with graffiti. To my left, I saw a fire...and I found myself staring at a girl.

Well, I guess she wasn't really a girl. She was probably about the same age I had been when I made my choice. She looked older, though—hard lines carved into her face, an unsmiling set to her mouth. But oddly enough, her eyes had a strange vulnerability.

That vulnerability was going to get her killed. Or worse, considering the things I saw hovering around her.

None of the demons had managed to manifest into physical form, a fact that was both good and bad. Once they took physical form, they were easier for me to fight. But as luck would have it, most demons took on physical form by taking over the body of a human and sometimes the only way to kill the demon was to kill the human too.

Demon possession is a sad fact of my life. I liked to get involved before things progressed this far—if I'd met the girl earlier, as in days, weeks or months ago, maybe this could have been prevented.

Right now, I was going to have my hands full keeping her from giving in. She had two very hungry *orin* hanging around her. The *orin* are the closest thing to vampires in existence. They literally feed on souls. They settle inside a person's subconscious and slowly, oh so slowly drain the life away. If the *orin* isn't evicted it can lay claim to the body once the victim's soul is truly gone. What separates them from the rest of the demons is the fact that once the host is truly gone, the body becomes demon property and as long as they continue to feed, the *orin* will continue to live, to grow stronger.

Most demons have to vacate the premises once their victim's soul dies.

I could hear the whisper of their voices inside my skull, bouncing and echoing around. I pushed them aside and focused on the girl. She'd built a fire inside a metal drum and she was staring into the flames like they held the answers to the universe.

In one hand, she held a knife.

In the other hand, she had a book. There wasn't a lot of light to see by, but I didn't need that much light. Another one of those neat little things that happened to me all those years ago—I've got eagle eyes.

My blood turned to ice as I stared at the symbol on the cover of the book.

It wasn't the kind of book you could buy at the local Borders or Barnes and Noble. Not even on Amazon or eBay. It had no title and was basically an omnibus of evil. I'd destroyed quite a few just like it in my time and I could have happily lived out the rest of my years, however many that may be, without seeing another one.

Of course, I wouldn't *be* that lucky.

It was a demon tome. The bitch of a book was handmade, and probably almost half as old as I was. Well used and crafted by somebody that had known their stuff.

Stupid, stupid girl, I thought, glaring at her.

It pretended to be a book of witchcraft, a book of spells. It didn't precisely lie either. It promised a chance at a long, youthful life, of great physical strength, beauty.

Those things could be had, and by almost anybody who wanted them. No mystical powers required, no months and months of training. All it required was a willing body and you could have youth, strength and beauty.

It didn't explain the flipside.

It didn't explain the price.

The price was taking a demon into your soul. Say the invocation to call an *orin* and you could live to a ripe old age and spend all your years looking like you were in the prime of your life. It didn't explain that you'd slowly fade away and then the *orin* would suck the soul out of all of those around you.

There were invocations for all sorts of demons—*orin, paraisei, glamori, vankyr, succubae, incubi.* Some were lesser known than others. Some were harder to kill than others. But they were all bad news.

The girl stared at the book like she was trying to memorize it—it was written in bastardized ancient Latin, so the chances of her understanding the words were slim to none. She was butchering some of the words as she sounded them out. Not in order, thank God.

It didn't matter if her pronunciation was off. If she started to chant, if she read the words out loud and in some semblance of order, the process started—a demon slipped in and if it wasn't one that I could extricate without killing her, she had to die.

"Wow."

She jerked her head up, staring at me like I was the one about to turn my body and soul over to some faceless evil.

I gave her my idea of a charming smile and nodded to the book. "That's a wicked looking book. Where did you find it?" It wasn't just a stalling tactic. I wouldn't mind knowing the answer to that. Those damn demon tomes were all over the place—every time I destroyed one, I hoped it would be the last. It never was. I'd destroyed several hundred in my lifetime and I'd probably destroy several hundred more before I gave up.

She wasn't interested in being distracted. Her eyes were a weird shade of purple and the eyeliner she had on nearly matched the shade of her irises. It also matched the purple streaks she'd added to her thick black curls. "Go away," she said.

"Sorry. Didn't mean to interrupt."

She looked back at the book and as her eyes fell away from me, I reached inside my shirt and tugged out the medallion I wore around my neck. I was hoping the demons would see it and maybe decide she wasn't worth the trouble.

On first glance, it was a plain silver disc. On second glance, one might see what looked like wings etched into the surface, sweeping out from the center of the disc. For a human, it would take a much closer glance, and a magnifying glass, to see the letters carved into the disc.

But demons had killer eyesight.

I'd kind of been relying on that.

They noticed, all right.

Their voices rose—high-pitched chitters that echoed inside my head. But nobody else could hear them. At least not right now.

The girl couldn't hear them. Until she called one of the demons, she wouldn't be able to see the things hovering in the air around her. Not until it was too late. Not until they were inside her.

One of the *orin* focused on me. I smiled at it and said, "Go away."

The girl jerked her eyes up and snapped, "Excuse me—I was here before you were."

"Wasn't talking to you." I kept my eyes on the *orin*.

Off to my left, I could see the other *orin*, its aura darkening to near-black, shadows hovering in the shadows. They didn't disappear.

Too bad. But I hadn't expected anything else. *Orin* weren't easily dissuaded once they had a victim picked out.

They ignored me and focused on the girl. They hung in the air, one on either side of the girl. Their voices grew louder and I knew they were projecting themselves into the girl's mind too.

Say it...read the spell.

You'll have power. You'll have acceptance. You'll have the life you want to have...instead of the one that's been given you.

"Now that's called false advertising, my friends." I rolled my eyes and laughed.

The girl jerked back. She shot a wide-eyed look over her shoulder and then looked back at me. "Who are you talking to?" she demanded.

"Not you." I advanced, and to my satisfaction she was suitably freaked out and scurried backward, using her hands and heels...and leaving the demon tome. I stooped down and grabbed it.

The *orin* wailed. They pushed their commands on her, hard and fast. *Get the book...you must get it or she will claim your power.*

"Oh, puh-leeze." I tossed the book into the fire and had the pleasure of listening to them screech. I also had the pleasure of smelling the book burn, listening to the pages crackle as the flames gobbled it down. It might have words of nasty power scrawled all over it, but it was just a book.

The girl didn't mess with screeching—she lunged for me. She had a good six inches on me, but probably only about thirty pounds heavier. I come from good solid, German stock—the short and stocky variety. She was strong, though. Strong and very pissed off.

I caught her under the chin with the heel of my hand, watched as her head went flying back. She didn't let go, though, so my next target was her throat. A quick jab there and she was too busy choking for air to worry about me as I rolled her off. I reached behind me to touch the knife I had tucked into the back of my jeans. It wouldn't hurt the demons now, but it made me feel better. I'm all for security blankets.

"She can't call you now. The book's gone and somehow I don't think she gets your particular brand of ancient Latin," I said, facing the two *orin*.

They still hovered. They watched me, body-shaped shadows, with a faint red glow that passed for their eyes. One of them drifted forward, hovering closer to the girl. *She doesn't have to read the words. She just has to say them. And we can tell her the words...*

Good point. She was trying to get to her feet. I grabbed her from behind, applying pressure. Contrary to what it seems like on TV, putting somebody under with a sleeper hold is not all that quick. As she sagged in my arms, I muttered, "Sorry." After I eased her to the ground, I smiled at them again. "She can't say the words if she's unconscious."

How long do you think you can keep her unconscious? For the rest of her life? We have the time. You have the time. But does she? Can you truly watch her until she dies? We've already been inside *her. She's already tasted our power.*

It was pissed. I could feel it. I was getting pissed, though. Inside her—shit. Shit. Shit. This was bad and getting worse. They'd been inside—that meant one of them had been close to taking her over. Close. Not the same thing as complete control, but it did give them power over her. That taste of power—most likely, they'd shared just enough of their experiences of draining a soul. It was entirely possible that all she felt was the rush of power, without realizing what it was.

"I don't really have anything else going on right now," I told the *orin.* "I can always use company."

I didn't turn my head to look at her, but I was tempted.

If she had known, if she had any idea the misery and pain she could unleash by using that book, would she have still done it? Illogical as all get-out, if you ask me, but people do crazy things for youth, strength, power and beauty. Plenty regret it later on, but when it came to demons, regrets didn't do much good. You were already gone, past hope by the time you realized the danger.

We want the girl, they told me, their voices as one, a low, vicious snarl inside my head that made my skull ache. *We will have the girl. But we can wait.*

They started to fade, returning to the netherplains where the demons resided.

Enjoy your...company. The last word was followed by a laugh that sent shivers down my spine. They disappeared, and immediately the air became easier to breathe and the ice in my blood thawed ever so slightly.

I blew out a breath and crouched down by the girl.

She was breathing. I could hear both her heartbeat and the soft, steady sounds as the air passed in and out of her lungs. She might have had her eyes closed, but she looked every bit as hard now as she had a few minutes ago when she'd been about ready to rip into me for interfering.

A hard life.

She'd led a hard life. I could see it in the stiff, rigid way she held herself, even in unconsciousness. I needed to touch her, but I was reluctant to do so. This could really only go one of two ways—either she wasn't too far gone to save, or she was. If she was too far gone, I had to kill her.

Even after all this time, it leaves a bad taste in my mouth. Even after all this time, it leaves me sick for weeks after.

But my role in this was clear—it had been almost from the first. I am the way I am because I'm meant to help people. That means protecting them, from themselves, from demon predators and from the monsters that walk around in human skin.

My hand shook as I reached out to touch her, but before I could make contact, I heard something.

It hissed.

Something brushed against the back of my neck, a hot,

fetid breath of air. I didn't wait another second. Rolling to the side, I scrambled to my feet just in time to face what had to be the biggest damn *bocan* I'd ever seen—nearly twice my height and easily three times as wide.

Bocan—it's the Irish name for the bogeyman and oh, holy hell, if you've ever faced one you'd understand why people feared the dark for centuries on end.

"How in the hell did you get here?" I muttered.

But I already knew.

Somehow, the *orin* were responsible. Responsible or involved. It was the only thing that made sense. The *bocan* weren't strong enough to manifest in this world. They dwelled in the netherplains and they could only come from there to here if some being strong enough forced open a doorway.

I hadn't ever heard of any *orin* opening actual doorways, but they had known about this behemoth.

Enjoy your...company, they'd said.

They hadn't been talking about the girl.

They'd been talking about the *bocan*.

Chapter Three

In his two-hundred plus years on earth, Rip had done some hard things, some ugly things. Ugly...like walking around with blood coating his face and hands like war paint. It wasn't the first time he'd been this way, but it was as distasteful and depressing now as it had been the very first time.

He wanted a shower, desperately.

He left the dead human in the alley, slipping away and using the shadows to hide himself.

The *paraisei* had almost gotten away. At the last second, it had realized it wasn't going to win against Rip and it had tried to flee. Rip had seen the black tendrils emerging from the host's bodily orifices. He'd stopped it in time, in a very bloody fashion, and now he had a human's blood staining his hands.

It wasn't the first time.

It wouldn't be the last.

But he hated it all the same.

The entire night was shot. By the time he got cleaned up it would be too close to dawn and his particular prey preferred to sleep during the day.

Another night. Wasted.

Another day where he'd spend the hours thinking about what he had to do.

God, I wish somebody else could do this one.

A harsh wind picked up. Although it was mid-April, winter hadn't totally given up and the wind had a cold edge to it. Rip might have enjoyed it, might have let it carry away some of death's stink, except, over the blood and sweat and dirt, he scented something else.

Greta.

And—*shit.*

I was pretty sure I hadn't felt this kind of terror in a long time.

I'm not really afraid of dying. Or at least, normally, I'm not. Remember that hard to kill thing I mentioned?

I *am* hard to kill, but a *bocan* is strong enough to tear my head from my shoulders, and they are fast. That doesn't sound like a fun way to go.

They are killing machines. Big, dumb killing machines and I was facing this one totally unprepared. The knife I carried wasn't long enough to kill the thing unless I was really, really lucky. I'm good, but with these things, being good with a knife isn't enough.

A sword would be better.

A *cannon* would be better.

Warily, I backed away, circling around and trying to lead the *bocan* away from the girl. I didn't know if she'd be able to see it when she woke up. It depended on how far she'd dipped her toes into the waters of evil and death. I could hope that when she saw it, *if* she saw it, it might scare her straight, but I'm not really big on hope right now.

Not the way the night was going.

And to think I'd been bored just a few hours ago.

"So how long have you been hanging around this plane?" I asked.

The *bocan* didn't speak. Their race didn't have vocal chords. Other than the sibilant sounds they made when they breathed, they were quiet. They moved quietly, they attacked quietly and they killed quietly. Big, dumb, ugly...and quiet. They ought to be loud—only seemed fair. Something like this breathing death down your neck, there should be some sort of warning.

It cocked its head. The dim light danced over the dull gold scales that covered it from head to toe. Those scales were like armor. It had been a while since I'd faced a *bocan*...probably two or three hundred years, but I hadn't forgotten how big they are, how strong they are or how hard they are to kill. At least the last time I'd faced one I'd had a for-real sword.

It came at me, a silent rush of death. At the very last second, I spun out of the way and felt the blast of air as it swiped out at where I'd stood only a heartbeat earlier. The thing's hands ended in claws that measured close to three inches long.

The skin along the back of my neck prickled as I once more started to circle away from the *bocan*, weaving around it in nonsensical patterns. It made another rush and this time, instead of moving aside, I went down and sliced upward. Black, bitter blood covered me as I managed to break skin. It shuddered, but I figured out very quickly that while I'd hurt the demon, I hadn't slowed it down. It slashed out as I scrambled away. Those claws got closer that time.

And then again. This time it caught me. I bit my lip to keep from screaming as the claws managed to get me in the belly, slicing me open. Blood flowed.

Shit—

A hand came out of nowhere and grabbed me, hauling me aside.

Dazed, I fell against the crumbled rock wall at my back and watched. I was in a state of shock, I think. I didn't recognize the man at first...well, not consciously. My body probably would have, if I hadn't been losing huge quantities of blood through the gashes in my belly. I whimpered and shrugged out of the blood-soaked jacket I wore and balled it up, pressing it to my wounded stomach.

The flesh was already knitting back together. I could literally feel it, deep, deep inside. It was a bad injury. If I was still wholly human, I'd be dead already. As it was, I was losing a lot of blood. Even us pseudo-immortals get weak when we lose too much blood.

Sinking to the ground, I watched as the man fought the *bocan*.

He was a lot more equipped to handle the thing than I was, that was for sure. The *bocan* tried to gut him with those lethal claws but the man moved away, quick as a wish. I saw one hand disappear inside the long coat he wore—something about that coat, the way it stretched over his shoulders, tickled a memory. I wouldn't look at his face. Thinking about it now, I know why I wouldn't look, because I knew in my heart who he was, and I needed to prepare myself a little bit more before I actually *looked* at him.

Instead, I focused on his hands...and on the very awesome weapon he'd drawn from inside that long, black coat. It was a black cylinder, maybe two, two and a half feet long. Yeah, I know, that doesn't sound too flashy. It would do some serious damage to a human, probably even a number of manifested demons.

But a nine-foot-tall *bocan?*

Nope. Right up until he twisted it, I wasn't impressed. But then he twisted it. I heard the whisper of metal as two edged blades appeared, one out either end of the metal cylinder.

Now it was five feet long, and bladed on both ends.

He used it like an artist. He moved like a dancer of death. The silver flashed through the air. His body barely seemed to touch the ground before he was moving off again. Eerie, deadly and oh so lovely to look at. In a rather morbid way, of course.

Black blood stained the metal as he sliced through the *bocan*'s scales.

The *bocan* hissed.

The man just laughed. That laugh. I knew that laugh.

Rip...

Just before I passed out, I finally let myself look at him. I found myself staring at his familiar profile. An ache settled in my heart and it followed me as I went under.

Rip had problems.

He had all sorts of problems. He had one dead demon on his hands. He had one unconscious, young adult female on his hands. He had one unconscious, not-so-young adult female on his hands—and she was injured.

His body screamed at him as he crouched beside Greta. Along his left arm, he had a series of gashes, three of them, each one of them a good seven inches long and deep. Very deep, because they weren't healing fast. The *bocan* had managed to tear into his muscle, and the muscles had to knit together before the skin could. So he was still bleeding.

But not as bad as Greta.

She was pale, even paler than normal. That milky, fair complexion was ghostly and even though he knew she couldn't die from the injury she'd taken, his heart skipped a few beats and then took up residence in his throat. To reassure himself, he laid a hand on her neck, felt the warmth and the life of her.

It didn't help much.

He was going to relive the night's events a thousand times over in the years to come—the nightmare of seeing the *bocan* come this close to gutting her, and he had been too far away to do a damn thing.

What were you thinking?

She had faced down a *bocan* with pretty much her bare hands. She'd had a knife. A paltry blade in her right fist as she'd circled around the demon. *Bocans* were too fucking big, too fucking strong, and that hide of theirs was like armor. Knives just didn't cut it.

He shot the dead creature a nasty look and wondered where in the hell it had come from. *Bocans* were uncommon in the world because they didn't have the abilities a lot of other demons had—they couldn't manifest, couldn't possess. They just killed.

A *bocan*. The *paraisei* he'd faced earlier. Something weird was going on. Demonkind didn't ever gather together in one place for long—it attracted too much attention, the sort of attention that ended up them being sent back to the netherplains.

What in the hell was going on?

Greta shifted under his hands. Under her breath, she whimpered quietly and Rip, without even thinking about it, bent over her and pressed his lips to her brow. "Hush, angel. You're safe now...you're safe. Sleep...heal."

His heart broke a little as she burrowed close to him. Rip let her, even though he had to get to work—figure out what to do with the *bocan*. And the human—shit.

Not having much choice, he reached up and fished his medallion out from under his blood-stained, black T-shirt. Fisting it in his hand, he sent out a broadcast call. *I need help.*

He couldn't take care of Greta, the human and the *bocan*. Not without getting noticed. It would be morning soon, and a man carrying a couple of unconscious women around was going to catch some attention.

He was going to have his hands full just getting Greta someplace out of sight.

The disc warmed in his hand, then there was a flash, a circle of light. A man emerged from the light, staring at Rip impassively.

Rip didn't flinch under the steely weight of the man's gaze. "Morning is coming. I won't be able to hide under the cover of night much longer and I don't have time to deal with the *bocan*, the girl and Greta."

"You were not sent here to deal with the *bocan*, the girl or Gretel. Gretel can deal with the girl."

"*Greta* is hurt," Rip snapped. "And I don't walk away from those who need me—job or not."

"You've already wasted too much time on this job."

Rip bared his teeth in a mockery of a smile. "I'm sorry. If my performance has been less than satisfactory you could always fire me."

No, he couldn't.

Narrowing eyes that glowed like molten steel, the man shifted his gaze to the *bocan*. Another flash of light, but this was a dark flash. A circle formed in midair and on the other side of the portal, Rip could see into the netherplains. Dark, barren...a midnight desert that never saw the sun, that never saw any relief from the endless heat.

The man inclined his head. Rip swallowed back his growl. The bastard was perfectly capable of getting the *bocan* through the portal on his own, but Rip knew he'd already helped as much as he was willing.

"You're too kind," he muttered as he hauled the monstrous creature to the portal. Uneasy, he glanced at the huge doorway and then at the man who waited in silence. "You wouldn't close that thing on me, would you?"

No answer.

Grimacing, Rip muscled the *bocan* through the portal and then dashed back through. The second he cleared the portal, it collapsed—so close behind him, Rip heard a strange, sucking sound, kind of like the sound a wine bottle made when the cork was pulled out. But louder. A *lot* louder.

Something caught hold of his coat and he jerked away, only

to fall to his knees as the material came free easily. It was also missing quite a bit of material in the back. The buttery, soft black leather had scorch marks all along the end.

"You bastard," he snapped, glaring at the man.

"Help has been given. Waste no more time, Rip. This has gone on long enough."

"That's not my doing," he said through gritted teeth.

But the man was already gone, the circle of light closing down behind him in the span of heartbeat.

"Bastard," he muttered. Striding across the grass, he knelt once more by Greta.

Now if he could just figure out what to do about...

But even as he started to try and figure that one out, Greta stirred. Then her lashes lifted and he found himself staring into bottomless blue eyes.

"Rip?" she murmured, her voice husky.

"Shhh. Take it easy," he said as she started to sit up. "You've been hurt. You're going to be down a few more hours, probably."

Greta frowned. "I feel fine," she said. "Just kind of tired."

Rip shot a look at her belly. Through the ragged, bloody tears in her shirt, he could see her belly. Soft, white...and whole.

Well, hell. The bastard had helped a little more than Rip had thought.

Unable to stop himself, he reached out and touched her, stroked his fingers along her smooth, unscarred flesh. "He healed you."

"Who did?" she asked, her voice low and hoarse.

Rip just shook his head. "This helps. Now we can deal with your human..."

They turned to look at the unconscious woman.

But she was gone. Since the *bocan* was dealt with and there was nobody else around, they had to assume the girl had escaped.

"Shit." Greta sagged in his arms, a scowl tightening her face. "This is bad, bad, bad..."

"The *bocan* is dead," he said gently. "She's safe enough."

A ragged sigh shuddered out of her and she stared at him from under a heavy fringe of lashes. "She had a book, Rip. And I don't have any idea who gave it to her."

A book. He didn't need to know what sort of book. There was only one kind of book that would have Greta worried.

"She has one of the demon tomes," he muttered, furious. He closed his eyes and rubbed at the back of his neck. "Bloody hell. Bad doesn't quite cover it then, does it?"

Chapter Four

So that's how Rip ended up back in my life.

The demon tomes were a big deal and none of us liked it when they were being passed around like candy. I'd have to deal with this and I was desperately hoping Rip would be willing to help me out.

"You are certain?"

We walked down the sidewalk, keeping to the shadows. Me in my torn clothes, Rip in his bloodied ones—it wouldn't do to catch a whole lot of attention. Sliding a look at him from the corner of my eye, I said, "Hmmm. I don't know...let me think."

I pretended to do just that, tapping my lips with my finger. "There was a young woman—hardly more than a girl—trying to say some words that haven't been legitimately used in like...oh say, forever. She had a couple of *orin* hovering around her. Oh, and she also had a book that looked like one of *the* books. You know, the ones we don't really like? Yeah, I'm pretty sure it was one of the bad books and we really do need to address it."

Rip didn't appreciate my sarcasm.

Or maybe he did. He just didn't say anything about it.

"This is a problem," he muttered.

"Tell me about it." Although it wasn't likely, it was possible there were other books close by and if the girl got to one, she wasn't going to waste time on proper pronunciation. I had very little time to get to her and I had no clue where to look. "Hey...why are you here?"

"Working," he said tersely.

I rolled my eyes. "Wow. That's vague. That's pretty much what we do, isn't it? Any more detail than that?"

"Why?"

I jerked a shoulder in a shrug. Man, he couldn't be easy, now could he? Couldn't just up and offer to help me find her? *No.* I was going to have to ask. Sighing, I rotated my neck. I had a mammoth headache creeping up on me, I was feeling more than a little nauseated and I needed some sleep. And a shower. So bad did I need a shower. "I could use some help finding the girl, if you're free."

I shot a look at him from the corner of my eye.

He was watching me. The minute our gazes locked, he reached out and caught my arm. "Do you wish for my help?" he asked, drawing me to a stop.

I couldn't even go into detail about what I wished from him. There just wasn't enough time in the day. Or strength in my legs—they were wobbling and threatening to give out on me at any second. I licked my lips and strove for a casual tone as I replied, "Well, yeah. That's kind of what I said. Are you free?"

"Free?" he murmured. Then he stroked his fingers over the rips in my shirt, tracing the skin where the *bocan* had sliced me open.

I remembered that, a fiery pain, followed by numbness. The *real* pain hadn't started until a few seconds later, when my blood was pumping out of me. It had been bad. Really bad.

But the flesh was already healed and I had no idea how that had happened.

"I'm not certain I understand what *free* is," he said, staring at his hand as he touched my belly. "But yes...I'll help you."

"Thank you."

"You sound relieved." A smile tugged at his lips. The fingers grazing over my belly shifted course, traveling up, up, up until he could hook a hand over the back of my neck. My breath caught in my throat.

"Did you think I would say no to *you*?"

I swallowed. Ah...well, I hadn't ever thought about it.

And I couldn't exactly ponder it in this moment either, because he was looking at me in a way that made my heart race, in a way that stole the breath from my lungs, in a way that made me forget we had some potentially big problems.

He was close, so close I could feel the warmth of his breath on my face. So close I could feel *his* warmth...

Is he going to kiss me?

Damn it, he couldn't kiss me. I was covered in *bocan* blood. I felt so sick to my stomach I thought I might pass out again. My head hurt. My heart hurt.

Damn it, what if he *didn't* kiss me? I missed his kiss, although that didn't really make much sense. We'd spent a couple of weeks in each other's company—and one hot, wonderful night that I hadn't been able to forget. It had been years ago and I still couldn't forget.

I didn't need to be thinking about kissing. I needed to think about the girl. Had to think about the girl. Had to…

This is why you left after that night, girl. This is why you avoid him.

Rip has always left me in a mess, a nasty, tangle of a mess, totally incapable of any sort of coherent, rational thought. But I didn't affect him like that. Hell, *nothing* seemed to affect Rip. When I walked away from him, he had just stared at me with that blank, noncommittal expression on his face. I'd seen him kill demons with that same look on his face. I'd seen him hold the door for little old ladies with that same look on his face.

Nothing affected Rip.

Everything about Rip affected me.

He didn't kiss me. He just kneaded the tense muscles of my neck and murmured, "There is very little I wouldn't do, if you asked, very little I wouldn't give. Anything that is within my power is yours."

"Wow, Rip. You haven't changed much. You still know how to charm a girl, don't you?" I pulled back. I had to. It was either that or collapse into a mindless drooling puddle at his feet.

That smile tugged at his lips again and he asked, "Am I charming you?"

Man, I'm in so much trouble.

That was the last clear thought I had for a while. Between the blood loss, the adrenaline rush and Rip, my head was very, very fuzzy. Fortunately, Rip was in better shape. Somehow, he got us both to the house I was renting, and somehow, he got me into the shower—I'm not entirely sure how. I don't remember unlocking the door, much less taking a shower.

Hell, for all I know, he ended up getting into the shower with me. Even thinking about that makes me get all hot and tingly.

Somehow, I got through the shower, and then I was on the bed, trying to find the energy to deal with my hair. All I wanted to do was sleep. For a week.

"Let me help," Rip murmured.

"I can do it," I told him. My tongue felt thick, about three times its normal size. I didn't really see *how* I could do it, because when I reached for the comb, I almost poked myself in the eye.

"Sure you can." He nudged my hand back down into my lap and finished with my hair. Then he was tucking me under the covers like a child.

"You know, I'm a big girl. I've been putting myself to bed for a few hundred years now. I can take care of myself." I glared at him, or at least I tried to glare at him. I had a feeling it came off about as threatening as a pair of bunny slippers.

"I know you can." He grinned as he settled down on the edge of the bed.

"I can," I argued. My lids felt heavy—heavy as in elephant-heavy. "I'm just kind of tired."

"I know...go to sleep, Greta. You're safe." He cupped my cheek and stroked a thumb across my lower lip. "You're safe."

I never felt safe when I slept with somebody else close by. The remnants of a past I can barely remember, I guess. But I fell asleep...and I felt safe. I fell asleep thinking of him.

It wasn't a big surprise when I found myself dreaming about him.

I've spent quite a few nights dreaming about him, more than I like to admit. It's been years since that one night, years since I've seen him. And still, I keep thinking about him. As many people as I've met in my life, it's hard to believe there's still room in my head for this obsession.

In my dream, we were on the beach. Warm sun, soft sand and a hard man...sounds like bliss for a woman, doesn't it? As long as the hard man is Rip, it pretty much fits the bill for paradise, in my opinion.

He kissed me, kissed me soft and gentle, then harder, deeper, like he'd swallow me whole if he could, like he couldn't possibly get close enough. I returned the favor—it simply wasn't possible to get close enough to Rip, not even when he was moving inside me.

In reality, he may not be affected by me.

But in my dreams, he seems to need me as much as I need him. Miss me the way I miss him. In my dreams, I really do matter to him. I'm not just a willing woman...I *matter*.

"I miss you," he rasped against my mouth. He had his hand fisted in my hair, using it to hold me still as he took the kiss deeper.

"How can you miss me?" I smiled at him. Even in my dreams, I had to keep it light, had to. "I'm right here."

"Not really, you're not." He stroked a hand down my side, cupped my hip and circled against me. "I'll wake up alone...this is just a dream."

"Hmmm." I nipped his shoulder. "If it's just a dream, we should probably make the most of it, don't you think?"

Nudging at his shoulders, I pushed until he moved away and lay on his back. I rolled on top of him and took him inside, shuddering in pleasure. His hands gripped my hips and his eyes, those dark, sinfully sexy eyes, stared at me, rapt on my face.

Like nothing else existed for him...just me.

"Nothing else *does* exist for me," he muttered. "Not when you are near me."

Part of me wondered how he knew I was thinking that. The other part didn't care—the other part was too lost in the pleasure to comprehend thought. He lifted me up with his strong hands as though I weighed nothing. Slow...steady...

And not enough.

Reaching down, I wrapped my fingers around his wrists. "Faster," I said, staring down at him. "Harder."

Rip's lashes lowered. "I don't want to hurt you. I don't want to scare you."

"You wouldn't ever hurt me. You couldn't ever scare me."

As I said it, the dream shifted around me and we were no longer the beach, but in a bed. A big, soft bed that cradled me like a dream as Rip moved over me.

"Say my name," he whispered. "Let me hear it."

"Rip..."

"Tell me you've missed me," he ordered, kissing me hard and rough. His voice was just this side of desperate, something I wasn't prepared for, not with him. "Give me something, damn it."

But I couldn't ignore that plea—it was just an echo of my own need, anyway...right? That's all dreams were.

"I've missed you," I told him. Then his mouth came down on mine and he was kissing me like he could drown in me.

One second I was dreaming, lost in Rip's arms, lost in his kiss and hovering on the edge of climax, and the next second I was awake, brutally awake and all too aware of the fact that I was being watched. I jerked up in bed, clutching the sheets and blankets to my chest.

Rip was standing in the doorway with one shoulder propped against the door jam. He had a look in his eyes that sent my skin to tingling all over. I mean *all* over—I felt it in my lips, my toes and every square inch in between.

"Hey," I said. My voice cracked.

He continued to stare at me.

It was very, very unnerving the way he watched me.

"Ahh...is everything okay?"

He didn't answer. Nope, what he did was push off the door jamb and come over to the bed. He knelt down by the bed, resting one hand on top of the blankets. He had such damn nice hands...the hands of a poet, a warrior...a lover. One of those lovely hands was only an inch away from my thigh too. I thought I could even feel the heat of it, through the blankets.

"You were dreaming," Rip said, his voice low and rough.

Oh, shit. Swallowing, I dredged up an innocent smile. "Was I?"

"Yes." His eyes, that dark, melted-chocolate gaze, locked on mine and I felt frozen in place. Unable to move as he laid a hand on my cheek and stroked my lower lip with his thumb. "Do you remember it?"

Oh, man, did I remember. But I couldn't really tell him that, now could I? Self-preservation is a lovely thing, and I looked him dead in the eye and lied. "Nope."

Self-preservation is a lovely thing, yeah, but it doesn't make me a better liar.

He smiled, a wolf's smile. "You don't remember?" He leaned in and nuzzled my neck, his breath teasing across my flesh like a caress. "Maybe I could jog your memory."

The hand on my cheek stroked down, over my neck, across my collarbone, down, down. The tips of his fingers brushed against the curve my breast and I realized I'd dropped the blankets and was sitting there as naked as the day I was born.

"I'm good. No need to jog the memory."

"You whispered my name," he murmured, nipping my earlobe. "Then you moaned. You sounded exactly like you did the first time I made you come."

As he cupped my breast in his hand, I whimpered. Heat...oh, sweet, blissful heat, hurtled through me and I pressed against his touch. Needed more. Needed him.

"Do you remember now?"

He lifted his head and stared at me, eyes glittering.

Dazed, I whispered, "Remember what?"

"The dream." He slid his hand up and cradled the back of my head, his fingers tangling in my hair as he tugged. "Do you remember?"

I blushed. I could feel my face burning, my cheeks flaming hot. *He'd have to be here when I'm dreaming that kind of dream...* Then his mouth came down and against my lips, he whispered, "Yeah, you remember."

It's been years, but I still remember. I still remember what it did to me when he kissed me. When he kisses me, it's like...flying. Like dying. I can't even describe what it's like to be kissed by Rip. When he kisses me everything else falls away and there's nothing but me. Nothing but him. His mouth on mine, his hands on my body and my hands on his.

I tugged him closer, desperate to feel him against me, but he held back. Then he was pulling away from me. I fisted my hands in his hair and tried to hold him—closer, closer, needed him so much closer.

"Greta."

He caught my wrists and pulled. I let him, even as I arched my neck to try and kiss him again.

"Stop," he muttered.

"Stop?" I repeated. Stop—wait, he wanted to *stop*? He kisses me and now he doesn't want me kissing him? I narrowed my eyes and glared at him. "If you don't want me kissing you, then maybe you shouldn't kiss me...maybe you shouldn't be snooping around while I'm sleeping, or listening in when you shouldn't."

The hands on my wrists tightened. Something flashed

through his inscrutable eyes. "You think I don't want you to kiss me."

"Well, you just told me to stop." I glared at him and tugged half-heartedly against the hands on my wrists. Once more, I was blushing, that hot, nearly painful blush, but it was just as much frustration and disappointment as embarrassment. If he didn't want me kissing him, why had he kissed me?

"Greta."

I scowled at him and pulled against his hands again. Harder this time. "Let me go."

He dipped his head and nipped my lower lip. "No."

"You know, there's a name for people like you—I'm not entirely sure what it is, but there has got to be a name."

I glared at him and turned my head away so he couldn't brush his mouth against mine.

"Tease—yeah, that's the word. You're a damn tease. You kiss me, then tell me to stop kissing you. Then you kiss me again. It's not nice to tease people, Rip." Especially with something like this. Especially when I was already so hungry for him I ached.

"I'm not trying to tease you." He nibbled on my lower lip again and whispered, "I could kiss you forever. That...and more." He reiterated the *more* by letting go of one of my wrists and stroking me. From my neck, down along between my breasts, along my belly and down, resting the heel of his hand low on my belly with his fingertips resting just above the curls between my thighs.

So close...so close...

I whimpered as he rubbed his lips against mine. "Yeah, well, telling me to stop is great way to prove that."

"You don't want me kissing you forever, though." He straightened, pulling his hand away from my belly, letting go of the wrist he still held. "You walked away from me—didn't want the complication."

He stood by the bed and stared down at me.

For once, those inscrutable brown eyes weren't quite so inscrutable. I saw a flicker of something. He was acting edgy too. Restless even. That's kind of weird for him. He's very much not the restless sort of person.

He shoved his blond hair back from his face and then

pushed his hands into the pockets of his jeans. It drew the material of his shirt tight across his shoulders and if I wasn't so busy trying to puzzle him out, I might have taken a moment to admire the way his shoulders looked under the soft, faded black cotton.

"You left, because you didn't want a complication. That's what you called it...a complication. I wanted you more than I've ever wanted anything or anybody, but you didn't want the complication." A strange, tired smile curled his lips as he watched me. He sighed and shook his head. "Sex with me was just a complication."

I'd hurt him, I realized. It had been a hundred years since that night. One hundred years, and I thought about it a lot. But this was the first time I'd ever even considered that maybe I'd hurt him when I'd walked away...and I'm an idiot.

Because it was right there in front of me.

It was in his eyes as he looked at me—because he *did* look at me. When he was around others, he barely paid them any attention unless he had to. But he watched me. He always had.

It was in the way he watched me, the way he watched over me, the way he spoke to me...

Did you think I would say no to you? He'd said that to me, late last night...or early this morning, to be precise. *Say no to* you—

To me—like maybe I meant something to him. A little more than...well, I don't know. A little more than others. That was part of why I'd walked away from him. In the few weeks we'd spent working together before, he'd somehow come to mean something to me—something more—I couldn't really say what.

But I didn't want to be just...well, just anybody to him. Most of our kind end up drifting in and out of relationships, casual ones usually because most of us are too damaged for anything more involved.

I'm not casual. I can't do casual. Trying to make myself do casual, to pretend to feel casual when I already felt a lot more than that, not knowing if he felt anything at all... I just couldn't see myself doing it. Add that to the chaos that reigned in my head and heart whenever he was near and you might be able to understand why I didn't think it was smart to get involved with him.

Then there's the fact that I'm something of a coward. I've

never been able to get involved in any sort of relationship. The few casual ones I'd had left me feeling rather incomplete and after a few decades of that, a girl learns to be happier just on her own. And I had been doing just fine, right up until Rip.

Slowly, I sat up in bed, staring at his back as he walked away. He was walking away, right out of my room, leaving me alone... I could go back to my dreams, I could go back to my decidedly uncomplicated, *lonely* life.

"Rip, wait."

He paused in the doorway, but he didn't look at me.

"You... I mean... Well..." I snapped my mouth shut. Words were sort of blurring up in my head and running together and nothing made sense. Except—well, I didn't want him to walk out. I really didn't want that. "Do you... I mean, did I...?"

Rip sighed and turned around, staring at me. Once more, his eyes were shuttered, revealing absolutely nothing. "Just out with it, Greta."

Out with it. Right. Just take a deep breath and calm down, think of a nice, diplomatic, preferably humiliation-free way to ask—

"Did I hurt you?" I blurted out.

Oh, good job, Greta. Way to avoid humiliating yourself...

"Hurt me?" he repeated slowly. Emotion flickered in his eyes yet again before he hid it.

"When..." I swallowed. "Well, when I told you I didn't want to...well, have a relationship."

He was staring at me like I'd sprouted another head.

"Look, forget I said anything," I said after he continued to look at me like that for about another thirty seconds. I stood up, using the sheet to wrap around me toga-style.

Clothes. I needed to get some clothes, and then maybe a blistering-hot shower to clear the cobwebs from my head, and coffee. Lots and lots of coffee. But of course, he was still standing there looking at me and my invisible second head, like he couldn't quite figure me out. I shuffled around the bed and headed for my dresser. Get the clothes. Get the shower. Get away from that dark, brooding gaze—

"I'm just tired," I told him. "I think I'm still a little off from the blood loss. That would explain why maybe I'm seeing things that aren't really there—"

"For months after you left me, I'd see you. Everywhere I turned. Every time I closed my eyes to sleep. Every time I saw a woman with dark hair, I'd stop and stare, hope that maybe it was you."

I stopped—no, that's not exactly right. I *froze*, unable to move. He was coming up behind me, I could hear him, then I could feel him because he was so close the heat of his body warmed mine. Then I could feel his hands on me, resting on my shoulders, then stroking down my arms until he could cover my hands with his own.

"I dreamt of you every night for years and even now, I can't go more than a few nights without seeing your face in my dreams. And you ask me if you *hurt* me when you walked away."

My heart was racing. So damn fast... Hell, if I could have a heart attack, I'd probably be in desperate need of CPR. And I ached. There was pain in his voice, and I had done that. I'd hurt him. Tears pricked at my eyes as I forced myself to turn around and look at him. "I'm sorry." It came out in a pathetic little squeak and I made myself clear my throat before trying again. "I'm sorry. I never thought... Well, I mean, you know, we only worked together for a few weeks. And there was just the one night. I didn't think we really had anything... Well, I mean...one night, you know?"

I was rambling. Man, oh man was I rambling. I can't help it. When I'm nervous, I blabber. A lot.

"One night." He smiled. But it was a sad smile. "Yes, it was just one night. Perhaps *we* didn't have anything. But I didn't need the one night, Greta, to know *I* had something. You didn't feel it—that isn't your fault."

He cupped my cheek and stroked a thumb across my lip, staring at me in that way of his—the way that makes it seem like nothing and nobody else exists. "You didn't want the complication of a relationship—I can understand that. Respect it. But I won't just be a distraction whenever we have to work together."

His lids drooped low over his eyes, shielding them from me as he pressed against my lip with his thumb. "Why don't you get dressed? We've got work to do."

His hand fell away and he turned around. Walking away.

It made my heart freeze to even think about it. He was

walking away—

"You're not a distraction."

He didn't stop.

"Damn it, Rip. I walked away because I don't know how to do relationships *period* and I figured you were just wanting..."

Now he stopped. Now he turned around, staring at me and oh, shit, I couldn't breathe. It was like something had gone and sucked all the oxygen out of the air and I was suffocating on the words trapped in my throat.

"You figured I just wanted...what?"

"Ah... Well, you know...one of those friends-with-benefits relationships." I gave him a weak smile.

"And you didn't want to be friends with me?"

"Yes. No. Damn it, I'm even confusing myself right now." I stared at him. The strength went out of me and I sank down to the floor. The sheet pooled around my legs and absently, I smoothed it down around my legs. "It's not that I didn't want to be friends—it's that I didn't think I could *just* be friends with you. You turn me into a mess. You have pretty much from the first time I met you and I can't think straight around you."

"The feeling is mutual," he muttered under his breath.

I frowned as he crossed the floor and sank, kneeling over me with one knee on either side of my legs. "You're a confusing woman, Greta. I don't know if I should walk away, if I should stay, if I should run like hell while I still have the capacity for thought."

"I'm rather lacking that capacity myself," I whispered. Then I reached up toyed with the button of his shirt. It was a rather faded black polo, one that stretched over his excellent chest and clung to his excellent arms in the yummiest way. I bit my lip and said, "I loved being with you. Loved talking to you, just being you. If I'd thought for five seconds you were hurt when I decided to leave, I would have... Well, I don't know. I might have still walked way, but I would have probably tried to talk to you first."

He threaded a hand through my hair and tugged, forcing me to look at him. "So what do we do now?" he asked. He massaged the back of my neck, his strong fingers digging into my knotted muscles and turning them to putty.

"I don't know. Maybe... Well, maybe we should take care of business, and then see how this plays out?" I suggested.

"I've got a better idea."

His idea involved untangling my hands from the sheet I held around me. It also involved urging me back until I was lying beneath him. And his mouth—it involved his mouth, running over me, along my shoulders, my neck, down over the curves of my breasts, my belly. And his hands—his hands pushing my thighs apart until he could lie between them and kiss me.

It involved his tongue and his hands and a lot of moaning from me.

It involved me climaxing—

I whimpered and gasped out his name, trying desperately to breathe and failing. I couldn't breathe, not when he touched me like that, not when he licked me, teased me, tortured me...

"Rip, please." I fisted my hands in his hair and tugged until he lifted his head and stared at me.

He didn't say anything. He just pushed up onto his knees and tore his shirt off while I fought with the zipper of his jeans. I wanted him naked. Naked and on top of me.

He shoved his jeans down and I decided naked wasn't an absolute necessity—he didn't bother taking them off and right now, I was fine with that. As he came over my, I lifted my knees and wrapped my legs around his waist.

He couldn't remember how to breathe.

It was a damn good thing he wasn't exactly mortal any more, because he would have suffocated by the time he got his lungs working again. But who in the hell cared? Rip slanted his mouth over Greta's as he reached between them, fitting the head of his cock against her entrance.

She was silken hot, wet and tight, closing around his aching flesh like a glove.

As he sank deep inside her, she whimpered in her throat and arched, wiggling under him and rocking her hips. Tearing his mouth from hers, he stared into Greta's eyes and saw the edge of pain she tried to hide. Easing back, he cupped her face in his hands and kissed her gently. He kept it light and easy, waiting until she relaxed. Then he sank deeper inside. Each time she tensed up on him he pulled back until finally, she reached down and cupped his butt. Staring up at him, she whispered, "Stop being so careful with me."

"I don't want to hurt you."

"Then make love to me, damn it." A pout formed on her soft, full mouth. Her blue eyes burned into his as she added, "I hurt for *you*. Holding back is killing me."

It was killing him too. *She* was killing him. A groan vibrated out of him and he pushed his hand into her hair, tangled the gleaming brown strands around his fingers. "Mine." He rasped it against her lips as he pulled back...slowly...so slowly.

Greta arched underneath him, her nails biting into his arms. "Damn it, Rip!"

He drove inside, forcing his way through the tight, clinging tissues of her pussy, deeper, deeper until she'd taken all of him.

"Oh." Her lids drifted down.

"Greta?"

With a smile curling her lips, she said, "Do that again."

He did. Again. And again. Even when she tightened around him and came with a cry, he continued to ride her, taking her deep and hard and fast and it still wasn't fucking enough—

The soft, warm weight of her breasts pillowed his chest, her nipples tight and hard, pressing into him. He kissed her again, desperate for the taste of her, the feel of her...desperate for her. All of her.

Need.

Need.

Need.

It was a burning inside him, this need for her, one he'd had to live with for so long. Even meeting that need was excruciating. Touching her, taking her, it was a painful pleasure that just might kill him.

It just might undo him.

It just might make him...

She came a second time and as she clenched around him, shuddered and wiggled and rocked beneath him, he came as well. His climax was another one of those painful pleasures—he wanted it to last forever, and at the same time, he didn't know if he could handle another second.

By the time it ended, his muscles were limp and he barely

had the energy to keep from collapsing on top of her. She breathed out his name on a ragged sigh and slid a hand down his sweat-slicked back, urging him closer. Unable to fight it, he sank down against her body.

His heart raced as he lifted his head, stared into her eyes.

A smile curled her lips and she sighed, a drowsy, content little sound.

Stunned, still struggling to breathe, he buried his head between her breasts. She felt something. She'd said as much, right?

His head was something of a mess, though, and he barely knew up from down.

He needed to know. That was one thing he did understand.

He needed to know...

A soft, steady sound reached his ears and he lifted his head and realized in the span of a few heartbeats, Greta had drifted off to sleep.

"Greta?"

She hummed under her breath and wiggled, arching closer like she wanted to disappear inside his skin.

Okay, so his need to know would have to wait a little while.

Chapter Five

He was already awake when I woke up.

It was the first time in years that I woke with a smile on my face and I couldn't stop myself from pushing up on my elbow just so I could see his face better. I could feel the dopey smile spreading across my face and I didn't care.

Reaching up, I toyed with the medallion he wore around his neck. It looked exactly like mine. But it was more fun to toy with the one he wore. Man, I had it so bad.

"How are you feeling?" he asked, stroking a hand down my arm, then running the tips of his fingers across my belly.

"Wonderful." I smiled. "A little tired, but I feel wonderful."

He cupped his hand over my breast. "Yeah, you do."

The gleam in his eyes faded as he sat up and urged me onto my back, eying my belly. I wiggled and tried to pull away. "I'm fine, Rip. Good as new."

He frowned and rested the palm of his hand just below my navel. "You were cut up pretty bad."

"Couldn't be that bad." I shrugged and tugged until he lay back down beside me. "I healed up quick enough. Hey...where did you get that staff thing of yours?"

"God."

"Seriously...?" I stared at him. The deadpan expression on his face never would have given him away. But there was a faint smile glinting in his dark brown eyes and it wasn't so easily hidden. His gaze locked on my mouth and all of a sudden, I realized what he was referring to.

He caught my hand and guided it down and I blushed even as I closed my hand around him. "I wasn't talking about *this staff, hotshot. I'm talking about the one you used on the *bocan* last night."

"I had it made. I could get one for you, if you'd like."

I grinned at him. "Hell, yes."

One of his rare smiles appeared and he shook his head. "Such a strange lot we are. I offer to buy you a tool of death and you smile like I'd offered to give you a puppy."

"I would make a lousy puppy mama. Tools of death are much more useful for us anyway." I dipped my head and kissed him, paused just long enough to nip his lower lip. He was reaching for me as I pulled away. "And speaking for tools of death, we really do need to moving. We've got work."

"Where do we look?"

"I can find her," I said, blowing out a breath. I had no doubt of that. She was a weight inside me, a dark presence in my heart.

Is that what I'd felt like to Mary?

Don't go there. Not right now—I couldn't let my thoughts go wandering down those paths right now. I sometimes get lost in my memories. After you've lived a few hundred years, it's easy enough to do. But I couldn't afford to get lost when somebody out there needed me.

Even though she wouldn't be happy about it, that girl from last night did need me. I could hear her need, calling to me.

Calling...

A hand closed around my arm and shook me. Dazed, I had to force myself to focus. Had to force myself to focus on Rip's face. He was half-lost to the shadows, staring down at me as we stood on the porch of the small house where I stayed.

"You in there?"

I gave him a wan smile. "Where else would I be?"

He didn't say anything, but he didn't have to. I jerked a shoulder up, shrugging restlessly. "I'm feeling a little out of it, I guess. Feel a little off from last night and now I've got *her* in my head."

I didn't have to say anything more than that. He understood.

"You up for this?" He curled a hand around the back of my neck and eased me close. I could feel him toying with my hair while he did it and I took a moment to just revel in it, in him.

"Greta?"

"I don't know if I'm up for this or not." I grimaced. "Not that it really matters. It's calling me." *She* was calling me.

"Then focus. If it's that strong, we may not have a lot of time."

We didn't. With every step we took, my urgency grew. Miles passed and we drew nearer. Closer...closer...almost there. But we were already too late. There was a dark cloud in my mind. Dark and suffocating.

She wasn't alone.

There was somebody else with her...and it was too late for that person.

Choices.

We all have to make them. Every day. Some are important, some are almost inconsequential.

But we have to make them and tonight, somebody had made a choice that was going to end in death.

We were outside a rundown house. It looked abandoned. It wasn't. The darkness didn't affect my vision. I could see perfectly fine and more. I could hear voices. Faint and muffled. She was in there.

And there was a book.

"Rip?"

He paused and glanced at me. "She's not alone," I told him, staring at him morosely. *Too late...*

"Neither are you." He dipped his head and kissed me.

I wish I could say all my fears and misgivings disappeared, just like that. I wish I could, but I'd be lying. It was a comfort, though. Having him with me. Now at least I wouldn't have to guard my back from one while I dealt with the other.

As we mounted the crumbling concrete steps, the stink of evil flooded the air. Demons, in their incorporeal form, don't smell. But once they settled in a human, it was kind of like the stench of decay came with them. Humans wouldn't smell it, but animals did. So did we. It was faint, cloying and enough to make me glad I hadn't taken the time to eat anything earlier.

I doubt I would have puked it up, but fighting the urge to

hurl can be kind of distracting.

I didn't need to be distracted right now.

It was an *orin*.

Orin—fucking soul stealers. The *orin* could probably make dealing with a vampire look like a walk along a moonlight beach. At least with vampires, when they move in for the kill, the typical person realizes there's something *Abby Normal* going on. With the *orin*, the typical person isn't going to realize something is going on until it's already over and done.

Of course, maybe it's not that big a deal—after all, either way, you were dead.

Somebody inside that house was dead.

God, please…don't let it be somebody young.

It wouldn't be a child. Children have their own sort of guardian angels that keep the demons at bay, but these days, childhood was lost earlier and earlier. True innocence came with a protection against demonkind that awes me even as it saddens me. If only we could spread that protection out to everybody.

The door creaked as we pushed it open. I recognized the girl from last night, although she hadn't seen us yet.

The other one had.

It was—*had* been a teenage male. Seventeen, perhaps. Maybe eighteen, but not much older. His body was still in that long, somewhat awkward phase, and now it would look that way forever. Or at least until the *orin* died. He had one of those poetically beautiful faces, the kind that made teenage girls sigh with longing.

His eyes—

I swallowed and made myself look into those eyes. I didn't like doing the dirty work, but I'd accepted it. I wouldn't hide when I had to do it.

The girl was seated on the floor, bent over one of the demon tomes. He sat next to her and stared at me over her bent head. As our gazes locked, he lifted a hand and rested it high on her back. There was a threat in his eyes, one I understood loud and clear. He didn't have to say a word.

His gaze dropped to the medallion I wore around my neck and a smirk twisted his lips.

"I'm terrified."

The girl jumped as he spoke. Her head swung around and she glared at me. "*You.* What in the hell are you doing here? How did you find me?"

"Get away from him," I said softly.

Rip stood beside me and as I spoke, I saw him move, saw him slip a hand into his coat. He pulled out the staff and twirled it in his hand. It danced there—like he was some sort of lethal baton twirler.

"Lady, what in the hell is your problem?" she demanded.

"Get away from him," I said again.

She stared at me, like I'd lost my mind. *God, please...just get away from that monster. Don't make me make you—*

The matter was decided for us, though. The boy reached for her and hauled her back against him. She shrieked, startled, then she whimpered. He was holding her with too much force, causing her pain. His fingers dug into her arms, squeezing tightly, so tightly, the skin tore—blood began to drip down her arms in dark rivulets.

In general, humans aren't strong enough to draw blood just by squeezing really hard.

Even though I hated seeing her hurt, it was the best thing that could have happened, I guess. It caught her off-guard, which effectively pulled her attention away from that damn book. The adrenaline rush from the pain would hopefully clear her head a little.

And if she caught a look at her boyfriend, it just might terrify her into running. I could handle her running. Then I'd just have the possessed boyfriend to deal with.

"Damn it, Joey, what are you doing?" she demanded, jerking against his hold.

All he did was tighten his grip, although I don't know how. He was already holding her so tightly, his fingers had gone white. Where they weren't stained with her blood...

She whimpered again and finally, she looked over her shoulder at him.

The *orin* was showing in Joey's eyes—eyes gone black as onyx. Other than that, his features hadn't really changed, but he looked *other*, at least to my eyes.

The girl screamed. Okay, so he looked *other* to her as well.

"He's got a demon inside him," I said. I waited until her

eyes came back to me.

"A demon...what are you taking, lady?"

"I'm not on drugs." I shook my head and started to pace around the edge of the room. Rip did the same, mirroring my movements. He went left while I went right. The *orin* couldn't defend itself against both of us *and* still hold onto the girl. "Neither is Joey. But he did get caught up in some very, very bad things."

"Shut up, Grimm," the *orin* said, grinning at me.

Grimm.

It served as an unneeded reminder—I knew what I was. What we were. There are hundreds of us. Maybe even thousands. Fighting the good fight, doing what we can to help. We were put on this earth with a specific purpose—to deal with monsters like this. I focused on that, focused on the weight of the medallion against my skin as I watched him.

I would save her. I hadn't been put in her life for nothing. "Let her go, *orin*. If you let her go, you might live another couple of days."

"But she's such fun..." He let go of one of the girl's arms and trailed his bloody fingers up, over her biceps, along her collarbone. He used the blood on his fingers to paint an "X" on her cheek. "I don't want to let her go. I want to keep her, make another like me. Although it would be fun to just kill her right now, right in front of you."

"If I don't get her away from you, she's dead anyway," I said, shrugging. My stomach clenched as I said it, but none of my turmoil showed on my face. I'd been doing this too long, dealing with his kind too long. I might be scared, I might be pissed, but I controlled it.

"But if I kill her now, you won't have a chance to save her."

"Saving her isn't my main concern," Rip said, joining the conversation as he moved to intersect us, using his body to hide me from the *orin*. "My main concern is getting rid of you...and the book."

The *orin* laughed. "Nice try, Grimm. You can't really expect me to buy that you don't care if I decide to gut her in front of you."

Rip moved closer. Closer. I stayed just behind him. Not sure what he was planning, but whatever it was, I was ready to improvise.

"I didn't say I didn't care. I said she wasn't my main concern."

Rip glanced down at the girl's face as he said it, felt his heart twist. Despite the heavy makeup, despite the hard veneer she projected to the world, she really was just a girl. Eighteen, maybe a year or two older. And she looked utterly terrified.

But demons knew how to exploit weakness and when it came to situations like this, showing any sort of fear or worry would definitely constitute a weakness.

Instead of trying to reassure her, he focused on the *orin* who held her life in his hands. Rip was fast—it would take him just seconds to reach the demon's present body. But a demon-possessed human could rival him for speed and it would take just seconds to snap the girl's neck or rip her heart out.

So he waited.

He lifted a shoulder and shrugged. "I'll save her if I can, but if I can't... Hell, she brought this on herself. If she dies, it's through her own actions. I'll be satisfied with killing you, getting rid of the book."

The *orin* sneered.

And backed away.

The girl struggled against his hold and he placed his bloodied hand on her neck, squeezing lightly. "Be still, bitch."

Tears gleamed in her eyes and she struggled harder. Terror was taking over. Low in her throat, she made animalistic little sounds and panted. She tried to jab back and hit him in the stomach with her elbow. All it did was irritate the demon.

"Shut up," he snarled, his voice deeper, rougher—utterly inhuman.

"They don't listen so well when they are terrified," Rip said.

The *orin* growled and locked his arm around her neck, squeezing until the girl's eyes fluttered shut, until her body went limp.

Finally.

"Greta," he said quietly, hoping she was ready.

"Thank God. I was getting a little bored."

In a moment of perfect synchronicity, Rip dropped to the ground. Silver flew over his head. As the blade buried itself in the demon's left eye socket, Rip grabbed the girl and jerked her towards him. The *orin* howled and reached up. He still fought, although the body he inhabited was dying. No...no longer dying.

Dead.

The heart no longer beat.

The lungs no longer breathed.

"They don't make very good shields when they are unconscious," Greta said, moving around to stand over the *orin*.

The mouth moved—it was a macabre sight. "Fuck you, Grimm."

Even having seen a show like it before, it was hard to watch. The human's body was dead, but the demon was still fighting to control it. Fighting to live—it was a useless fight. The *orin* couldn't take over an unwilling body. It couldn't touch Rip or Greta, and the girl—the one person that could have served as a host—was unconscious.

"Knocking her out was just plain stupid." Greta knelt down and grabbed her knife, drawing it away. She wiped the blade on the mortal's shirt, leaving blood, brain matter and gore. "You didn't really think you'd get away from us, did you? But you had to go and put a sleeper hold on the one chick who could have taken you in."

"Fucking...bi..."

Then it was gone. Just like that, the demon ceased to exist.

"Well, that was fun," Greta said. She stared down at the lifeless body at their feet, with a somber, unhappy look on her face.

"Fun." Rip moved to stand behind her, resting a hand on her shoulder.

She lifted her knife and stared at it. Gently, he reached around and covered her hand with his, easing the blade back down. "It was too late for him. There was nothing we could do."

"We could have gotten to him sooner."

"And he could have not used the book."

In the end, it was that simple. The boy might not have understood just what he was getting into, but a demon tome *felt* wrong. It gave off bad vibes and anybody who touched one would know, somewhere inside, that it was wrong. They'd know using it was wrong. If they made the choice to do it anyway...

"He made his choice, Greta."

Chapter Six

Choices.

That's what it all comes down to in the end, I guess.

I sat on the couch and watched the girl. She still hadn't woken up. I don't think she wanted to. Somewhere inside, she knew she was in a world of bad, bad things and she wasn't ready to deal.

Easy to understand.

But still, I needed her to wake up.

I needed to know how far she'd gone with the book, I had to look into her eyes and *know*—that was all I'd need. A look into her eyes, and I'd know if she had gone too far. If she had...

God. I don't want to think about that. Yep, I understand all about not wanting to deal. I sighed and leaned my head against the back of the couch. I was tired. I didn't know if it was from the injury the other night or if it had something more to do with something else.

I felt stretched thin and I certainly didn't feel equipped to handle whatever lay before me. Even if she wasn't too far gone—

How disgustingly weak is it of me to admit that it would actually be easier in the long run if she *was* too far gone? If I had to kill her and just deal with the grief and guilt? She was different.

Something about this girl was different, and I had a bad feeling I knew what it was.

It was something I didn't *want*. Especially not right now.

I wasn't ready to take on the responsibilities that Mary had taken with me. Talk about pathetic. Talk about weak. Five hundred years of living and I still wasn't ready.

I found myself thinking about Mary, thinking about her and wondering. Had she been ready? I'd been younger than this girl when I'd been thrust upon her, and not only had she saved me from Hans and my stepmother, she'd been forced to raise me. Not to be just mentor, but mother as well.

Closing my eyes, I let my thoughts drift. Found myself remembering...remembering a life that had ended long ago. A life where I had been called Gretel—

Germany, 1520

"I know this place. My father's home is near."

Famine had spread across the land and many, many people went hungry. But Gretel lived happily in the small house in the deep of the woods. Every week, they walked to town with baskets of food that they gave to those in the most need. The baskets held bread and flour, sometimes some meat, eggs and seedlings.

Gretel hadn't ever asked Mary why they did this. Questioning Mary simply never occurred to her. Mary was like a mother to her—no, more. An angel. Her guardian angel. Mary taught her to read, taught her other languages, taught her kindness...and forgiveness.

True peace cannot be easily found without forgiveness. Without true peace, one cannot be happy.

If nothing else, Mary wanted Gretel to be happy.

With her heart racing, Gretel stared through the trees to the house. Her hands were cold and clammy with sweat and her belly was a horrid tangle of nerves and fear. She wished to leave, run away and never come here again.

Stricken, she looked at Mary and whispered, "Why are we here?"

But Gretel already knew.

"You know why." Mary stopped and turned, looking at Gretel. "Your stepmother and your stepbrother haven't fared well over the years. They have run out of food, out of money. Your stepmother is too ill to work and your stepbrother... Well, Hans never was one for a hard day's work, was he?"

Gretel swallowed. Her mouth was terribly dry.

"You may give them that basket." Mary nodded at the basket on Gretel's arm. "You may walk away from them. It is your choice."

"What happens if I walk away?" Gretel asked.

"They will starve," Mary said simply.

Gretel squeezed her eyes closed. The basket on her arm felt even heavier now and there was a bitter, ugly taste in the back of her mouth. "What should I do?"

"I cannot tell you that, dear one. You must decide for yourself."

"But I do not know what is the right thing to do," Gretel said, shaking her head. She looked at Mary and pleaded, "Please. You have been like a mother to me. You have taught me, you have cared for me, you have loved me. I'm asking you—what would please you more? Simply tell me and I will do whatever you ask."

"Gretel, I have loved you like a daughter." Mary laid a hand on Gretel's shoulder. "You have always pleased me. From the very first day you arrived on my doorstep, you have pleased me. And whatever choice you make, please know that I will not be disappointed. But this is your choice, and it's one you must make for yourself."

Memories of the nights she'd cried herself to sleep haunted her. Nights when she had gone to bed hungry. Nights when she had gone to bed with her back aching from one of her stepmother's beatings. Nights when she had lain in bed, hot with shame, sick with pain and tormented by the things her stepbrother had done to her.

Leave them to starve, a voice whispered in the back of her mind. *She never cared if you were hungry. She never cared if you were in pain. When you tried to tell her what Hans did to you, she slapped you and called you a liar. The world will be better off without them.*

Gretel shook her head. "But that is not my decision to make." She lowered her eyes and studied the basket on her arm. There was food enough for a good week, if they were careful. As well as seedling plants, a bit of flour and salt.

She took a deep breath and then looked at Mary. "I will give the basket to them. But I do ask that you walk along with me. I cannot go to that house alone."

They were not greeted with open arms. Gretel was not given any apologies for their treatment of her, although she knew they recognized her. But she had not done this for apologies and she did not wish for them to welcome her.

She only wanted to give them the basket and then return home to the small house in the deep of the woods.

"Your stepbrother follows us," Mary said some time later as they walked along the path that would lead them home.

Fear gripped Gretel. "He does? How do you know that? Why does he follow us?"

"Now, Gretel, you are not a dim creature." Mary gave Gretel a bland look. "Why do you think?"

She patted Gretel's shoulder and for some odd reason, that simple touch comforted her.

"I told him, you know, when he left you with me that day, he was never to return to my home again. Never." Mary sighed and reached up, toying with the silver medallion she wore. It was something that Gretel had never seen the woman without. She wore it always. "I so despise it when I am disobeyed."

Letting go of the piece of silver at her neck, Mary smoothed a hand down her skirt and then turned the lone basket over to Gretel. "Take this and go home. Whatever you do, you mustn't come back here. No matter what you hear as you walk, you must go to the house. Do you understand me?"

Gretel frowned. "Go home? But...I cannot leave you here alone, Mary. Come, let us hurry. If we hurry, we can reach the house before he gets close. We'll be safe there."

"I do not fear him," Mary said, reaching for Gretel and pulling her close in a hug. "He is no threat to me. Now, do as I say."

Gretel did not want to leave.

But she could not make herself argue, not with Mary. Not with the woman who had been so kind, so good to her.

She left. Even as part of her wanted to grab Mary, cling to her, she walked away.

She walked away from Mary, following the path as it curved through the forest. Mere seconds passed before she heard him speak.

Then Mary's voice, clear as a bell, her words echoing around Gretel. "I told you not to come back here, Hans. You were warned and you ignored my warning."

Hans' laugh echoed.

The sound of it terrified Gretel down to her very bones. She heard the sound of branches breaking. A slap. The thunder started. A cold rain began to fall. It seemed only seconds earlier she'd seen sunlight filtering through the leaves. Behind her, she heard their voices, Hans' hoarse bellow, underscored by Mary's quiet, level tone.

The wind began to whip through the trees, howling eerily.

Gretel began to run. She ran so fast, and the farther she ran the more trouble she had remembering *what* she was running from. By the time she reached the small house in the deep of the woods, she had utterly forgotten why she ran, what had frightened her so.

It would be years before she remembered that day. It would be years before she could think of it clearly.

By the time Mary reached home sometime later, Gretel had already started preparing dinner and the two women sat down, as if nothing had happened.

The following week, as was their custom, Mary and Gretel set off for the village. They hadn't been there long when Gretel noticed how very many people were staring at her. Some appeared to offer her looks of sympathy, while others gazed at her with avid curiosity. Uneasy, Gretel smoothed a hand down her skirt.

"Mary, do you know—"

She was unable to finish her question, for at that moment, one of the villagers approached them.

"Gretel, you poor thing. I am so sorry for your loss."

"My..." Gretel looked at Mary and then back at the villager. "My loss? Whatever do you mean?"

"Child, have you not heard?" Shocked, he looked from Gretel to Mary, and then back. "Your brother Hans was found dead last week. It must have happened shortly after you left his home."

Hans was dead?

Staring at him with stricken eyes, she whispered, "Dead?"

"Yes. He was in the forest. It would seem he was killed by wild boars."

Hans.

He was dead.

Gretel turned away and raised a hand to cover her face. Tears stung her eyes. Her heart raced. A wave of nausea struck her.

Hans was dead.

She did not know whether to weep or rejoice.

The question burned inside her, but she did not give voice to it until they were safely away from the village and on their way back to their home within the forest.

But finally, she could hold it back no longer.

"You knew about Hans," she blurted out.

Mary continued to walk.

Gretel could not move. Her very legs felt frozen, her feet too heavy to lift.

"Mary?" she whispered.

The other woman stopped and sighed. She returned to Gretel's side, smiling sadly. "You have been like a daughter to me, Gretel. I've told you that, haven't I?"

"You have. And you know you have been like a mother to me. I love you. With all of my heart, I love you. But please, tell me—did you know about Hans?"

Mary inclined her head. "I knew."

"How long have you known?" She could hardly see through the tears in her eyes.

"A week." Mary gazed at Gretel with somber, serious eyes.

"You knew for a week, and you did not tell me?" Gretel spun away and pressed a hand to her mouth. "Why?"

"I chose not to."

"You would rather I hear it from people who are but strangers to me?" Gretel cried out. "Mary, how could you be so cruel?"

"I did not do it to be cruel." She looked away and when she looked back at Gretel, there was unhappiness in her eyes. "I did not tell you, for I worried what you think of me."

"What I would think of you?" Gretel shook her head. "But he was killed by wild boars. Why would I think badly of you over that?"

Mary said nothing. She reached up and toyed with the medallion she wore—it was something she often did when she was sad.

There was a look in her eyes.

That look turned Gretel's blood to ice.

"Come. We must talk." Mary looked around the forest and said, "But we cannot do it here."

Chapter Seven

"Come back to me." Rip's voice whispered in, filtering past the memories and finding me. Lost inside the memories, I latched onto his voice and let him pull me out.

I came to and realized we were on the loveseat, with me perched on his lap and his strong arms wrapped around me, his lips at my temple. "Come back to me," he said again.

"I am. I did." I swallowed and my mouth was painfully dry. I felt like I'd been asleep for days—weeks. "Was I sleeping?"

"No. But you weren't here either." He pushed my hair back from my face and cupped my chin, tilting my head back. His brown eyes, warm and concerned, stared into mine. "Where were you?"

"Remembering." I caught sight of the bottle of water on the couch next to us and I reached for it. He rested a hand on my back and stroked up and down. I took a sip of water and snuggled against him. I tilted my head back so I could see his face. "Do you ever get lost in your memories?"

"Not often." He shook his head, then lowered it and pressed a kiss to my lips. "But my memories are not as dark, are not as grim as yours."

"Grim." I smirked at his unintentional pun. "But you're a Grimm...aren't *grim* memories kind of required?"

"No." He smiled and stroked a finger down my cheek. "Some of us were lucky and didn't have to walk one of the darker roads to get where we are."

There was a low, rough sigh off to our side and I turned my head, staring at the girl. She was coming out of it too, I realized.

"She wasn't one of them." I moved off his lap and perched on the edge of the loveseat, watching her. She had so much pain inside her, even unconscious, I could feel it. I licked my lips and looked at him. "She's supposed to be one of us. I think maybe I'm supposed to guide her."

"I figured as much." He rested a hand low on my back. It managed to be both comforting and bolstering, giving me some very much-needed strength.

"What if I'm not strong enough?"

On the couch, she started to move around. Rip leaned in and murmured into my ear, "Don't be an idiot." He gave my back one last stroke and then stood. "You can't do what you do without strength. We both know that."

He left the room just as the girl sat up. She took one look at me and screamed.

I didn't do anything.

She stopped screaming and bolted for the door. Then I did something. I shoved off the couch and got between her and the door. "Sit down."

She swung out with her fist and I blocked it, caught her other hand as she tried to hit me from that side. Her arms were covered with bruises and dried blood from where the *orin* had torn her flesh. I was as careful as I could be, trying not to touch any of the open wounds, but the way she was fighting, it wasn't that easy.

Rip intervened. He emerged from the other room and wrapped his arms around her, hauling her back. "Calm down."

She elbowed him in the gut. He grimaced and shifted his hold until he could pin her arms to her sides.

"Let me go!" she screeched.

And damn—she could really shriek. My ears felt like they were going to split open and bleed. I rubbed my left one and said, "If you'll stop fighting, he'd be more than happy to let you go."

But she just wasn't inclined to take our word for it. She continued to struggle, using her foot to slam down on Rip's instep, trying to ram her head into his nose. Rip stoically took all of it while I stood there and pinched the bridge of my nose. There was a headache building behind my eyes and it was only getting worse.

Finally, I had enough.

"Let her go, Rip."

Without a word, he did so and when she lunged for me, I hauled off and punched her in the nose. I pulled it—I'm a lot stronger than I look, stronger than her for certain. I didn't want to seriously hurt her, but I did want her attention. Blood fountained out of her nose and for a few seconds, she was too blinded by the pain and the tears to fight.

"It's time for you to calm down and listen to me—I don't want to hurt you. Neither does he. But you're not leaving here either."

Silence. Save for the odd hitches in her breathing, she didn't make a sound as she sat there and held a hand to her heavily bleeding nose.

"Rip, do you have a handkerchief?"

He produced one from somewhere—the man could probably whip out an AK-47 and a can of whipped cream if you asked him. Prepare for everything, that was Rip. I took the handkerchief and held it out to her. She grabbed it away, glaring at me like I'd forced her to take a poisonous snake by the tail.

"Now...are you ready to talk?"

The answer to that question was no.

It continued to be no for the next hour or so.

Damn it, she was stubborn.

"Damn it, you can't *keep* me here." She was scared, she was pissed and she looked like she was about ready to make a run for it—again. She'd already made two attempts. I'd stopped her the first time. Rip had stopped her the second time. After that, she hadn't tried to run again.

Somehow, I suspected she was more afraid of Rip than me. She sat in the chair, trying hard not to look at him, and trying hard not to look terrified.

I stared at the girl without a lot of sympathy.

She glared at me and repeated, "You can't keep me here."

"You keep saying that. And you sound so convinced," I mused. Then I shrugged. "Maybe the correct phrase would be I *shouldn't* keep you here. But I can, and I will. I can't let you go right now. You have no idea the kind of trouble you were messing with last night and until I know you're safe, you and me are going to be like best buds," I told her.

She sneered at me. Okay, the tough girl was back. "And what are you going to do...watch me twenty-four seven for the rest of my life?"

"Not necessary." She hadn't completely fallen for the dark evil promises the book offered, but that didn't make my job easier. I still didn't know what I was going to do with her. She wasn't too far gone, but it was still possible she'd take that final step. If that happened, I'd kill her. If that didn't happen, I could fail and she would die anyway.

No matter what happened, she wouldn't need a twenty-four-seven guard. Either we'd both win, or we'd both lose. I was prepared to handle either outcome, but I was really, really hoping I wouldn't fail. Of course, if we both lived, I had a feeling she and I weren't done. If she lived—and learned the error of her ways—then she had a choice to make and there was a lot of information she'd have to get before that.

But none of that was going to come any time soon. She wasn't listening, she didn't want to listen, so until we could *get* her to listen, we would have to watch her like a hawk. I don't know about Rip, but I was hungry and I was tired. I needed to get some sleep and try to think of where to go from here.

Across the kitchen, he stood by the back door, playing the not-so-subtle bad cop. He had his arms crossed over a wide chest. He was wearing his devastated black leather coat—he'd have to buy a new one. From the front, it mostly just looked a little battered, a little worn. But the back had a huge piece of material missing by his legs, like it had gotten caught in something. It wasn't cold enough to need the coat, but that wasn't why he wore it. The coat hid a number of weapons and other surprises. He probably felt naked without all of his toys.

Speaking of toys...

An idea hit me. She wasn't going to like it, but I needed to get away from her for a few minutes. I doubted Rip wanted to play babysitter either. We both needed a break. I asked him, "You got any sort of handcuffs on you?" If I knew anything about the man, he'd have a dozen different weapons hidden somewhere, as well as a sundry of other gadgets and devices.

Rip lifted a brow. Then he dipped a hand inside the coat and withdrew a pair of cuffs.

Our guest freaked.

"Oh, shit, no." She lunged for the door and terror gave her both speed and strength. I ended up with an elbow in the gut. Although the injury from the *bocan* was gone, the area was still tender. I grimaced as pain jolted through me. Unwilling to take any more abuse, I used my foot to take her legs out from under her. She struggled to get back up.

I was weaker than I'd realized because she almost got away—if Rip hadn't been there, she would have. He caught her and hauled her to the table. She tried to rack him and he narrowed his eyes.

"Try that again and I'll get upset," he said, his voice flat, his eyes colder than ice.

She went still, staring at him in utter terror.

Man, I wish I could inspire that sort of terror with just a few words, a cold look. I usually had to draw a weapon, kick a little butt before anybody showed me any kind of respect. I glared at his back as he cuffed her to the chair, running the cuffs through the ladder back rungs.

"I'll find something to tie her legs to the chair," he said, straightening up and looking at me.

"Thank you."

As he left, the girl started to cry. "Please...please don't hurt me."

Guilt jabbed needles into my heart. There was a look in her eyes, one I'd seen before. One I'd worn before, as well. Sighing, I dropped into the chair across from hers. "We're not trying to hurt you. We don't *want* to hurt you."

She didn't believe me. I've got to admit, I can't say I blame her. But my options here were very limited. Silence stretched out between us. Rip was in the other room, waiting. I didn't know whether he'd found anything to tie her legs with or not, but he'd been standing outside the room for a couple of minutes, not doing anything, not saying anything.

"What...what happened to Joey?"

Joey...? The memory of a young face flashed through my eyes. Young face—demon eyes. Oh, yeah. The boy the *orin* had possessed. This was not going to help matters any. But I'd be damned if I lied.

"He's dead."

She started to cry again, deep, ugly sobs. I rested my elbows on my knees and stared at the floor, waited for the storm to pass.

Finally, she asked, "Why? Why did you kill him?"

"Because he was going to hurt people," I said flatly. I nodded towards her arms. "Don't you remember what he did to *you?*"

What little color remained in her face washed away as she lowered her gaze and stared at her arms. I could see the memories in her eyes, fighting to surface.

"*He* did that," I said. "He did it. He used you to protect himself and if he could have done it, he would have killed you to protect himself."

"*No!*" She shook her head. The cuffs rattled as she jerked against them, fighting to get free. "That's not true."

"Then you're telling me you don't remember how he grabbed you? Held you between himself and me? You remember. I can see it in your eyes."

"He loved me...he wouldn't hurt me."

She needed so desperately to believe that.

Heaving out a sigh, I said, "He might have loved you. But the man who hurt you last night wasn't the one you knew. The book saw to that."

Shadows skittered across her face. "What are you talking about?"

"You know what I'm talking about. The book."

"You burned my book...and besides, it's just a *book*."

"No." I held her gaze and repeated, "No. It's a lot more than just a book and I think you know it. Your friend wanted power. Well, he got it and it killed him—and make no mistake, that power is what killed him. The power comes from the demon that takes over your body and once that happens, *you* cease to exist. Your friend was dead long before I showed up."

I pushed up from my chair and left the room. I caught Rip's gaze and shook my head. I didn't want to mess with the rope for now. She couldn't get out of here without making noise, and if we heard her, we'd stop her. Right now, she needed to think and I needed to get away from her pain before it choked me.

It was going to be a long day, I decided.

Three hours later, I was back in the other room. I'd lain down for a little while for a nap, not that it had done me any good. I'd also showered, and that had helped. I no longer felt like I had the stink of demon death clinging to me.

Now if I could just get through to the girl.

"If you're not going to hurt me, then just let me go," she pleaded.

"Why?" I leaned back in the chair. Yeah, I felt bad for her. I didn't like scaring people or freaking them out. But I didn't feel bad enough to let her go either. Even if I didn't have this gut-deep knowledge that she was one of us, I couldn't let her go. Not until I knew she was safe from the *orin*, which meant convincing her those books were bad, bad news. Which meant convincing her of her own strength, her own worth.

"Why should I let you go? So you can go back to what you were trying to do the past few nights?"

"I wasn't *hurting* anybody."

"Not yet." I cocked my head and studied her. "But if you had succeeded, you would have. Or at least the things inside you would have, would have used your body to hurt quite a few bodies."

She stared at me blankly. "What are you talking about?"

"Look at your arms, girl. A *human* couldn't do that to you—not so easily. Humans just aren't that strong—humans can't *tear* flesh with just the strength of their grasp. But he did. Remember his face. Remember how his eyes looked...he wasn't human anymore, and that book is part of the reason behind it."

She shook her head. "That's insane."

"Is it? Apparently you believe in stuff like witchcraft, magic. Why is so hard to believe in monsters? Demons? Soulstealers?"

"Soulstealers?"

I nodded. "Yes. Soulstealers. That's what took your friend over—that was what killed him. That was what you were summoning the night I found you. You were getting ready to help them manifest and the first thing they would have done was set up housekeeping inside you and you... Well, you would have ceased to exist after a while."

"That's not true." Her voice shook as she said it and she

wouldn't look at me.

"Yes, it is. They didn't tell you that part...but then again, why would they? They promised you power, didn't they? Let me guess...you just want some power so you can have a little more control over your life. Make good things happen instead of the bad things." I lifted a brow. "How close am I?"

She shook her head. "You're wrong. Nobody promised me anything."

"And I bet the book just dropped right out of the sky, didn't it?"

She flushed and looked away. Abruptly, the passive and submissive prisoner disappeared. She snarled at me and jerked against the cuffs. "Let me fucking go!" she shouted.

Rip chose that moment to join us. I gave him a faint smile as I eyed the rope in his hands.

"Took you a long time to find it."

Rip shrugged. "I was kind of hoping we wouldn't need it. But she's not listening, is she?"

"No." I had no idea where he'd found the rope, but then again, I hadn't been in the house that long. For all I knew, the landlord could have had some stashed down in the basement.

She tried to kick him as he crouched down in front of her. He shot me a look. Rolling my eyes, I joined him and crouched down out of kicking range, and forced one ankle back, held it still. He tied it and then we repeated the process on the other side. I had to fight a wave of weariness when I stood. Leaning against the table, I let him finish up—using more of the rope just above and below her knees. Rip might have been the original boy scout. He believed in covering all the bases.

"If you don't want to hurt me, then why are you doing this?"

The headache pounded behind my eyes. I rubbed at my temple and sighed. I was feeling seriously exasperated at this point. "Look, I've already explained that you were getting ready to dive into something you couldn't possibly handle—"

"You don't know me!" she screamed at me. She jerked so hard against her restraints that she managed to make the chair clatter on the ground.

"You sure about that?"

"Fuck you."

I made a face at her. "I'm so sorry, but you're a little young for me and you're also female."

She opened her mouth, going to yell at me again, I was sure. Lifting a hand, I cut her off. "Look, here's the deal. I know you. A lot better than you think. You're angry, you're pissed off. You've had bad shit happen to you and it's usually because of things you don't feel you can control. So you want to take control. You've always been different…" I paused and looked her over. She had that Goth-girl look going, but that wasn't what made her stand out. It was something only certain individuals can see…people like me. And demonkind. She had some sort of gift and that gift made her different. "You feel like you're on the outside looking in because of it. You hated it. Until you realized you could use it. So you started using it a little. Then a little more. Maybe you started needing it, maybe *it* started using you."

She stared at me, that strange purple gaze darkening to twilight. She didn't speak, but I saw the answer in her eyes.

"Where did you get the book?"

She looked away.

Rip leaned by the counter just behind her, a small smile on his lips. I glared at him. I felt like I was beating my head against a brick wall, not getting *anywhere* and I was damned tired of it.

He shook his head a little and shoved off the counter. He bent down and murmured, "What's your name, girl?"

Under the warm gold of her complexion, she went pale. "Muh…Mandy."

"Where did you find the book, Mandy? Did somebody give it to you?"

But she wasn't going to share that answer with him. Even if he did terrify her.

"Don't worry about it right now, Rip," I said. "Right now, it doesn't matter. We'll figure that out later…assuming she lives through this."

Her eyes popped wide, but I was done dealing with her for now. Stupid girl doing stupid things, messing with forces she couldn't even begin to understand, and being too stupid to realize that we were trying to help.

Rip followed me into the other room, closing the door behind him. "This wasn't exactly how I'd expected things to play out," I told him as I headed for one of the chairs. "You know, a few days ago, I was going out of my mind with boredom."

"Well, at least you're no longer bored."

"I'd rather be bored." I closed my eyes and leaned my head against the back of the chair. Everything was in sheer chaos. I'd fallen into a bit of a rut lately, and now that I was out of the rut, part of me wanted back in.

Even if it meant no more Rip.

I stared at him and tried to figure out just how he'd ended up back in my life. How he'd already managed to become such an important part of that life. Yet again. I'd managed to avoid him for the better part of the last century and I'd planned on keeping to that pattern indefinitely.

You know what they say about best-laid plans.

He glanced around the cottage. "At least you have some privacy here," he murmured. "Since she's not being…"

From behind him, we could hear her screaming, "Damn it, let me out of here."

"Cooperative," he finished.

When I'd gotten into Ann Arbor a few days earlier, I'd found this little cottage within a few hours. At the time, I'd thought I'd really lucked out. Most people don't want to rent out to people for short, indeterminate periods of time—I'd told the owner I may be there a few days or a few months. As long as I paid by the week, the owner hadn't cared.

Yep, I thought I'd gotten really lucky, but as we listened to my unhappy guest, I decided luck had nothing to do with it. Fate, God, take your pick had everything to do with it. Instead of living in some microscopic, long-term efficiency-styled hotel room, I had a modicum of privacy, a for-real bedroom and a sofa bed in the living room and plenty of room for my unexpected guests.

I rested my elbows on my knees and watched as Rip straightened and shrugged out of his coat. The back of the coat was seriously messed up. Like it had gotten caught in a meat grinder or something.

"That used to be a very nice coat," I said, biting my cheek to keep from smiling as he stared at the back of the coat in disgust.

"Yes. It did." His voice had a clipped edge to it—he was younger than me and hadn't completely lost his accent. Back when he had been born, Americans didn't sound like they do now—it was a softer version of a British accent. Even in the older ones like me, when we are angry or upset, something of it still bleeds through. Personally, I think it's going to be a shame when Rip loses his accent altogether. It's sexy.

Hell, Rip is sexy. Rip is mouth-watering. Rip is...staring at me like he knows exactly what I'm thinking, I realized. Of course, I'd been staring at his mouth so it wasn't like I'd been practicing much in the way of subtlety, I guess.

He threw the coat down on the coffee table and started to approach me. I tensed up and then made a concentrated effort to relax. It seemed rather pointless to get worked up when he got in my personal space. After all, last night we'd spent a decent amount of time getting in each other's personal space.

"This isn't over," he murmured as he knelt down in front of me and rested his hands on my thighs.

Was he talking about us? Or the mess with the girl? I really wasn't sure.

I reached up and ran a hand through his thick blond hair, watching as the strands fell back into place.

"She had a book and you said you'd burned it. Her friend had a book. That many close together spells bad news."

Okay, so he was talking work. I continued to play with his hair and closed my eyes. "Seriously bad news."

It was my mess, though. I'd stumbled into it and it was my obligation to see it through.

Screw obligations. I opened my eyes and looked at him, getting lost in the soft, velvety brown of his eyes. "Will you stay? Help me with it?" I cupped his cheek in my hand, felt his rough stubble graze my palm.

"I'll stay. For as long as you need me." He turned his face my hand and kissed it.

I found myself thinking wistfully, *How about forever? Can you stay forever?*

Chapter Eight

Rip stuck his head under the piss-poor showerhead and rinsed the shampoo from his hair. He had the water on cold in the hopes that it would clear his mind. He had a job to do and he was letting himself get distracted—

Hell. Greta was more than a distraction.

To him, she was everything.

The silver medallion around his neck grew warm against his skin as he reached for the soap. Rip ignored it. The warmth faded. But ten seconds later, it did it again and this time, it wasn't warm—it was hot. Hot enough that when he glanced down, he saw a faint red mark where the metal had rested against his skin. Swearing, he finished scrubbing off and rinsed off. He reached up and closed his hand around the bit of silver and closed his eyes.

What?

Rip didn't bother wasting time with pleasantries. Not with this jerk.

You are on assignment. The voice echoed inside his head.

Yes, I am. But I've also got an obligation to help my brethren.

Helping your brethren...is that what you call this? That is why you linger? It has nothing to do with Gretel?

There was a sly undertone to the words and Rip curled his lip, wished he wasn't just communicating via mind, wished the bastard was there so he could punch him. *She doesn't go by Gretel anymore.*

That is no answer.

I know my job, Rip answered. *I've never failed yet, have I?*

There is always a first time. There was a pause and then,

So you expect me to believe you'll resume your duties tonight? That you will leave this mess to Gretel?

Her name is Greta, Rip corrected. *She hates the name Gretel and you know that. Don't worry. I remember my obligations. I'll see to them.*

I hope you do.

The presence withdrew and Rip was alone in his head once more. Scowling, he let go of the charm and looked down at his chest. The faint redness had already faded, his body soaking up the small injury like a sponge.

He needed to get some sleep. His head was all cloudy, from fatigue, from worry...from Greta. He needed sleep and he needed to think, to plan.

He remembered his obligations, all right.

And taking care of Greta was obligation number one.

Rip stared out the window, watching as the sun sank ever closer to the horizon. Behind him, Greta straddled a chair, facing Mandy. No softness, no warmth glinted in her eyes as she said, "The book, Mandy. I want to know where you got it, and I want to know now."

Mandy replied with the same answer as before. "Fuck you."

Inwardly, Rip winced. Greta had pretty much stretched her patience as far as it would go. As night drew closer so did the risk to others. If there were any more of the books come nightfall there was a chance another foolish human was going to try and use them.

They needed to know more about them, and they needed to know it *now.*

He could feel Greta's urgency, and her disgust.

If the girl had known anything about Greta, she might have given a different answer. She might have just told Greta what she needed to know—they'd all be better for it.

Greta was still for a moment, still and quiet. Then she came out of the seat and came to stand in front of the girl. Her face was expressionless.

His heart ached as he watched them. Ached for Greta.

When each of them came to the Circle, they were granted

with gifts—increased strength, speed, near invulnerability. And each of them received a gift that was uniquely their own. Some of them became better hunters. Some were gifted with empathy, an ability that let them connect with those they would try to help in their new lives.

But not all of the gifts worked the same. Some were less desirable than others, and Greta's was one of the worst. She had been gifted with coercion, an ability that let her force her will on others. That gift could get ugly and it had its own built-in controlling mechanism. She couldn't use it without pain and the more she used it on the same person, the worse the pain got.

"Tell me what I need to know about the book."

Her voice had an edge of command in it, the sort of command that simply wouldn't be ignored. Hell, if Rip knew anything about the book that Greta didn't already know, he would have been singing like a songbird. Even though he didn't know anything, he was still hard-pressed to keep his mouth shut.

Grinding his teeth together, he closed his eyes and tried to block Greta out.

He was successful.

Mandy wasn't. She was all but screeching out her answers.

Over and over. Louder and louder.

Greta said, "Enough."

The coercion was broken and Rip opened his eyes, drawing a deep breath to dispel the lingering effects.

"You make any sense of that?" Greta asked him as she settled back down in her chair.

Rip lifted a hand. He was still trying to recall just what Mandy had said.

Once the words settled into some sort of cohesive order, it was like somebody had just doused him with a bucket of cold water. He didn't realize he was gaping at Mandy until Greta cleared her throat.

"Any way she could be making that up?" he asked, forcing the words out.

Greta just stared at him.

"I'll take that as a no."

Mandy gaped at Greta in horror. "What did you do to me?"

"Only what had to be done."

Rip waited until Greta had left the room before he moved to the girl. She stared at him with dark eyes, fear written all over her. It clung to her. "What did she do to me?"

"As she said, only what had to be done."

Mandy shook her head. "She *made* me tell her. I felt it, it was like she ripped it out of me and I couldn't stop her."

"You're right. You couldn't. I imagine it hurt."

Her throat worked as she swallowed. Bending down, he studied her face closely. Yes, she hurt—he could see the line of pain between her eyes, see it in the tense way she hunched over in the chair. With a cool smile, he said, "Good. Perhaps next time, you will just tell her what she needs to know when she asks you, instead of making her force it out of you."

He found Greta in the bedroom, sitting on the edge of the bed. She looked at him, her eyes dark in her wan face.

"Is it bad?" he murmured, kneeling in front of her.

"Not too bad." She gave him a weak smile. "She's already so scared it didn't take much to force the answer out of her. I'll be good in a minute."

And she would. He'd seen her in action before, knew how quickly she recovered from the pain. But he hated it. Hated every second that she had to suffer when she used the coercion.

"She said one of her friends gave her the book," Greta murmured, closing her eyes. "Now I have to find this friend of hers—this Fae chick."

"*We* have to find this friend of hers," Rip corrected. He settled on the bed behind her and laid his hands on her shoulders. She tensed at first and then, as he started to knead the tight muscles, she relaxed and leaned into his touch.

One good thing, though, at least his loyalties no longer felt divided. His need to help Greta, his obligation to his duty—they were one and the same now.

"You sure you're good to keep hanging around?" Greta studied his face, reaching up to trace her fingertips over his mouth. "Not that I don't love having you here, but you were on the move when we met up. You were trailing somebody, weren't you?"

"Yes." Unable to stay still, he got up and moved to the window, staring out in the fading light of day.

Greta was staring at him. He could feel it. Glancing over his shoulder, he said, "I'm on the trail of a Grimm named Fae."

Greta's jaw dropped. Stunned, she gaped at him. "Did you say you're on the trail of a Grimm? One of *us*?"

I've been living this life for close to five hundred years. I've seen a lot of things, heard a lot of things, done a lot of things. Not much managed to take me by complete and utter surprise, but Rip had just done it.

For the first time, I found myself wondering if I maybe I just needed to call it quits. I'm not stuck in this life. I've got an out option I can exercise when I see fit. Right now might be a good time, because if Rip was on the tail of another Grimm, maybe it was time to turn in my wings, so to speak, and just live out the rest of my life as a human.

I wasn't entirely certain I wanted to be in a world where the good guys weren't the good guys anymore. I didn't want to live in a world where the guardian angels were no angels.

"What do you mean you're trailing after a Grimm?"

He stared at me, his dark brown eyes unreadable. "You heard me well enough, Greta. I've been trying to track her for the past two months and every time I get close, she slips away."

"Why are you trailing after her?"

"To see if she remembers how to make hot-cross buns— nobody makes them like she used to," he said. Broad shoulders rose and fell in a sigh and then he turned away from the window to pace the room. "You know why I'm after her, Greta. I wouldn't be assigned to this if there wasn't a problem."

"Could there be a mistake?" I really wanted him to say, *Yeah, I think there's a mistake and once I find her, we can clear all of this up.* But he wasn't going to do that. I could see the answer in his eyes.

If Mandy had gotten the book from a Grimm, there was no mistake.

"What do you do when you find her?"

Rip shot me a look over his shoulder. "When did you make the choice, Greta? Do you remember the year?"

I scowled. "What does that have to do with anything?"

"I'm just wondering. You're older than I am—you were doing this before I was even born. How can you possibly have any bit of naiveté left inside you?"

Naïve?

I gaped at him. He'd just called me naïve.

I was born in 1501. I didn't have a *naïve* bone left in my body, and hadn't for some time. "I am *not* naïve," I snarled.

"Then you know what I'll do when I find her. I'll do the only thing I can do."

I rubbed the heel of my hand over my chest. My heart...it hurt. I fisted my hand around the medallion I wore. It was just like the one Rip wore. Just like the one this "Fae" would be wearing...if she really was a Grimm. I didn't know her. I hadn't heard of her, but that didn't mean anything. Like I said, there are a lot of us.

"You'll take her wings," I murmured.

"Yes." He crossed his arms over his chest.

"Will you kill her?"

Rip just stared at me.

"Of course you'll kill her," I muttered. "It's not like she's likely to see the error of her ways. It's not like she's going to relinquish her immortality or face the consequences. Dear God, maybe I am naïve."

I looked at him from the corner of my eye. He sighed and crossed the floor to stand in front of me. "No...you're not."

"You just told me I was."

He cupped my face in his hand, rubbed his thumb over my lower lip. Just like earlier, that simple gesture had my knees going weak. It had my heart racing. It had me wanting to press my mouth to his and find some measure of comfort, some measure of heat to ease the cold ache in my heart.

"You're not naïve. You just like to see the best in people. It's why you're so good at what you do, why you've been able to do it for so long. You always see the best in others."

"Not always." I grimaced. There had been plenty of times in my life when I hadn't seen anything but the worst. Like Hans. Like my stepmother...no. Not going to think about them. At least not right now. I had enough gloom, doom and despair weighing down on me.

"Well, I guess this means we're partners for the time being."

Rip stared down at me. He shifted his hand from my face to my neck, his long, talented fingers working the muscles there. "How is your headache now?"

"Gone." It hadn't been a bad one. Barely more than a pinch. It wasn't the pain that bothered me—it was actually having to use the damned gift. If there was one thing about my existence that I would change, it would be the coercion. Having a so-called gift that let me force my will on others was something that left a bad taste in my mouth, even after close to five centuries.

I'd been at the mercy of somebody stronger before. I knew what it was like to be forced into doing things I didn't like. Now I was in a position where I often had to do the same to others. Maybe that's why that gift had been given to me, though. Since I knew how awful it was to have all choice stripped away, maybe I was less likely to abuse it.

"I've got a feeling though the headaches are only just beginning. Somehow I don't think Mandy is going to happily offer up the rest of the information we need."

I finished strapping on my weapons and slid out of the bedroom.

Mandy huddled on her seat, refusing to so much as look my way.

"I'm sorry," I said quietly.

She flinched at the sound of my voice. If she could have covered her ears, she probably would have.

I sighed and turned away, staring out the window. Night had fallen. It was time to head out, but I still didn't know what we were supposed to do with Mandy. It didn't seem wise to leave her here tied to a chair, but I couldn't trust her to stay if I untied her either. If she left, she was a sitting duck.

"How did you do that?"

I glanced back at Mandy's face and before she could look away, I caught a glimpse of the stark horror in her eyes.

"It's just part of what I am."

"What do you mean—a part of what you are?"

"Just that." I turned and faced her, tried to decide what to tell her, how much I even had time to tell her.

"Joey…" Her voice caught on his name and she blinked away the tears that threatened to fall. "He called you Grimm. But the guy calls you Greta—is that your name? Greta Grimm?"

"Heaven, no. Greta Grimm sounds like some sort of Goth strip act." I smiled at her, hoping to put her at ease.

But how could she be at ease when she was tied to a chair? Soberly, she stared at me. "Then why did he call you Grimm?"

"It's what I am."

She was confused. I could see it. I wanted to explain, but I couldn't. Not right now. Sighing, I said, "Look, I can't explain right now. But I will—it's stuff you need to know."

Rip entered the room. I glanced over my shoulder at him. He had his black leather coat on, his long blond hair pulled back and an expressionless mask on his features.

"Time?"

He nodded curtly. His eyes slid to Mandy and I blew out a breath. "I think we need to untie her."

"She'll run."

Tucking my hands into my back pockets, I turned and stared at her. "I'm hoping she won't. Because if she runs, we'll just follow her. You're in too deep now, Mandy. You can't get away now. Besides, if you run and we *don't* find you, you'll end up wishing we did in the few seconds you have once you realize you're about to die."

As I spoke to her, I felt something dance along down my spine.

A whisper of danger.

The promise of pain.

The hunger for death.

The muscles in my back went tight and I reached for my blade. Shooting Rip a narrow look, I said, "They've found us. Undo the cuffs."

Rip shook his head. "Bad idea."

"We don't have a choice. If we don't untie her she's a sitting duck."

"Even untied, she can't hope to face them."

I glared at him. "No, but she can *run*. The cuffs, Rip. *Now*."

The girl looked back and forth between the two of us. Apprehension skittered across her face as Rip stalked around her. Metal links clinked and then he dealt with the ropes. The second she was free, she lunged to her feet only to freeze in mid-step as I cut her off. "Bad things are coming, Mandy, and they are probably looking for *you*."

"Me?" She shook her head. "But I haven't done anything."

I sighed in disgust and turned my back to her. "Just a word of warning. If you take off running, I'm going to be too busy to come after you." I shot her a look over my shoulder and added, "So if you want to live, I suggest you stay put. Whether you want to believe it or not, whether you like it or not, you're safe with us."

"Yeah, because being handcuffed to a chair for hours on end is just so very safe, so very comforting," she mocked. Shaking her head, she started to back away, keeping Rip and me in her line of vision.

Something slammed into the door.

The solid oak shuddered in its frame.

I gave Mandy one last look. "Don't say I didn't warn you."

Then I braced myself. I had a bad feeling that whatever was on the other side of that door, Rip and I were going to have our hands full. Incorporeal demons couldn't bang on a door—at least the ones that were strong enough to find their way here.

Unless of course it was yet another *bocan*—something that had been *brought* here.

Great. So we were either facing fully manifested demons in full possession of bodies, or monsters like the *bocan*.

There was another blow and then the door was knocked clear off its hinges. Man, I was going to have to give the landlord some serious bucks to make up for this. Staying on the balls of my feet, I waited.

Two *orin* came through. The bodies they wore were young, about Mandy's age. They hadn't had the bodies long, I don't think. One came for me. The other went for Mandy, only to be blocked by Rip. He pulled out that wicked, double-edged blade of his and went to work. I waited until mine was close enough and then I struck. I was rather limited by the knife. I really needed to get one of Rip's little toys.

Blood flew. The air was thick with the sounds of my labored breaths and the grunts, snarls and swears from the demon-possessed. Rip barely made a sound, save the way the wind whistled as he cut through the air. He had his *orin* down in under a minute. Then he came up and skewered the one who had faced off with me.

It wasn't over, though.

I heard a sibilant hiss and turned my head. As I found myself staring into the flat, dead gaze of a *bocan*, I muttered, "Why me?"

The *bocan* had damn near gutted Rip this time around. He sucked in a deep breath of air and tried not to collapse. The wound in his side was bleeding sluggishly. His heart hammered somewhere in the vicinity of his ears and he cast one final look around the room before stumbling over to lean against the wall.

Greta stood in the middle of the room, splattered with blood. One of her shirt sleeves was half torn off. The other sleeve had a long slice in it. Through the slice, he could see a narrow red mark where the flesh was knitting itself together. She had a black eye, but her body was already absorbing that injury. In a few more minutes, he wouldn't be able to see it.

All in all, she was in much better shape than he was.

She turned her head, staring at him, her blue eyes unreadable.

The girl was huddling against the wall, splattered with blood and gore, her face locked in a mask of terror.

Rip had only two clear thoughts in his mind—*Thank God, Greta isn't hurt.* Followed closely by *Thank God, that silly girl at least had the presence of mind not to get in the way.*

The rest of any coherent thought was lost as hot blood pumped out of his wound. His head spun in dizzying circles. Even with the wall at his back, he could barely stay upright and ended up keeling over onto the floor.

Blood roared in his ears. Dimly, he thought heard Greta. *Panicked*, he thought to himself. *She sounds like she's panicking...like she's scared.*

But he'd be damned if he could understand why.

The darkness was getting heavier and heavier. Greta touched him. He'd know her touch anywhere. Cool, soft and strong. He wanted to cover her hand with his, but he realized he couldn't move his arms. Or his head. Not even his eyelids...

Chapter Nine

He can't die. I've lost track of how many times I said that to myself in the past fifteen minutes. Dozens. Maybe even hundreds.

Still, I kept looking at him, kept listening to the fragile beat of his heart and waiting for it to fade. The wound on his belly was deep. Very deep. If Rip had been wholly human, he would have died almost immediately.

As it was, the blood's flow had slowed to a sluggish pace, but not because the wound was clotting. He was bleeding out. Could we bleed out? I really didn't know.

I heard footsteps behind me and I drew my blade, spinning around. I made a sound I didn't even recognize—I think I must have growled. It sounded nothing like me. Nothing like my voice. It took me a second to realize who it was standing there.

Mandy. The girl responsible for this mess. The girl with the weird purple eyes and a penchant for finding trouble.

"Leave me alone," I snarled at her.

She stared past me, her gaze locked on Rip's face. She shook her head and said, "This isn't right—this is really fucked up, lady. How can he still be alive?"

"You don't hear very well, do you? *Leave. Me. Alone.*"

She swallowed and took a deep breath and when I went to turn back to Rip, she grabbed my arm. "I can help him. I don't know how in the hell he's still alive, but I can help."

I didn't waste my time asking how. If she was willing to help... I stood off to the side and watched as she looked him over. "I need to get his feet elevated—he's got to be going into shock," she told me.

"He..." I blew out a breath and then finally just said it.

"He's not a normal guy. You can't treat him like he is."

Mandy shot me a narrow look. "I figured that much out when he didn't drop to the ground after that...thing did this. But he's lost blood, everybody needs blood or we wouldn't have it, so I'm going to treat him like I'd treat anybody who'd lost a lot of blood."

I ran and fetched and carried for her, and watched while she used the pitiful first-aid kit and clean rags to staunch the flow of blood. I threatened to rip her head off when she said we needed to call for an ambulance. There was no way. She probably couldn't tell yet, but his wound was already healing from the inside out. If a doctor got Rip in his hands, there would be all sorts of questions we couldn't answer.

"I said no hospital." Then I glared at her. "Do you even know what you're doing? You sure as hell aren't old enough to be a doctor."

"I'm a...look, I can help him." Her eyes skittered away from mine. "I can help. Do you want me to try or not?"

"Yes. Try." I was getting little curious about just how she thought she might help. Very curious.

A few seconds later, my question was answered. She pushed Rip's tattered shirt away and laid one hand on either side of the gaping injury. The warmth I felt coming from her was staggering—it was like her body had suddenly become a furnace. It blasted off her in waves and she stared out into the distance, her eyes opaque and unseeing.

Then, quick as a wish, she was done. The wounds on his belly were still open, but they looked days, maybe weeks old and his bleeding had stopped. She sagged over him, bracing her body upright on her hands as she sucked air in and out of her lungs.

"He needs a hospital," she finally said. "I took care of the bleeding but he's weak from how much blood he lost."

I knelt down beside him and stroked my fingers down the side of his face. He was cool. But he breathed. And his heartbeat, though thready and faint, sounded a little stronger. "Thank you."

I shot her a look and murmured, "I never would have guessed you for a healer."

She didn't answer, just stared off over my shoulder. "You need to get him to a hospital."

"No. But he'll be okay now that the bleeding has stopped." We couldn't do hospitals. Too many questions. Too much paperwork. Too many gaping holes in our background.

"He's not *fine*. He nearly bled to death and he needs to replace that blood."

I glanced at her. "He'll be fine, trust me."

"Fine. Let all my hard work go to waste." She shook her head and then smirked at me. "Well, here's the good news. I'm leaving, and you can't stop me, because you really do need to keep an eye on Superman there."

She started for the door.

I was between her and the exit before she had taken two steps. She jerked back, startled.

"Sorry. You can't leave."

Her eyes narrowed. "You can't stop me without hurting me and I don't think you're going to do that."

"A few hours ago, you were pretty damn certain."

She jerked a shoulder in a shrug and said, "That was before... Well, whatever *that* was. I'm leaving, So unless you're willing to knock me out and tie me down, get out of my way."

I smiled. "Oh, I'm perfectly willing. And *that* is something you and I need to talk about. But not now."

"You can't make me stay here and watch that guy die." She had a wide-eyed look now, an expression of remembered horror that dug at me. "If you won't take him for *real* help, he's going to die from shock alone and I can't watch it. Let me leave because I can't watch this."

"He isn't going to die." She wouldn't believe me. But I could prove it to her. Taking a deep breath, I asked, "If I could prove to you that he's healing, that he'll be okay, would you stop trying to leave? You'll be in more danger than you can understand, being alone right now."

"How are you going to prove he isn't dying?" She folded her arms around her middle. She tried to sound defiant, but she just sounded...broken. "You have some kind of life support around here you're going to whip out any second? Can you get an IV going on him? Restore some of the fluids he's lost? I stopped him from losing more, but I can't do anything else than that. Only time, rest and medical care can do that."

"You're wrong." I reach for my knife and held out my left

arm. Holding her gaze, I slashed it down my forearm.

She yelped and went to grab the knife. I pulled it back and held my bleeding arm between us, watching as the blood flowed, watching as it dripped down my arm, watching as the blood stopped.

She saw it too.

Her eyes were so wide the white showed all around her pupils. She hadn't blinked, hadn't breathed since I'd cut myself. I grabbed one of the rags we hadn't used for Rip and wiped the blood away, revealing the scar underneath. My flesh had already knit itself back together and now all that remained was a dark, vibrant red line that faded with every heart beat.

"He's like me. He was already healing before you touched him. You stopped the bleeding, so now his body can focus on healing. He will be fine."

She didn't want to believe me.

But I think at that point, she was too overwhelmed to run.

It was hours later. Rip slept. He'd woken twice and each time, I forced a bottle of water down his throat. A little before noon, Mandy had checked the bandage on his abdomen and she'd ended tossing the filthy rags in the garbage.

He had three shallow wounds on his abdomen, but every second that passed saw them healing more and more.

"So what are you?"

I looked up from my place at Rip's side. I'd been brushing his hair back from his face without even realizing it. Touching him made me feel better—reminded me he was alive. He would heal. Even though my *head* knew that, my heart needed the comfort. My heart is still very much one-hundred percent human, no matter how old I am. He was no longer quite so pale, so I knew his body was repairing the damage. I really needed to wake him up and make him eat, but I hated to disturb him.

"Are you going to tell me or just keep petting him?"

"Tell you what?" I blushed but didn't stop stroking his hair.

"What are you? You aren't one of those...things. But you sure as hell can't be human. People don't heal like that."

"I'm not *not* human," I hedged. I'd been mentally prepping

myself to have this talk with her, but I still didn't know where to start.

She was watching me with those weird purple eyes, her gleaming black hair hanging in her face. "What in the hell does that mean? You're either human or you're not. Are you like...I dunno...an alien? Because *humans* don't heal like that."

"It means that I *am* human. Or at least I used to be." I held out my hands and shrugged. "I *was* just like you...once. But it was a very long time ago and it's a very long story."

"He's not going anywhere." She glanced at Rip and then back at me and added, "Apparently, neither am I. Entertain me."

Rubbing the back of my neck, I wondered if I really wanted to mess with this right now.

You don't have a choice.

I worried that might very well be true. I rested my head against the headboard of the bed. We'd hauled Rip into my bedroom once I was convinced the bleeding had stopped. Mandy had come with us—I didn't trust her not to leave, but I couldn't tie her up again either. It just didn't seem right.

"One of them called me a Grimm," I said softly, reaching up and folding my hand around the medallion I wore. "That's what I am. That's what we both are."

"A Grimm?" Her forehead puckered as she scowled. "What in the hell is a Grimm?"

"It's just what we're called."

She glanced at Rip, then back at me. Fear sparked through her eyes and she opened her mouth to ask me something, only to stop. Then start again. It took her three minutes to finally ask me anything. "We... You mean more than just you and him, don't you?"

"Yes." I toyed with my medallion as I worked my way through possible explanations, discarding them almost as quickly as I considered them. "There are a lot of us. And we're here to protect people from creatures like the things we faced earlier."

"You mean that big...what in the hell was that thing?"

"It's called a *bocan*—it's an old Irish name for what Americans call the bogey man." I stared into the living room. Most of the blood had been cleaned up. For now, the bodies were wrapped in blankets and waiting by the door—it wouldn't be long before I had to deal with them, though.

The *bocan* would be the hard part, though. How had Rip gotten rid of the first one?

I made myself focus back on Mandy. I was having a lot of trouble staying focused right now. "But the *bocan* wasn't the only monster. The other two were monsters as well. The *bocan* could just kill you. The others—by the time you realize you can't get away, you only *wish* they would just kill you."

"But they were just...people."

"No." I closed my eyes. "They used to be people, and then they did something stupid—like using a book to call up an *orin*. Or maybe they were just weak to begin with. They are worse than the *bocan*. A lot worse."

"That thing damn near tore your friend to shreds. It could kill me in a heartbeat. What could be worse that that?"

"A quick death can be a blessing," I said. Then I shrugged.

"You won't find quick with the others. They are called *orin*—they feed on souls. And that's much, much worse than just dying." I watched her now—it was important that she understand, that she realize. Her soul wasn't weak, so the only way the *orin* could take her was if she let them. "You know the legends about vampires—how they need blood to live. Well, an *orin* is like a vampire, but you can't *see* it. It has no physical body on this plain and it uses its magic to take one."

"What do you mean, on this plain?"

"There are different plains—different levels of existence, so to speak. You and me, we live in the mortal plain. Then there's the demon plain—the netherplain are where the demons are trapped." I lifted a brow at her. "Do you believe in God?"

She snorted. "As in the biblical one? Hell, no. It's just crock."

"You need to rethink that line of thought." And she probably would. If she decided to become one of us. It's hard to ignore what's right in front of your face. "Anyway, the netherplain is where the demons are trapped and most of them will stay trapped there, physically at least, until the end of the world. Then they will be given free reign, for a time."

I drew my legs to my chest and rested my elbows on my knees. With a sigh, I said, "Unfortunately, a lot of demons are smart. Their physical bodies can't break free, but the strong ones can manifest for short periods of time on this plane. If they can get themselves a body, they can even walk among us for as long the body lives. In the case of the *orin*, they can make that body live a very, very long time."

That's what would happen to her—if I failed. "That is what they want you for, Mandy. They want your body, and they want your soul. If you give them half a chance, they'll take it and once they do, I can't help you." *All I can do is kill you.*

"How?" she demanded. "How can they take my body?"

"With your permission."

"Like I'd give it." She gave me a bizarre look, her eyes full of doubt and skepticism.

"But you were getting ready to do just that when I first found you with the book. It's bastardized Latin, but basically you were getting ready to toss out the welcome mat for one of them."

She didn't want to believe me. I could see it. But my gut told me she did. Or at least she was starting to. Poor kid. The warm gold of her skin went white and her throat worked as she gulped.

She looked away for a minute then looked back at me and asked, "What happens once one of them gets inside you?"

"You die." There's no soft, easy way to explain that. "It feeds on your soul and once everything that is *you* is gone, the body becomes demon property and then it starts reaching out and munching on the souls of those in your life. Anybody and everybody you come in contact with. For as long as the body lives, and that can be a very, very long time."

"That's crazy." She surged to her feet and started to pace the bedroom. She didn't go far from me, though. She kept sending skittish looks into the living room and I suspected that as much as she might want to run, she didn't want to risk coming in close range to the dead bodies. "This is all crazy. It's all insane. Demons aren't real."

"I bet there are a lot of people who would insist that a girl healing a man with just her touch isn't real either," I said quietly.

She shot me a sidelong look.

I gestured towards the living room where the *bocan*'s corpse awaited disposal. "Go tell that to the *bocan*," I offered. "Explain what that thing is, if it's not a demon. I'm kind of curious how you'll rationalize it away."

She just shook her head and continued to pace.

"Mandy."

She stopped in her tracks to look at me.

"Tell me where you got the book."

"I told you that already. A friend gave it to me. Her name's Fae. She... Well, she looks out after people."

I looked her over from head to toe and then snorted. "Darling, it's been a long time since you've let people look out for you." She was diamond-hard, through and through. Or at least that was the image she projected and if I hadn't seen her in very dire predicaments, I might have even bought it.

She might need a good slap on the head but she didn't need somebody holding her hand either. Nor would she allow it.

"I don't exactly *let* her look out for me. She just... Well, she was always around. Always willing to listen." As she spoke, her features got colder and colder, her gaze darkening with anger.

She fooled you, didn't she? She sucked you in. I think I felt sorry for her. Whoever this Fae was, Mandy had believed in her. And somehow, Fae had convinced Mandy that she'd returned that belief.

Having illusions shattered can be so very painful.

It was nearing dawn when she spoke again.

"So what exactly is a Grimm? I mean, where do you come from? Why are you here?"

"Didn't I already explain that? We're here to protect people from the things that try to escape from the netherplains."

She shook her head. "But where do you come from? You said you were like me once. What made you like you are now? And why in the hell are you called *Grimms*? Of all things."

"Because guardian angels just sounds so...theatrical." I smirked inwardly at the look on her face.

"Guardian angel. As in wings. Harp. That kind of thing?"

I jerked my shoulder in a shrug. "Do you see any wings? They would kind of stick out here, don't you think? And I couldn't play a harp if I tried. But yeah, guardian angel—that's the general idea."

Now she really wanted to think I was crazy. I smiled.

She glanced at the door. I could all but see the wheels spinning in her head. She wanted to make a run for it. The night was pretty much gone. She'd feel safer in the daylight.

Who knows—maybe if she ran long enough, hard enough, and didn't get her hands on another book, she just might be safe.

But she didn't make a break for it.

"Let's say I buy the guardian angel bit." She didn't want to. But something wasn't letting her just brush me off either. I wonder what?

"Okay. Let's say just that."

"Explain why a guardian angel would be called a Grimm—it sounds kind of... Well, I don't know...morbid, or freaky or..."

"Grim?" I offered with a smile. I shrugged again and said, "It wasn't my idea. Up until a couple hundred years ago, we didn't really *have* a name. Then stories about us started getting out. Not the real story, though. Just a few details, here and there. Stories started getting passed around, handed down from one generation to the next. One of the older ones had an idea on how to hide us—in plain sight. Fictionalize us—so to speak."

She stared at me with a dumb, blank look on her face.

"You ever heard of Hansel and Gretel?"

She ran a hand over her hair and shook her head. "You mean like with the bread crumbs, candy houses and all that? The wicked witch?"

"You don't know your fairy tales very well. In the story, it was a gingerbread house. But in reality, it was just a little house. No wicked witch. Hans, though..." I grimaced. I didn't want to go into detail about Hans. Even though time has faded those memories quite a bit, it still took me back to a bad place.

"You're fucking kidding me."

Chapter Ten

Rip drifted awake slowly. He could sense Greta was near. Feel her hand on his brow. The soft, gentle touch of her fingers stroking his hair. She wasn't scared or worried, so that must mean they were safe—which meant he could enjoy waking up next to her.

They were talking.

Caught in the twilight between sleep and waking, he could hear Greta talking to...somebody. What was her name? Mandy—yes, that was it. Mandy. They were talking.

"You ever heard of Hansel and Gretel?" Greta asked.

"You mean like with the bread crumbs, candy houses and all that? The wicked witch?"

"You don't know your fairy tales very well. In the story, it was a gingerbread house. But in reality, it was just a little house. No wicked witch. Hans, though..." her voice trailed off, but he knew her well enough to sense the pain, the remembered fear that lingered even after all this time.

He forced himself to come completely awake. He opened his eyes and stared up at Greta's face.

She wasn't looking at him.

She was watching the girl.

From the corner of his eye, he could see Mandy, see the disbelief on her face, the edge of cynical laughter trying to work its way free.

She shook her head and snapped, "You're fucking kidding me."

She started to pace, her heeled boots thudding dully on the floor. "Insane. Why in the *hell* do I always end up with insane people around me?"

"She's not insane," Rip said softly. His throat was dry—dry as a desert. Damn, he was thirsty. He didn't even have to say anything though. Greta pushed a bottle of water into his hands and he eased halfway up in the bed, wincing as the healing muscles in his belly screamed a reminder at him.

Like he could forget that he'd been gutted not that long ago. He downed half the bottle before lying back down.

Mandy was watching him like she expected him to come after her at any second. Pale and spooked. She stared at his torso with an intensity that had him shifting on the bed until he realized what she was staring at. His healing wounds. Almost already completely healed. He pressed a hand to his stomach and shot Greta a look. He knew how bad it had been. He should have spent another day or two, at least, healing.

"How long was I out?"

"Only six hours."

Glancing at his stomach, he looked back at her. "I don't heal this fast."

"Mandy helped you." She glanced at the girl and smiled faintly. "Apparently, she's got a healing gift."

"She's a healer."

"Yep." Greta slouched over the bed, bracing her elbows on the mattress as she slanted a look at Mandy. "She's got a gift that lets her heal some damn bad wounds, but she doesn't believe in demons, in God, in us."

Mandy sneered at them. "I'm in the room, hello? And the jury's still out on the demon thing. The guardian-angel bit, though, that is messed up. No way."

"Doesn't it stand to reason that if demons exist, so do angels?" Rip asked. He couldn't stand being flat on his back—left him feeling too vulnerable. He eased back up and shifted until he could rest against the headboard. It helped. Some.

"I still haven't decided on the demons. And what does one have to do with the other?"

"Balance?" he suggested. "If there's good, there's evil. If there's evil, there's good."

She just glared at him for a few seconds before looking back at Mandy. "So if you're Gretel, who is he supposed to be? Hansel?"

Rip snarled and almost came out of the bed. Greta reached out and rested a hand on his thigh, stopping him. She gave him a gentle smile and shook her head. "Take it easy, darling. She doesn't know."

Darling... Rip wasn't one from pet names or endearments. So why did it sound so wonderful for her to call him *darling*? He reached down and covered Greta's hand with his, lacing their fingers. The sight of their joined hands mesmerized him. Glaring at Mandy from under his lashes, he said quietly, "Hans was a sick dog that should have been put down long before he was."

Greta squeezed his hand. "His real name was Hans. Not Hansel. He was called Hans but my name really was Gretel. I just changed it after...after Hans died."

"This is so confusing," Mandy muttered. She rubbed her temples and slumped against the wall. She looked exhausted, like a stiff wind would blow her over. She wouldn't let it, though. She had a well of strength in her.

Rip could feel it. At least now he understood why Greta had been so drawn to the girl.

"If you're not Hansel—Hans—whatever, then who are you?"

"My name is Rip."

A frown darkened her face. Squinting at him, she said, "Okay, so I'm not as up to date on my fairy tales as Gretel of breadcrumbs and candy houses, but I can't think of a single fairy tale with a guy named Rip."

"That's because I'm not from a fairy tale." Rip shrugged restlessly and took another drink of water. His stomach was starting to rumble. He needed food and he needed it yesterday. His body could heal damage, but it still needed fuel. "Not all of us are."

Greta grinned at him. "No, he's not a fairy tale. He's more of a folk tale. Think of Rip Van Winkle."

He scowled at her. It shouldn't surprise him that she knew, although he hadn't shared that story with others. It wasn't one of the shining moments in his life. The only people who knew were those responsible. Himself...Fae. And probably the bastard in charge of them.

"Isn't that the guy who slept for like a hundred years or something?"

Rip rolled out of the bed. His legs were still unsteady, but he needed food, and he needed out of the damn bed. "It wasn't a hundred years. It was only five months—and I didn't *sleep*."

He had been hypnotized. There was a very big difference.

"Washington Irving put his own little artistic touches to the story," Greta said, watching him as he reached for his jeans. They were blood-stained and torn, but clean. Somebody must have washed and dried them.

His shirt was done for, though. Unless he wanted to walk around with gaping tears in it. He wadded it up and tossed it on the bed and then turned to look at Mandy. She still had the horrified, yet entranced look on her face. Like she didn't want to hear more, but needed to. "I didn't sleep," he said again. "I was already..." he reached for the words, wondered how much Mandy had been told.

"A Grimm," Greta said, as though she'd read his mind. She gave him a small smile. "I've already explained that part—or most of it."

He nodded. "I was already a Grimm, working with my trainer." He closed his eyes and then opened them, staring at Greta. He hadn't ever thought he would love again. Not until he met this woman.

"I met a woman. Fell in love with her. We had been married for a year when the war started. You'd know it as the Revolutionary War." Folding his arms over his chest, he stared out the window. "She didn't know about what I was. I never told her. She wouldn't have understood. Wouldn't have believed me. I left to fight in the war without telling her what I was. I wrote her letters. All the time. She would write back, telling me how she missed me, how much she loved me, how she longed for me to come back to her, safe and whole. And I did."

He closed his eyes and remembered what happened the day he returned.

His beloved wife had been with another man. A man who Rip had loved dearly, like a brother. "I came home and found her longing and loving another man—my best friend."

He'd nearly killed them both.

He might have if Fae hadn't been there.

She'd been drawn there—much the same way Greta had been drawn to Ann Arbor. With the knowledge that she was needed.

He hadn't seen the other woman in nearly forty years, not

since she had trained him.

"Not the nicest homecoming," Mandy said. Then she shrugged. "But that's people for you. You can't trust anybody. Especially those who claim to love you."

"You're awful young to have that outlook on life," Greta said softly. She moved up to stand behind Rip. She slid her arms around his waist and pressed a kiss to his spine. In a voice too quiet for Mandy to hear, she whispered, "I'm so sorry."

He covered her hands with his and squeezed. Turning in her embrace, he wrapped an arm around her shoulders and held her close. "I wanted to kill them. I believe I would have killed them. But others had different plans. There was one of us there—a Grimm who had the ability to hypnotize others, with just a look. You look into her eyes and the whole world falls away."

Mandy's eyes widened.

"She used her gift to get me away from there and she kept me under until she knew I wouldn't act out of temper. I was gone for five months and when I came back, I found out the two of them, my wife and my friend, had died the past winter. I left, and I never returned." He grimaced and said, "How some fool writer managed to come up with the idea that I was some layabout who slept away twenty years, I don't know."

Mandy gaped at him.

"You seriously expect me to believe that. That you're really Rip Van Winkle, that's Gretel from Hansel and Gretel, and that there are freaks out there that can hypnotize you—keep you under control for five months? You are *nuts*."

"Possibly." Rip jerked a shoulder in a shrug. "After you've lived to see centuries come and go, you don't see reality the same way."

His stomach chose that moment to growl, very loudly. Glancing down at Greta, he said, "I've got to get some food in me if I expect to be any good when she comes looking for us."

"Who?" Mandy demanded.

But Rip didn't answer. He needed food about as much as Mandy needed to breathe in that moment. His healing body demanded it.

She trailed along after them into the kitchen, watching as Greta nudged Rip to one of the stools at the breakfast bar. "Sit. Rest. I can do up some food—we could all use it at this point."

He would have rather done it himself, just to get away from Mandy's inquisitive stare. But he didn't argue, especially not when Greta dropped a couple of packages of peanut butter crackers in front of him. It wasn't anywhere near enough, but it would help while she got together a real meal.

"Who's coming after us?"

"The woman I told you about—the one who kept me from killing my wife and my friend," Rip said, popping a cracker into his mouth and munching on it.

"Why would she come after us?" Mandy just stared at him.

"Not us." He drank the rest of the water from the bottle and then braced his elbows on the smooth wooden surface of the bar. "You, Mandy. She's coming after you."

"*Me?*"

Rip watched her intently. "The woman who saved me—the woman who trained me—the woman who kept me from making the worst mistake of my life—her name was Fae."

I wondered if he was aware of the pain reflecting in his brown eyes. He wore an expressionless mask, his face cold and remote. Like an ice sculpture. But the pain in his eyes... I hurt for him.

I hurt for Mandy, as well. And I thanked God I had Mary in my past, instead of Fae. Mary had made the choice to give up her wings, live a mortal's life, die a mortal's death.

That's the out option, you know. If it gets to be too much, if we get to be too lonely, or just too damn tired, we can give up our wings and live a completely mortal life. We'll age, and we'll die. That's what Mary did.

Even after all this time, I still miss her.

She was one of the truest people I'd ever known. She'd made me, and I'm not talking about her making me into a Grimm—she'd helped me become who I am. After all the things Hans did to me, if there hadn't been Mary, I don't know who I would have become.

She was more than a mother than to me, even before she'd brought me into the Circle.

I can't imagine how hard this must be for Rip. We all

tended to bond to those that brought us into the Circle. Sometimes a parent-child bond, sometimes a sibling bond, but always close.

Fae had been that to Rip. And then she'd turned on us all.

"Fae," Mandy echoed, her voice faint and reedy. She shook her head and backed away, staring at Rip with horror. "This is a sick fucking joke. First you tell me you're guardian angels. That you're the good guys. Then you tell me I'm trying to conjure up demons, and the woman who's been a dear friend to me—one of my *only* friends—is a guardian angel too, but if she's one of you, and if those books can really do what you say, why would she give me one?"

"I don't know," Rip said. "Perhaps she's lost any and all grip on reality. Perhaps it got to be too much."

"Wouldn't guardian angels be above that?"

Rip pinned her with a flat stare and said, "We're hardly perfect. Our bodies heal, our bodies don't age, but in our hearts we're human. We have every human weakness that any other human has, every other strength. I don't know why. But she's coming after you, and if she can't get you to do what she wants, she'll just as soon kill you."

I stopped messing with the meal when Mandy threw something at Rip. He knocked it out of the way, his reflexes only marginally slowed by his injury. He stared at her, and there was sympathy and sadness in his gaze now.

"You're lying," Mandy said, shaking her head. "This is all some kind of fucking sick joke—or you're just so fucking crazy, it's not even funny."

She disappeared from the room and I braced myself, expecting to hear the front door open. But her footsteps didn't even go near the door. I heard another door open, then slam shut.

The basement door. She was hiding down there. Away from us. Away from the truth. Poor kid. She probably even knew she was hiding.

Rip looked at me and sighed. "Should you talk to her? Should I?"

"Neither." I shook my head and went back to the food. "Just give her some time. It's one hell of a load we just dropped on her."

After I fed him, I urged him back to bed and then settled in beside him, stroking my hand up and down the hard, smoothly-muscled planes of his abdomen. I felt my way along each of the fading scars.

In a day or two, they'd be completely gone, but I don't think I'd ever forget how they looked, those hideous, horrible open wounds, pumping out blood in rhythm with his heart.

"I thought you wanted me to rest," Rip said, his voice drowsy.

"I do." I pushed up on my elbow and looked at him. I loved looking at him. His face was so unbelievably beautiful—perfect, even. And his eyes—melted chocolate. I could get lost in those eyes.

Resting a hand just above his heart, I whispered, "I'm sorry about your wife and your friend. I more or less figured out who you were a while back, but I didn't know... Well, I didn't know. That must have been hell for you." I smirked and added, "And to think you tried to tell me that not all of us have such shadowy, dark stories."

"Mine is nothing compared to what happened to you." He covered my hand with his, stroked his thumb along the back of it.

"Do you know? I mean, all of it?"

He shook his head. "No. If you want to tell me, I will listen. But no, I don't know all. I just know enough."

"How?"

He glanced away and then back at me. "Through Fae. She knew your Mary, you know. They were close at one time. Fae knew of you because of Mary, and then after that night, I learned of you from her."

"So the psycho Grimm who is out hurting people instead of helping them is spilling out my life story?" I winced. I could do without that. Seriously.

He stroked a roughened fingertip along my jaw. "Not to everyone. She told me. I suspect, only me. Would you rather I not know?"

"I don't know. No. Yes." I blew out a breath and sat up, drawing my knees up and hugging them to my chest. "I just don't know."

He stroked a hand down my back. The warmth of his touch, the care, the passion he held in check, made me shudder. I shot him a look over my shoulder and said, "If I'm supposed to let you rest, then you really need to quit touching me like that."

"Like what?"

I rolled my eyes at him. "Like at all. Any time you touch me, all I want to do is get naked with you."

He waited a beat and then responded, "I don't mind you getting naked."

"You need to rest." I tried to mean it. Really.

But when he caught one of my braids and wrapped it around and around his wrist, drawing me closer, I knew I didn't.

We needed each other more than he needed rest.

We needed each other.

I glanced at the door as I leaned over him, my mouth just a whisper away from his. It was mostly closed, open enough that we could both hear Mandy if she started up the steps or tried to escape.

"Should we be doing this?" I asked him as he pressed his mouth to my jaw.

"We should." He grabbed the waistband of my shirt and stripped it away.

I threw a knee over his hips and straddled him. Through the layers of denim, I could feel his heat, feel how hard he was. He throbbed against me and I moaned, rolling my hips against him.

"You're right. We should."

"Your clothes are in the way," he whispered, pulling me down and burying his face between my breasts. He ran gentle hands up my back and sought out the clasp of my bra, slipping it free and pulling the silk and lace away from me. When he caught one nipple in his mouth, I groaned and reached down, threading my hands through his hair. The dark gold strands tangled around my hands.

Rip surged up, uncaring of the wound in his belly as he tucked me under his body and levered up onto his knees. He stripped away my jeans, then his own. Just before he would have come over me, I reached out and traced the wounds on his belly. "Are you feeling well enough? We don't know what will come tonight. You need to be ready."

He caught my hand and guided it to his cock. I folded my fingers around him and stroked. He shuddered and arched into my touch. "Trust me, I'm fine."

Then he came over me. I spread my legs to accommodate him, whimpering as he stroked his fingers along the sensitive flesh between my thighs. He pressed his thumb against my clit and stroked. He alternated between teasing strokes there and dipping his fingers in and out of my sex, spreading the heated moisture around.

I rocked against his hand and tugged on his shoulders. "Stop teasing me."

"But it's fun," he murmured, nipping my lower lip.

I worked a hand between us and closed my fingers around his sac, tightening them and tugging—gently at first, then harder and firmer.

His eyes narrowed and he growled, thrusting himself against me. "Don't," he rasped.

"But it's fun." I gave him a look of mock innocence and then grinned as he eased up onto his knees, one on either side of my hips, staring at my hand on his flesh. He cupped his cock in his hand and started to stroke, his breath leaving him in ragged bursts.

I tugged lightly, staring at him from under my lashes.

His golden hair fell across his shoulders, into his eyes. With his face in shadow, I could just barely make out the hungry glitter in his eyes. I tugged on him again and he groaned, his head falling back. He stroked himself harder and reached down with his other hand, covering mine and squeezing until I tightened my grip.

I winced, certain I had to be hurting him, but when I looked at him he had this look on his face. It took my breath away.

"Harder," he muttered, tugging on my hand again. He moved faster and faster and then, with a muffled shout, he came. The hot, wet fluid coated his hand and my belly.

I smiled up at him, but the smile faded as he crushed my mouth under his.

He kissed me like he was starving for me.

110

I opened for him—I opened my mouth for his kiss, my legs for his body...my heart for his. I needed him. So much. I'd been a fool to think I could convince myself otherwise. Ever since I'd walked away from him, I hadn't been living.

I had just existed.

He entered me with one deep, hard thrust. I wailed his name against his lips and he immediately froze, his long, lean body stiffening over mine. He tore his mouth away and swore. "Damn it, Greta, I'm sorry..."

I grabbed his shoulders. My nails pierced his flesh. Wrapping my legs around his hips, I whispered, "Don't you dare stop."

"I'm being too rough—"

"I won't break." I stared at him, reaching up to cup his cheek in my hand. "You'd never hurt me."

I knew that. Like I knew my own name, I knew he'd never hurt me.

Arching my hips, I rubbed myself against him and then flexed my inner muscles around his throbbing length. We both shuddered.

"Rip, please..."

He kissed me again and started to move. Deep, rough strokes, followed by a slow, lingering withdrawal. It was a teasing, taunting rhythm designed to drive me mad. I panted and wiggled and rocked underneath him, flexing around him as though I could keep him from pulling out. I needed him—needed more.

He stared at me. I felt lost in that gaze, lost in him. I traced one finger along his mouth. He caught the tip between his teeth and bit down lightly. Then he caught my hand and twined our fingers together. Lowering his head, he pressed his brow to mine and stared into my eyes. Like that, with our hands entwined and our gazes locked together, he rode me. The time for teasing was gone.

I could feel it, my climax, moving up on me hard and fast. But I didn't want to go without him. I flexed around him again and watched his lids flicker, watched as a sexy little snarl crossed his face. "Come with me," I whispered. "Stay with me."

"Always." He moved higher on my body and each stroke had him rubbing against my clit.

Harder. Faster. It built higher and higher, twisted me

111

tighter and tighter. Then it broke and I came with a moan, shuddering and shaking under him while he growled in his throat and slammed home, deep, deep inside me. His cock jerked and pulsed and then he was coming too.

He collapsed against me with his head pillowed between my breasts, working his arms around me. With our bodies tangled, I lay there panting and sucking in air. Cool air danced over my heated flesh. I could feel his heart pounding against me. It echoed the rhythm of my own.

I was drifting ever closer to sleep when I heard him speak.

"I love you."

Until Greta tensed in his arms, he hadn't realized he'd spoken out loud.

Inwardly, he swore. Hard and furious. Outwardly, he didn't allow himself much reaction. All he did was push up onto his elbows and look up at her. Waiting.

She blinked at him.

"What?"

He ran a hand along her thigh and shrugged. "You heard what I said."

"No, I didn't."

"You did." He slid his hand back up her thigh and rested it on the swell of her hip. "If you didn't hear me, you wouldn't look so terrified."

"I'm not terrified," she lied. Her voice shook as she said it.

"You are." Then he caught her hand, drew it to his lips. When she didn't pull away, he let himself breathe a little deeper. He kissed it and then laced their fingers together. "I love you. I think part of me loved you before I ever saw you. I think part of me was born loving you."

From under his lashes, he looked at her. "You can't tell me you don't feel something."

She ran her tongue along her lips and he closed his eyes. If he kept looking at her, he was going to kiss her again. And they needed to do this—he needed to tell her. And he needed to hear—either she loved him, or she just cared. If it was the latter, he needed to know, because he needed to be away from her.

She combed a hand through his hair and pressed against his head until he had his head pillowed between her breasts once more. "Yeah, I feel something. And yeah...maybe I am a little terrified."

"A little?"

A weak smile curled her lips. "Yeah. Maybe a little. Maybe a lot. Guess that's why I worked so hard to stay away from you for so long. I don't understand the mess inside me, Rip. Not at all."

"That's okay. I don't either. But we can figure out together."

She stared at him, shaking her head. "You've been in love before. I've never wanted to love anybody. I don't like letting people close."

"I never loved my wife the way I love you." He pressed a kiss to the inner curve of her breast and murmured, "I've never loved anybody the way I love you. I don't think I ever could. I was made to love you, and only you, like this."

Tears glittered in her blue eyes. "Wow. I never thought you the poetical, romantic type."

With a wolfish grin, he murmured, "Oh, I can get very romantic." Then he slid a hand between them and cupped her, pushing one finger into her hot, swollen pussy. "Would you like to see?"

"That's not romance, pal." She groaned and pressed her hips against his hand. "But I don't care."

Chapter Eleven

I made him rest more.

He'd nap for a few hours, then wake up hungry and thirsty. I'd feed him and then he'd be hungry for me.

On the third cycle, he didn't drift back to sleep immediately. He lay there with me in his arms. I rubbed my fingers across his scarred belly. Already, the scars were white and smooth, completely flat. They'd be gone come morning.

"Do you think she'll come tonight?"

Rip shook his head.

"She won't wait until tonight."

I waited for him to elaborate. But he looked like he was done talking. Rolling my eyes, I pushed up onto my elbow and stared at him. "Why not?"

He shrugged and toyed with the ends of my hair. "She isn't patient. She sent the *orin* to retrieve the girl and they failed. So she'll come, and she won't wait for nightfall. She isn't a demon—she finds no added strength in the darkness."

"Is she strong?" Then I rolled my eyes and muttered, "Of course, she's strong. She's the one opening a door for the *bocan*, isn't she? It has to be her. At first, I thought maybe it was the *orin* somehow, but that just doesn't make sense. If the *orin* could open doorways to the netherplains, we would have known about it before"

"Yes." He stared up at the ceiling, brooding.

He did the broody-male bit so very well, his dark golden brows drawn tight over his melted-chocolate gaze, that very bitable mouth drawn into a tight, straight line. It made me want to lean over him and bite him, see if I couldn't kiss his scowl away. But instead of doing that, I made myself focus on the problem at hand.

If the *orin* could open doors, the world would have been overrun with demons from the netherplains long ago. God never would have given the demons the power to escape. Although, I've got to admit, I wonder why He gave *anybody* the power to open the doorways to the netherplains, why any of the demons trapped there were allowed to escape at all. Wouldn't life be easier if they were seriously, permanently and completely trapped?

It seemed that way to me.

One of the many questions I've got for when I finally meet my maker. I sent a brief prayer to the heavens that it wouldn't be anytime soon—not today, not tonight. Preferably not for a long time.

I don't really fear dying. It happens to all of us and I already know where I'm going. But all of a sudden, life was looking really interesting for me and I wanted to see where it takes me.

Where it might take us—Rip and me.

Plus, if I had my choice, I'd rather not get taken by some psycho Grimm who had to go and turn to the dark side.

"You got any idea why she's doing this?" I toyed with his medallion and stared off into the distance.

He sighed. I could feel the warmth of his breath skating along my cheek, dancing through my hair. "No."

"None?" Pushing up onto my elbow, I looked at him.

He had that broody look on his face again, and I wanted to kiss him again. But now I wanted to kiss him because I could feel the pain in him and I just wanted to take it away. He cupped my cheek and stroked a thumb across my lips. "No, Greta. No idea at all."

Hot tingles started dancing inside me any time he touched me. I wanted to bite his thumb, then suck on it. Then kiss my way up his arm, along his shoulder until I could bury my face against his neck and breathe him in.

But I didn't. Deep inside, somewhere past this mind-blowing hunger for him, somewhere past all the confusion and hope brewing inside me, there was something else. A part of me, getting ready for a confrontation.

I don't know if it was instinct, some foreknowledge given to me so I could prepare or what. But the time for lying with my lover had come to an end.

For now.

Only for now.

I wouldn't let myself think otherwise.

I huffed out a breath and made myself sit up. "We need to get Mandy up here. Talk. I need to know as much as you can tell me about Fae." I grimaced and looked down. "And I need a shower."

Rip sat up behind me and pressed a kiss to my shoulder. He slid an arm around me, pressing his palm against my belly.

We sat there like that for a long moment and then, as though by some unspoken agreement, we pulled apart at the same time. I rose from the bed and turned to watch Rip as he did the same. He winced as he stretched. I knew the feeling—the muscles in my belly still hadn't forgotten the damage the *bocan* had done.

A few minutes later, I was standing under the showerhead, scrubbing my hair, my body. I didn't linger. There wasn't any time. I finished in what might be record time for me. Water sluiced off my body as I grabbed a towel and rubbed myself dry. I hadn't no more than pulled on a pair of panties when Rip appeared in the door.

He didn't say a word as he stripped away his jeans and climbed into the shower. His shirt was trashed, but I'd gone through my clothes and found an old, faded, oversized blue T-shirt that I wore to bed sometimes. His jeans had been washed, just a few faint marks where the blood hadn't come completely out.

Blood can be damn hard to wash away.

I grabbed the blue T-shirt and tossed it onto the sink for him after I finished dressing. And I only peeked towards the shower once on my way out. Okay. Twice. No woman who has ever seen Rip could blame me for that.

I didn't mess with drying my hair, just quickly braided the damp mess and left it at that. Mandy was back upstairs, eying the bodies. They were starting to smell. We needed to get rid of them—hell, we needed to get rid of them yesterday, but I couldn't leave Rip alone and I wasn't about to let Mandy deal with it.

And now...now, I just didn't know if there was time.

Rip strode in the living after me and stopped abruptly to

stare at the covered corpses. I shot him a glance and asked, "How did you get rid of the last *bocan*?"

He tugged on his medallion. I grinned at him. "Bet he appreciated that."

His lips quirked in a smile.

"Think he'd take care of this one?"

"I don't know. But we'll worry about the bodies later." He had a strange look in his eyes. I don't know if he knew it, but his hand kept opening and closing. Flexing into a fist. He wanted his weapons.

I pointed to the chest I toted along when I moved from town to town. "They are in there," I said. "Even that staff thing, although I was seriously tempted to hide that one and keep it."

"It's not balanced for you. Weight's wrong. I'll have one made for you. After." He strode to the chest and crouched down in front of it. The moment he had one of his blades in his hand, I could see the muscles in his back and shoulders relax minutely.

Mandy stood in the doorway of the stairwell, staring at the bodies with revulsion. "How much longer am I going to have to stay in a house with corpses?"

"You won't have to worry about it after tonight," I told her absently.

Either we'd deal with Fae, win, and then deal with the bodies and leave town.

Or Fae would kill us.

Either way, our worries would be over.

"How strong is she?" I asked once Rip straightened up. He'd finished tucking away about half of his blades. The rest would go into his trashed leather coat.

"Very." He leaned back against a wall with his arms crossed over his chest. "Physically, she's only an average fighter."

Average for us was pretty much like me. I could tangle hand-to-hand with pretty much any human and survive. But the demons, especially some of them, I had to be faster, stronger and use long, pointed objects to survive.

Rip was the better fighter. He was kind of like the *supreme* fighter. Its part of his gift, I think—and I bet that's part of why he was sent after Fae. He knew her better than most, and he's a born predator. He'll hunt and hunt and never give up.

"What about the not-physical things?" My coercion only worked on things that were more human than not. Demon-possessed humans, once they were all the way gone, didn't react to coercion.

But Fae was still basically human. Just a little more. Like me. Like Rip. I didn't know if it worked on Grimms or not.

"Hypnosis. If she catches your eyes, that could be all it takes for her to have you."

I nodded. "Okay, so don't let her catch my gaze. When I use coercion, do you feel it?"

His lids flickered. "Yes."

"How much?"

"Depends on how hard you press, I think. I've only felt it twice." He glanced at Mandy. "You felt stronger when you pushed the girl, even though it didn't seem like you were using as much as before."

Before...back all those years ago when we'd worked together. A few weeks together. One night together. Then years of emptiness because I was too much a coward to hang around and see what happened.

"Will it work on her?" I asked.

Rip shook his head. "I don't know. It could be our best bet."

"I've got a better idea."

We turned to look at Mandy. She looked a little green around the gills. "Why don't we just run? If, and I'm not saying I believe you here, but if Fae really is that crazy and dangerous, shouldn't we just not be here if she comes looking for us?"

"You believe us," I said with a shrug. "If you didn't believe us, you wouldn't still be hanging around."

She desperately wanted to be gone from here. It was written all over her face—it might as well have been in neon. She wanted to be gone, wanted to run hard and fast and never look back.

But she couldn't, and even if she didn't admit it, I knew why.

"I *don't* believe you." She glared at me. "You don't know Fae—you don't know she's the same woman Mr. Rip Van Winkle is looking for or not."

"I do know." Rip stared at Mandy, his eyes intense.

Mandy edged out of the door. Keeping close to the wall, she

made a circuit around the room until she stood in the doorway to the small kitchen. "This is *insane*. You two want me to believe that I'm talking to *Gretel* from *Hansel and Gretel*, and Rip Van Winkle—who didn't go to sleep for twenty years, he was just being controlled by some guardian angel gone bad."

"She hadn't gone bad at the time," I pointed out.

Her purple eyes flashed. "This is *insane*. How can you expect me to believe this?"

"I don't." I shrugged. I hadn't believed Mary right away either, and I'd known her for a lot longer than Mandy had known me. I'd trusted her. Mandy didn't know me, and she certainly didn't trust me. "I don't expect you to believe—me— *yet*. But if you want to live, you're going to listen to what I say."

"How can I trust that?" she whispered, shaking her head. Tears blurred her eyes. "How can I?"

"Listen to your gut." She had the healing gift, so chances are she had some sort of empathic gift. Feeling the pain of others, being drawn to it, so she could heal. Healing and empathy went hand and hand. "What does your gut tell you? Does it say trust me?"

"She's here."

Rip could feel her.

Part of him, even after all these years, even after he knew what she'd become, part of him wanted to reach out and hold her. He reached inside his coat and drew his staff, palming it so the length of it was hidden by his arm.

They would have to take her out physically first.

Before she could use her gift.

Something thudded against the door. Hard. Mandy yelped. Then it was silent.

"What was that?" Mandy asked, her voice a soft, faint whisper.

Neither Rip or Greta answered. Greta was tucked in the corner, almost hidden from sight. She had to stay out of sight, because if he couldn't incapacitate Fae before she caught him, then Greta was the next option.

His ace in the hole.

There was another thud against the door. It rattled and the wood whined. The poor door had been all but decimated last night. He had done a quick-fix job on it, but the patch job wouldn't hold.

At the next thud, it gave way, half-ripped away from the wall. Rip found himself eye to eye with a *vankyr*. Another demon that took over human bodies, possessed them. It wasn't one that was in for the long haul, though. Not like the *orin*. It wanted as much blood and chaos as possible and during the fray, it would try to find another host.

It didn't feed on souls.

The soul ended up trapped inside, going along for the ride, an unwilling audience for whatever nasty trouble his demon stirred up.

Rip waited as it lumbered towards him.

Just before it would have reached him, he whipped up his staff and twisted it. Twin blades emerged. Metal whispered through the air as he struck. The body hit the floor and the head rolled away. Behind him, he heard Mandy scream.

"Get to the basement," he ordered. "Now."

He heard her feet moving, but he didn't dare turn his head to see if she was obeying him. He couldn't look at her. Couldn't worry about her.

A winsome, willowy blonde stood in the door, her arms folded across her breasts. From the corner of his eye, he could see the smile on her mouth, see her lips part as she murmured, "Hello, Rip."

"It's over, Fae."

She laughed. She had always had a beautiful laugh. One of those laughs that sounded like gently chiming bells. It made people want to look at her, to laugh with her and share her amusement. Rip focused on the busted door instead, keeping her in his peripheral vision.

"Over?" She clucked her tongue. "Now, you sound so certain. Arrogance has always been your downfall, precious. You know that, right?"

Shifting his body, he flicked a wrist. One of his custom throwing knifes dropped from a sheath into his hand. One shot.

He'd have one shot.

"Nothing else to say?" Fae asked softly. "No requests for

explanations? No impassioned pleas?"

"They wouldn't work." He chanced one look at her. Threw the knife.

But she'd been ready.

She wasn't there when the knife hit and instead of burying itself between her breasts, it was buried into wood.

With the speed and silence of their kind, she came around to stand just beside him. Her hand, cool and icy, touched his. "Let's not get so rough, Rip. You know I don't share you fascination for sharp objects. Look at me, precious. Let me see your eyes."

He jerked away. But she followed him.

A smile curled her lips—a devious, satisfied smirk. She wasn't looking at him. She was looking at Greta. She'd seen Greta.

"Well, well, well. They sent more than one after me? I'm impressed. I hadn't realized I was such a danger already."

Rip brought his staff up. Damn hard to fight when he could look everywhere but directly at his target. She was skilled at catching a person's gaze. He had to keep that from happening. Had to keep her from using it on Greta.

He struck and Fae moved—*towards him*, not away. Moving inside his strike and pressing against him.

Caught—

"Stop."

It was Greta's voice. Full of command. Heavy with it. Rip threw himself towards it mentally. Grabbing onto the sound of her voice, letting it jerk him away before Fae could command him.

"Close your eyes."

Chapter Twelve

They both froze when I spoke.

Mandy was down in the basement, safe away from this. Safe—so long as we didn't fail.

"Close your eyes," I ordered them. Rip had warned me. I don't know how her gift differed from mine. I had to actively work to keep people under my control, and I couldn't do it for long before the pain became too severe.

It worked best for short-term options.

Somehow, I suspect hers is more long-term. After all, she kept Rip under her control for five months.

Bad gift to put into the hands of somebody who no longer fought on the side of the angels.

Both of them stood there, still frozen, locked in mid-step. Rip's blade still hanging in mid-air. Fae stood pressed against him, one hand reaching up to touch his cheek.

"Let me go," Fae demanded.

"Be silent, Fae." I looked at Rip—saw the muscles contorting in his face, a muscle jerking in his jaw. Fighting me even as he needed me. "Rip, open your eyes and move away."

He did and the minute my attention was focused solely on Fae, I realized how fucking strong she was. I could feel her struggling against my mental control, could feel her heart racing, her muscles tensing as she fought to take control of her body. And she was winning.

Bit by bit, she was forcing her body to turn so she could face me. We can't have that, now can we?

"Fae, get on your knees. Keep your eyes closed." She resisted. I pushed harder and pain sliced through my head.

"*Now.*"

I felt something hot and liquid trickle from my nose. Nosebleed—absolutely perfect. I usually didn't hit this level quite so fast.

"You've lost your wings, Fae. Give them up. Now."

"Never." She snarled, breaking free of my hold enough to answer me.

She was trying to turn her head. Trying to look at me.

"Keep your damned eyes closed and *do not look at me,*" I bellowed, putting every bit of power I had into the words. I didn't dare look away from her. The pain in my head built and built. We needed to end this now, because I couldn't fight her.

"Rip. Just do it. Now."

Fae screeched and jerked against my hold as Rip circled around me and came at her from behind. "You'd stab me in the back?"

"No." He didn't stab her in the back.

He took her head in one swift strike.

And just as quickly as that, it was over. Metal clinked on the ground as I staggered back against the wall and fought to remain conscious. Something metallic glinted up at me. Tarnished silver.

Fae's wings.

Her power.

I wavered in and out of conscious, only vaguely aware of Mandy as she crept through the door to stare at Fae's body. She gave me a horrified look and then went back to staring at the corpse.

"You were right," she whispered, her voice thick.

Darkness swam in. I forced it back and listened as Rip spoke. Bit by bit, the pain receded. If I could just stay conscious, for a few more minutes...get this done. Then I'd collapse.

"I'm sorry, Mandy. Neither of us had much choice."

"I know. I...I can see it." She shot the dead bodies by the door a look. "I can feel it. Even dead, she feels...tainted. Just like they do. But she never felt like this before. Why didn't I see it?"

I had to make myself look at the girl. "You feel a taint?"

She nodded and swallowed. "It's evil. I can feel evil—the same way I can feel pain. But I can't fix evil. I can't fight it—it makes me helpless and I just have to deal with it.

"That's why I accepted the book." Tears filled her eyes and she looked at me. "She said it was a way to learn how to control my gift. It would teach me how to block out the things I didn't want to feel. That's why I took it. And when I looked at her, she never felt so...so dirty. Why didn't I feel it before?"

"Because she wouldn't let you." Rip used one of the blankets that covered the bodies to clean his blade. "I already told you that she can hypnotize with just a look. She looked at you and without saying a word, she told you what you would see when you looked at her."

The blackness was trying to push in on me again. My head didn't hurt quite as bad as it had a few seconds ago, but I felt weak. Ridiculously weak. Had to get up, though. We needed to deal with the bodies...and get out of here.

Now.

I slammed a hand against the wall to keep from hitting the floor as nausea swam up to join the pain, threatened to drive me to my knees. I didn't want to be on my knees in this house. Not on this floor. It was thick with blood, dark with death. Death, and its taint, would linger here.

Distantly, I felt ashamed, saddened. This had been such a nice little place and I had helped destroy it...

My legs were wobbling and I locked my knees to stay upright, concentrated on taking just one step. Then another. So focused on that, I didn't see what was happening off to the side.

A silvery light, gathering in strength. Gathering mass.

It flashed and then there was a man.

He gave me a vaguely disgusted look and said, "Gretel, do sit down before you collapse."

Mandy stared at him with wide, shocked eyes.

"Hi, Will. Nice to see you too," I muttered, swallowing the nasty, hot bile that was climbing up my throat.

He moved away from the circle and studied the house. "You made an utter mess."

Rip strode towards me and caught me in his arms. I have to admit, I was glad. The last of my strength drained away and in another second, I would have collapsed, I know it. "What in the hell are you doing here?" he demanded, glaring at Will.

"I'm here to clean up." Then he flicked a look at Mandy. "And to take your charge from you."

Mandy blinked and then looked at me, naked terror on her face. "Charge...is...is he talking about me?"

We hadn't ever gotten around to that part. I looked at Will. "Take her? Why?"

"Because she needs to be...enlightened."

"She has to choose it," Rip said.

Will shrugged. "In her heart, she already has. But don't worry, sleepyhead. I have not been gone from the field so long that I've forgotten the order of things. I'll do it all right and proper, I promise."

"But she's my charge," I said, shaking my head. "It's up to me."

Now Will smiled. It was a real smile too. And unless I was mistaken, there was some affection in it. "No, Gretel. You saved her—you and Rip. That's all you were sent here for. Well, that...and so you two would find each other."

My eyelids were too heavy.

I couldn't keep looking at him.

The darkness swarmed around me. I fought against it and made myself open my eyes. There was still work to do.

A hand touched my cheek.

"No. I'll handle it now... You rest."

It was Will's voice.

But it was Rip touching me. I turned my face into his hand, shuddered out a sigh and slept.

He didn't like trusting Will. But he knew he did. Knew he had to. Rip glared at the other man as he pulled Greta against him.

"What are you doing here?"

Will returned his stare, a mocking smile on his face. "I already explained that."

Mandy backed away from him. She looked like she was about ready to fly into a thousand pieces. This was too much for her. Way too much. "You aren't taking *me* anywhere."

125

"You'd rather walk in this world, knowing about the monsters but unable to fight them?" Will asked her.

It was the same question he'd posed to hundreds. Thousands.

It was the same question Fae had posed to Rip, all those years ago.

"Fight them?"

Will stooped by Fae's lifeless body and brushed his fingers against the tarnished silver medallion. "Yes. Fight them." He glanced at Rip, then at Mandy. "There is evil in the world. But it doesn't have to leave you helpless. You don't just have to deal. You can learn to fight it—you can learn to block it out so it doesn't sneak into your dreams at night. That is the choice I offer you."

"What in the hell are you talking about?" Mandy pressed fisted hands to her temples and squeezed her eyes closed. "None of this makes sense. I don't know what to do. I don't know what's going on."

"If you come with me, I'll explain all." Will stood and held out a hand.

Mandy shot a look at Greta. Somehow, she'd forged a bond with the other woman. It didn't surprise Rip. Softly, he said, "You can trust him. Greta does." He sneered at Will and then added, "I trust him. I just don't like him."

"How can I trust anybody now?"

Stroking a hand down Greta's pale cheek, Rip said, "Maybe you should just do what Greta said. Trust your gut. Somewhere inside, I think you knew you shouldn't trust Fae. You wanted to. Maybe you needed to. But you knew you shouldn't."

Hesitantly, she nodded.

"So what does your gut say now?"

Mandy looked from Rip to Will and then back. She closed her eyes. Will continued to stand there, hand extended and waiting, like he had no doubt what Mandy's choice would be. When she opened her eyes, she looked only Rip.

"If I say I want to just leave here, run away, change my name, maybe become a nun and walk around praying and playing with a crucifix, would you let me? Would *he*?"

"Yes." Rip held her gaze.

"Yes," Will echoed.

The tension eased from Mandy's body and then she turned and studied Will. She *looked*. Rip could feel the intensity of that stare, feel the raw, untutored power in it. And even before she placed her hand in Will's, he knew the answer too.

She'd made her choice.

"I'd look lousy in a nun's habit, anyway," she murmured.

As Will led her to the circle, Rip glanced around and muttered, "Leaving me to clean up again, you bastard."

Over his shoulder, Will called out, "You made the mess, lad. Not me."

The silver light flared. Bright and hot.

By the time it faded and Rip's vision wasn't so blinded by it, nearly a minute had passed. Weary, he eased Greta's body down onto the couch and then stood. Such a mess, a troublesome mess, and it wasn't going to be a pleasant task.

He glanced around the room. Stopped. He blinked his eyes a few times and then a reluctant grin came. "I'll be damned."

The room was impeccable. Even the busted door was restored.

And the dank, slimy feel of evil that should still linger was gone. No sign of the demons lingered. Not their presence, not their blood and not that lingering shadow of darkness.

I woke up to feel sun on my face.

There was a warm breeze blowing, toying with my hair, brushing against my body. My very naked body, I realized as I opened my eyes.

I didn't know where in the world I was.

It was bright, though, very bright. Lots of windows. Lots of open windows that let in that very nice, warm breeze. Frowning, I pushed upright and looked out one of those windows. My jaw dropped as I realized I was on a beach. Somewhere.

"Good morning, sleepyhead."

I swung my head around. Rip stood in the doorway, wearing a faded, worn-out pair of jeans, his medallion and nothing else. No leather coat, no arm sheaths that held five different knives. "Sleepyhead—isn't that your nickname?"

His mouth twitched in that faint smile. "Sometimes I really

hate the liberties storytellers take. That man didn't get a single detail right except my name."

"Well, the brothers Grimm didn't exactly get my story right either, but I'd rather the world not know it anyway." I shrugged and smoothed the cool, clean white sheets down around my legs. "Where are we?"

"Florida."

That would explain the sandy beaches, I guess. Blood rushed up to my cheeks as I remembered the dream I'd had about Rip and me and beaches just a few days ago. Was it even a few days? Yes. It had been at least two days...I thought. But then again, it could have been longer. I had no idea how I'd gotten here. How long I'd been here.

"How long was I asleep?" I asked him, stretching my stiff body out before I eased over the edge.

"Nearly thirty hours." He padded towards me and settled down on the bed next to me. "We needed to get away from Ann Arbor. It was a miracle none of the mortals saw us or called the police. I left some money for whoever owns the house, put you in my car and just started driving. Didn't know where to go so I just came here."

I glanced around and said, "Just where is *here*...besides Florida?"

"It's my home," he murmured. He laid a hand on my thigh. "And I was kind of hoping maybe you'd want it to be your home too."

A grin tugged at his lips, and if I wasn't mistaken he looked nervous. "Of course, it's not one of those candy houses or anything, but still, I'd like to share it with you."

"It was a gingerbread house, you dolt," I said, even as tears started to sting my eyes.

A home.

A real home.

I hadn't had one since...Mary. I could have—it was possible. There were arrangements that could be made, strings that could be pulled when one of us wanted to find someplace sort of permanent. Someplace safe. A home.

But nothing had ever felt like home since I'd left behind the little cottage in the woods where Mary had raised me. So many years ago.

One would think I might forget what it felt like to come *home.*

It's not something one forgets. Ever. I promise you.

I covered Rip's hand with mine. "Yeah. I'm thinking I'd like that."

He stroked his fingertips over my brow and murmured, "How does your head feel?"

"Wonderful." I leaned in and kissed him, pressing my mouth to his. I smiled against his lips and added, "I feel wonderful."

"Yes." He pulled me into his lap. I straddled him and pressed myself against the heat I could feel through his jeans. Hot and hard, already.

As he pulled me down on the bed with him, I whispered, "I love you."

He cradled my head in his hands, his dark eyes locked on mine. "I love you."

Later, I remember lying in bed and thinking, *Huh. I finally got that happy ending, didn't I?*

No
Prince Charming

A Time to Heal

Sometimes his job absolutely sucked.

Will stared sightlessly into the distance. In his mind's eye, he could see her face, see the broken girl he had nursed back to health all those years ago, the girl who had become his lover for a time. The strong, confident woman she had become...the woman he had fallen in love with.

She had settled inside his heart, quite to his surprise, and he realized the vague, itchy feeling swirling inside him wasn't concern.

It was jealousy.

She wouldn't be his.

Of course, he hadn't ever thought Elle would come back to him, but there were nights, long, lonely nights when he had hoped.

Those hopes were crushed now.

She wouldn't be his.

She had never been his.

No... Elle's heart now, and had always, belonged to her so-called Prince Charming.

Will smirked, knowing how much that moniker annoyed a certain man. "I only wish *I* had thought of that one," he murmured, stroking his medallion.

It pulsed under his hand and he sighed.

"I know," he said quietly. "I know. It's her time."

The medallion pulsed again, stronger. Hotter.

Will grimaced. But then he nodded and added, "Yes, his time as well."

Lucky bastard.

Chapter One

A cool wind whipped across the parking lot, carrying with it the acrid stink of smoke, the earthy tang of sweat and sex...and a miasma of death.

Not physical death. No, this was worse. Death of the soul, of everything that makes you who you are. Oh, the body will die. But the body dies anyway. The soul doesn't have to, unless you give it away.

The soul can go on. It's meant to go on. People aren't supposed to give their souls away. But they do it anyway.

Though people didn't realize it, that's what was going on. Inside that club, people gave away their souls or their bodies or both. I could feel it.

Idiots. There was a line winding around the front of the building, all these fools vying to get inside—there was fun to be had, after all. Dancing. Drinking. Maybe even some drugs, for those looking to score.

A party.

But the real party wasn't on the main floor.

"Are we going inside or what, Princess?"

I glanced over my shoulder at my partner for this current job and gave him a halfhearted smile. Ren was one of my best friends, and as such, he could get away with calling me *Princess* without the threat of bodily harm. Come to think of it, he was the *only* friend who called me that.

I didn't have many of them and most of the good friends I did have wouldn't call me princess just because... Well...they knew. At least, they knew enough. It was a nickname that brought back terrible memories.

The first time I'd been paired up with Ren he had caught

my hand and pressed a courtly kiss to my knuckles. As he stared at me over my hand, he'd murmured, "I must call you princess. Or perhaps empress. No...goddess. I'll call you goddess."

"How about just *Elle*?" I'd suggested.

"No. Too simple. Too mundane. I need something to remind me that I am in the presence of magnificence...perhaps it will keep me from making too big a fool of myself."

The other man with us had given a sigh of long-suffering patience and then, that patience at an end, he'd cuffed Ren across the side of the head. "You've a job to do, remember. If you can get it through that daft head of yours."

Looking back, I remember how those words had worried me. The last thing I'd wanted to have to work side by side with was an idiot.

But Ren wasn't an idiot. I'd learned that quick enough. Before that job had ended, we were friends.

By the time the next job was dealt with, we were lovers.

The on-then-off-again relationship was one of the few constants of my life. At any time, I knew I could go to Ren, find welcoming arms, a warm body, a lot of pleasure...and a decided lack of pressure. I'd drift away and he'd always be there—waiting until I drifted back.

His presence in my life was a comfort.

Sad, that. He's an amazing lover and the best thing I can say about him?

He's a comfort.

Like a beloved old blanket. I grimaced. Ren would utterly despise it if he knew that was what he meant to me. It was more than that, of course. But still...

"Well?"

Sighing, I said, "We might as well go in."

Ren cocked a brow. It was black, black as midnight, arching over eyes the same intense dark shade. His skin was swarthy and dark, his scalp smooth. He'd been that way for as long as I'd known him and I'd spent enough time around him to know that he wasn't taking a razor to his head every other day.

"Don't sound so anxious, lovie," he drawled, his mouth quirking up in an amused smile. "If I didn't have a healthy ego I might be a bit...concerned."

I opened the door and climbed out. He did the same and I looked at him over the roof of the car. "Concerned about what?"

"How *not* excited you are about walking into a sex club with yours truly at your side ready to do your every bidding." He wagged his brows at me as he brought his arms up, resting them atop the car. He dropped his chin down to rest on them and gave me a winsome smile. "*So*, my pretty little poppet, are you going to surprise me with a whip? Some chains? A simple pair of handcuffs?"

I rolled my eyes.

"We'll hold off on the props for now. Remember, we're just here to investigate."

"Oh, now you really don't believe that," he said, his voice sardonic.

No. I didn't. *Investigation* might be the official reason, for now, but it wouldn't be an investigation for long.

For now though... "Investigation, darling. Remember that." As I pushed away from the car, I smirked at him and added, "Besides, investigation or elimination, it doesn't matter... Sex clubs are not my thing. It's a job."

"Well, damn." With a forlorn sigh, he shoved away from the car.

Let it not be said that the man didn't get into his role.

There was a line of people just waiting to get in and we hadn't been in that line forty-five seconds when he started...well, feeling me up.

I'd been watching the others around us without appearing to do so, and I already knew these people were *not* the shy type. They weren't afraid to be seen, and they certainly weren't afraid to look.

I was standing with him at my back when he rested his hands on my waist, easing me closer so that I rested against his chest. He pressed a kiss to my shoulder and then he murmured against my ear, "We might as well blend."

That was all the warning I had before his hands came up, cupping my breasts. Warm hands...hard. Strong. He knew exactly how to touch me and despite the fact that I was extremely self-conscious, I didn't have to fake the pleasure as I arched into his touch.

I loved the way it felt when he touched me. I had no reason to pretend about that.

I just had to pretend we weren't being watched.

We didn't make it into the club that night, but that wasn't a big surprise, at least not to me.

"We're at capacity."

That was the line we were given when we finally got to the door.

Ren looked disgusted. I felt the same way.

At capacity, my ass.

On our way back to the car we saw him let in a few others. This wasn't exactly the sort of club I preferred to frequent, but clubs like this, whether they were sex clubs or not, tended to be very insular. We'd have to either find somebody to get us in there or hang around until we gained admittance.

"We'll just find somebody to get us in tomorrow night," I told him as we headed back to the car.

He opened the door for me but before I could duck inside, he slid his arms around my waist.

"How bad is it in there?" he asked quietly.

I looked over his shoulder back at the club. I lifted a brow. "Can't you tell?"

He shrugged. "I feel so much demon activity that it feels like I've got a hive of fire ants crawling under my skin. But it's not just demons we need to deal with here, is it?"

"No." Sighing, I dropped my head onto his chest. When his arms tightened around me, I let myself relax and snuggle against him. He stroked a hand down my back, resting it just above the swell of my ass. The wind tugged and played with the hem of the short, flirty skirt I'd worn but as long as I stayed close to Ren, I was warm.

Unless I started thinking about what waited inside that club.

"It's too late for some of them," I whispered.

Too late.

But then again, that wasn't anything new.

Back again.

Damn it, this time we were going to get inside that damn club no matter what.

We'd taken last night off, pretty certain we'd come over a little too eager if we camped out three days running.

"Relax, Princess," Ren said, resting his hand on my leather-clad knee as I put the car into park. "We'll get in there."

I made a face at him and tried to work up the enthusiasm to head inside so I could find the real party—and crash it. I didn't want to be here. Especially not tonight.

I couldn't understand why, but something inside me wanted me gone.

Back away...slowly...and nobody gets hurt.

That's what I wanted to do—back away. Actually, I wanted to run away.

Instead, I climbed out of the car and met Ren at the back. He smiled at me and stroked a finger down the chain I wore around my neck. It carried a simple medallion, one tucked between my breasts. I'd known what I'd be wearing tonight and I'd taken the precaution of wearing a longer chain, tucking my medallion inside the low-cut, tight-fitting bodice.

It just wouldn't do for it to come out and catch the wrong eye.

"Come on," I said with a grim sigh. "Let's get this done."

The sooner we finished, the sooner I could get out of here.

I needed a break...a break away from the job, from Ren, from everything.

Through the mess of bodies, the layers of concrete and the distance between us, I could feel them.

Succubi. Incubi. They were responsible for this little party. Who was the leader?

Succubus, incubus, it didn't matter—they all functioned the same. The lesser demons acted like drones and their sole purpose in life was to have sex as often as possible—it was their food. And the king or queen would feed through them. On occasion, when they found a tasty morsel, a king or queen would take a human, but they usually just let their drones do the work for them while they lay back in a semi-stupor, drunk from the sexual energy they absorbed.

And damn, there was a *lot* of that energy here. I hadn't even gone inside and I could feel it.

By my admittedly jaded eyes, there were a good three hundred people crammed inside a building meant for less than half that—at the most. I might not have seen inside the building yet, but I could feel them, sense them. After so many years of doing this, I'd developed a pretty good radar for the job.

A lot of people. All of them young, all of them looking to party.

Ripe pickings for the likes of the succubi and incubi.

The wind was cold again. Or still. It wasn't like it had warmed up an awful lot since the first night I'd been here—that was actually about ten days earlier, when I'd first landed this assignment. I'd waited a week to get started. The one look I'd gotten of this place had assured me that I didn't want to do this one alone and I'd had to wait a week for Ren to show his face and act as backup.

I barely managed not to shiver and wished I could have found something a little less revealing. Something warmer.

It was early May, but right here on the edge of Lake Erie, it was still cool.

This was *not* where I wanted to be.

Honestly, I really don't understand why anybody would come to Sandusky, Ohio, of all places, unless they had to. Or unless they were some of the strange people who flocked to the nearby amusement park to have their brains scrambled on the metal behemoth monsters. Roller coasters. Why in the world somebody would choose to subject themselves to that, I'd never know.

Now I'm not into roller coasters and all that, but I know some people love them. Other than the amusement park, I can't see the appeal. There's the lake, but I'm not exactly the outdoor-girl type. There's not much shopping, although there is a decent Borders, so at least I'd been able to pick up some books.

Still, I can't see the appeal of the tourist town. I just can't.

Ren though, had spent last night at the amusement park. I'd declined. Going into someplace packed with people and big metal rides that made you move way too fast? Not my idea of fun.

There wasn't much here to grab my attention, but I could see why it seemed to do so for the demonic.

It was the life.

The pulse, the throb, the rhythm.

The demons were drawn to the life.

"We've got to get inside tonight," I told Ren. Halfway across the parking lot, I picked up my pace. "It's getting darker in there. We're going to lose more if we don't move soon."

There was so much life…so much emotion.

Lust. Anger. Jealousy. Need. Love. Rage. Hatred.

Emotions—uncontrolled emotions drew predators. That's why the demons were here. Wherever there were people there would be emotion. And wherever there was emotion there would be demons.

Wherever there are demons there would be Grimms.

There would be us. Unlikely guardian angels trying to keep the unsuspecting mortals from making bad, bad and worse mistakes.

That was our job. We would do it. We would do the job. We would deal with the succubi and incubi. We would find the king or queen and eliminate them. Then Ren or I would hang around long enough to make it clear this area was now under the Circle's watch.

If I had my way about it, it would be Ren hanging around. If at all possible, I wanted to clear the hell out the second we dealt with the king or queen.

I was planning on getting out of Ohio as quick as possible.

Maybe head for New York this time. Or Chicago—

No. Screw that. I was going to Milan. And the Circle could pick up the damn ticket too.

I'd asked for a break and I'd ended up with an assignment instead.

They owed me that break, damn it.

I took a deep breath and glanced down at my clothes. Barbie goes badass. That was the look I'd been going for. I had on a black silk corset and, unlike some of the corsets I'd seen around lately, mine was the real thing—it pushed my boobs together and up, cinched my waist and kept my spine ramrod straight.

I was as comfortable in one as anybody could hope to be, but then again, I'd had a lot of practice. I'd grown up wearing these things when I had to—thanks to a doting father, I hadn't spent my entire childhood in one.

But I had worn them often enough.

Never one quite like *this* though. Black-on-black silk brocade with blood-red lacing. I'd paired it with leather pants and heels that would break my neck—*if* I fell, and *if* I could break my neck in such a mundane manner. Which I can't. I'd pulled my blonde hair into a high ponytail, gone a little heavy with the black eyeliner and red lipstick.

Barbie does badass, with a little bit of Dominatrix Barbie thrown in for good measure.

"You look delicious," Ren said as he kissed one bare shoulder. "You sure you don't have a whip lying around?"

"Oh, please." I smirked at him and took a few seconds to adjust the bodice. I had my pendant tucked between my breasts. Wasn't very comfortable, but I couldn't afford to have the wrong person see it, nor could I afford to be without it. There wasn't any room for weapons on me, but that had been intentional.

I wanted to look around this first trip in, not fight. I'd made that clear to Ren as well, but he'd have weapons on him. I knew that as sure as I knew my own name.

Still, I knew I could trust him not to draw them unless he had to.

I just hoped nobody forced his hand...or mine. I might not have weapons, but I'm pretty far from helpless.

The air closer to the building felt hot and heavy, a warning of what lay inside.

I'd known from the get-go this wouldn't be a quick, easy job. I might have been harboring hopes, but they were dying, fading, withering away with every second I remained close to this abyss of darkness.

"Should be a piece of cake," he had told me. Those had been my boss's exact words.

"Will, one of these days, I'm going to kick your ass," I said to myself.

"Hmmm?"

I shook my head. "Just grumbling about Will. The bastard had the nerve to say this should be an easy job."

"Well, so far all I've done is make out with you in view of others and watch other people making out as well," Ren shot me his trademark devilish smile and in a low voice added, "Seems remarkably easy."

"Your luck is about to break."

This wasn't going to be easy. It wasn't going to be quick. We would have to kill while we were here. Not tonight, but sometime before the job was over. I knew it as sure as I was standing there. Possession by succubi or incubi was subtle...a seduction. It started out as just a minor need. Sex—something pleasant...maybe even harmless.

But the more the victim fed that need—through sex, naturally—the stronger the hold. It was like an addiction.

In the early days it was possible to rid the victim of the demon's presence. Possible, but not easy, and the longer it went on the harder it would become.

Sooner or later, without intervention, the demon would be in control and the need for sex would dominate over anything else. Everything else.

Either the victim literally fucked themselves to death—forgoing food, water, anything and everything that wasn't sex. The other scenario—the need for sex became so overwhelming they lost all inhibitions and all sense of right and wrong.

I'd saved people in the past before one of the possessed could rape them.

Somebody in there was already too far gone. Either they were killing themselves without realizing it, or I'd have to kill them when they went too far. Personally, I'd rather find whoever it was and just end it *now*.

A waste. Such a waste. Somebody had given up everything, just for the fun of a few quick fucks.

Do I sound slightly bitter? Sorry. Can't help it. I'd lost my rose-colored glasses a few hundred years ago. Right about the time I lost my virginity and, shortly thereafter, my Prince Charming.

"Elle."

Speak of the devil.

I knew that voice. It was the last voice I wanted to hear right now. Unless he was saying something along the lines of, "Ow, that hurts!" as I beat him across the head with a heavy, blunt object.

I stood there, frozen. Although I didn't want to turn and

face the music, my partner had no reservations.

I dug my fingers into Ren's arm.

Why?

Will. Damn it. He'd done this—orchestrated this. The bastard.

Schooling my features, I turned around and I'm proud to say, I didn't feel the urge to swoon. Not even for a second.

That angel face of his hadn't changed at all in the past three hundred years.

He looked as perfect now as he had the day he kissed me for the first time.

Heat flashed through his grass-green eyes as he studied my clothes and despite myself, my belly clenched in response. Why is it that I can barely remember the name of my father, my stepmother, my friends growing up, but I can still remember the way it felt when he made love to me the first time? It had hurt...but then, after he'd cleaned me up, he'd lain between my legs and done things to me that had left me scandalized.

I can still remember the shock. I can still remember the pleasure.

And I can still remember the pain when I discovered the following night that he was engaged to be wed.

To my sister.

"Why...if it isn't my Prince Charming."

Chapter Two

Michael had been born a prince, the youngest son to the King of Geran, a small kingdom tucked between France and Italy.

Geran no longer existed, but Michael had not forgotten the lessons of his youth. He'd been born a prince, and he'd had all the arrogance one would expect.

In all his years there had only been one woman who could ever make him feel like a foolish young boy. All he'd ever wanted to do was please her, love her, protect her.

He had failed.

She was the only woman he'd ever met who could render him utterly silent. The only woman who made him want to forget duty, honor, pride.

The only woman who could push him so far past jealousy, well into murderous rage. He was there now, there, and fighting not to let it show as she stroked a hand down her companion's arm.

There was an intimacy between them, one that couldn't be mistaken.

The nights they'd been here, he'd watched them. Now, with her standing so close, and that bastard watching him with an insolent, arrogant smile, the rage inside him bubbled and burned, threatening to tear free.

But the rage wasn't the worst.

The worst was the pain.

Seeing her with another man, it hurt in ways Michael couldn't even begin to describe.

Elle turned to face him and for the first time, he got a good look at her clothes. A *real* good look. The air froze inside his chest. Need burned through him. He wasn't sure, but he thought he might have swallowed his tongue.

It was a cool night, but he was sweating under the black silk shirt he wore. His palms itched...itched to reach out, cup her hips and draw her close. At the same time, he wanted to pick her up and haul her close, carry her away so nobody else could see her.

Where that bastard standing next to her couldn't see her, couldn't touch her, couldn't kiss her.

She looked like a wet dream come to life.

Her shoulders and arms were bare, as were the mounds of her breasts. Red lace edged the top of the corset, drawing the eye to smooth white flesh. Her waist looked impossibly narrow and her hips flared out, round and perfect. She had a woman's curves and she'd cradle his body to perfection.

He knew that from experience.

Of course, those experiences were several centuries old. But some things a man never forgot. Some memories never fade.

Like those breasts. Those hips. Those long, leather-encased legs. The silken blonde hair that tumbled down from a tight ponytail, and the big blue eyes that had once looked at him as though he'd hung the moon. The way she'd teased him and made him laugh.

Another memory that didn't fade? The memory of the pain in her eyes the day she realized who he was. Her stepsister's fiancé.

Watching her walk away had been the hardest thing he'd ever done in his life. To that point.

Since then, his life had been a study of hard lessons. Watching as another man touched this woman was just the latest lesson.

Living a long, empty life without her. Watching her turn away from him. Running after her only to find her too late. By the time he'd caught up with her she was forever out of his reach—unless he made a choice.

"The day will come when she will need you. The day will come when she will die without you. But it will not be easy. You will spend a great many years alone...you may die saving her and even if you don't, she may never forgive you. What do you

145

choose...live for her? Or would you rather die?"

That was the choice he'd been given all those years ago by a strange white-haired man who went by the name of Will.

"How can she ever need me again? She is dead. I have failed her."

"Things are rarely as they seem. The woman you love is not dead."

Michael closed his eyes, banishing the memories. He couldn't think of that now, not here. Couldn't think of losing her, couldn't think of the night he'd come face-to-face with Will. Couldn't think about how he had plunged a knife into his own chest either. Through death's door...and back again. That was how one became a Grimm, and if he wanted to be there for Elle he needed to die.

So he'd died. And Will had brought him back.

All in the hope that one day she would need him. Love him. Forgive him.

Forcing his eyes to open, he gazed at her lovely face. This woman did not need him. This woman did not love him. This woman would never forgive him.

If he had known then what he knew now, he wondered if he would've made that same choice.

Will had warned him—*you will spend a great many years alone.*

Yes. Will had warned him. A great many years. More than three hundred to be exact. He hadn't expected to wait this long.

All these years, he had been waiting for a second chance. All these years, he had waited for her.

Waited—because he'd been told that she would need him. He'd held onto that, because he loved her, because he wanted to believe she would one day forgive him, one day love him again, one day *need* him.

And now, here she was...so lovely, so beautiful and strong. So out of reach.

He'd been a delusional fool.

She leaned against her lover and smiled at him. A golden brow arched and she said, "What's the matter, prince? Cat got your tongue?"

He skimmed his gaze over her once more, wishing he could move in and touch. Wishing he could take and taste. Instead, he tucked his hands into his pockets and inclined his head. "Just trying to understand your choice of clothing."

"Oh, well, now. I can help there." Elle gave him a devilish smile and leaned in, her voice a low, silken purr. "It's a sex club. I'm trying to blend."

Michael didn't think Elle could ever blend. No matter what she did.

She was close...so close. Closing his eyes, he took a slow, careful breath, flooding his senses with her scent, reveling in the warmth he felt radiating from her.

But then she pulled back. Gone. Her eyes stared at his and she had a blank, bored expression on her face. "So now that you know why I'm pretending to be S&M Barbie, why don't you get out of here?"

"I can't." Inclining his head, he said, "I was sent here. Told to find you, help you."

"Help me?" She shrugged. "Sorry, Michael, I've already got help." She inclined her head towards her companion and asked, "Ren, have you met Michael?"

"No." A cold smile curled Ren's lips and he stroked his jaw. "I don't believe I've had the pleasure. Although I've heard of you. Quite a bit, actually. But, as you can see, help is already taken care of. Run along now...go crawl back under a rock or something."

Michael bared his teeth in a grim smile. "I'll go on along when I'm damn good and ready...what was the name again...Ren?"

The other man opened his mouth to respond and Michael looked away, dismissing him. "He sent me, Elle. You're stuck with me."

Elle's lashes lowered, shielding her blue eyes from him.

But he didn't need to see her eyes to feel her anger, feel her confusion.

She hid it behind a cool smile just a few seconds later. "I suspected as much. Damn, apparently I went and pissed somebody off but bad, if I got stuck with you."

Michael managed to hide his wince, but just barely. "I'll be sure to let him know you didn't appreciate my presence."

She didn't need to ask which *him* he was talking about—it could only be Will. He was the only one who ever sent them anyway. All orders came through him. For the most part, those who served under Will's lead didn't have to follow orders—they knew their responsibilities and they did their jobs.

But every once in a while there came a special case.

Michael didn't know what was special about this particular job, but if there was a chance in hell that Elle might actually *need* him, then he'd walk through fire to help her.

And if that meant he'd have to stand by at the side while another man pawed her, so fucking be it. He'd be insane when the job was done, but if she might need him, he didn't give a damn.

If he was honest, he'd have to admit he'd walk through fire just to see her smile. Burns healed. Doing something that would actually put a real smile on her face? It would be worth a little pain.

He looked at her, itching to press his face against the warm mounds of her breasts. Itching to pull her close and feel her cuddle up against him and stroke his neck the way she used to do.

She was staring at him. Unable to stop himself, he lowered his gaze, rested it on her mouth. That pretty mouth, slicked with wine-red lipstick and curled in a sneer. He looked up and met her eyes.

"Let's get this done," she muttered.

Then she turned on her heel and stalked towards the club.

Michael fell in step next to her, ignoring the man on her other side and trying not to stare at her, trying not to growl as he noticed other men doing the same.

This was too much.

Under my shields, I was far too aware of him. Far too aware of the longing I sensed within him. It bore a close resemblance to my own need.

It reminded me of a time best forgotten. Seeing him brought back too many memories. Memories I couldn't afford to dwell on right now.

We needed to learn more about the succubi, the incubi, and we needed to see if the queen or king was here.

There *was* a king or queen. There had to be. I could feel the presence of ten demons, easy. If there were that many drones there would be one in control. There might even be more than that inside the club, but I couldn't tell from out here.

I slowed as we drew closer to the line of people, eying it with disgust. "I really don't want to wait through that line again, Ren."

"Nor do I, Princess," he murmured, toying with the ends of my hair.

Michael stood at my other side, watching the people in line with the same level of interest he'd show to bland watercolor. "We won't, then."

"You've a better idea, mate?" Ren asked.

"As a matter of fact, I do." Michael looked at me as he spoke, not Ren. He offered me his arm, a courtly gesture I recognized. The look on his face was the look only the truly *royal* could manage. It said, *I'm a fucking prince, you peasant. Yield and worship.*

Might sound arrogant as hell, but that's how things are with certain individuals. We'd both been born in a time when royalty was worshipped—hell, people still go all ga-ga over royal families. But when we'd been born, not showing a prince the respect he expected could get a man thrown in prison.

I eyed his arm and then looked up at him with a smirk. "You really think the Prince-Charming routine is going to work here?"

"I never was a Prince Charming...*Cinderella*. But I was a prince. It will work, and you know it as well as I." He gave me a regal nod, the kind only a prince could do.

I sighed. Hell. He was right.

"Come on, Ren," I said quietly. I held my arm out and he took it. On the other side, Michael did the same.

"This isn't going to work," Ren muttered. "Just walk right on up there like we own the sodding joint—not going to work. Mark my words."

"Does he ever shut up, Elle?" Michael asked.

"Not often." I straightened my shoulders and let him lead the three of us right up to the doorway.

If my body went slightly haywire at that light, near-impersonal contact, so what? Once upon a time I'd loved this man, dreamed of marrying him, spending my life with him...back when I still had the naiveté of the young and in love.

As expected, it worked. We were still five feet away from the velvet rope when one of the bouncers lifted it for us. A few people grumbled—I could hear it even over the throb and pulse of the music.

Ren was one of them.

"I don't believe it," he muttered. As we stepped into the darkness, he continued in a similar vein.

A faint smile curled Michael's lips. If his touch did bad things to me, that smile did even worse things.

I went to jerk away from him, but then I realized we had people watching us.

Michael had always drawn attention.

The last thing I wanted right now was to make a scene, so I followed, pulling Ren along as well, when Michael led the three of us to the dance floor.

Hey, I mean, it was as good a place as any to start casing the joint.

Not that I was actually thinking of work.

I had good intentions. Seriously. But then Michael's arms came around my waist, drawing me close. Ren was at my back and I wanted to press closer to him—lean against him and let him handle it. I'd relied on his strength before and the temptation to do so now was strong.

Keeping one hand on my hip as Michael moved closer, Ren dipped his head and whispered, "How come I never get the undercover work that involves being sandwiched between two lovely ladies who'd love to have their wicked way with me?"

Trying to relax, I smiled at him over my shoulder. "Well, if you start doing that in your free time, you'd start to have a hard time telling the difference between the job and your reality, sugar."

In front of me, Michael dipped his head and pressed his mouth to my shoulder.

So close. He was so damned close. I could feel his heat, his strength, his chest pressing against mine. All so painfully familiar. I tensed against him and he lowered his head, murmuring, "We're supposed to blend, Elle."

Blend, not fuck, I almost snarled at him. But then I caught sight of the people around us. I'd yet to pay them much attention—too distracted by Michael.

I *knew* what kind of club this was. I did.

I mean, Ren and I had spent a couple hours going just past third base, and with an audience.

But still, it was a fucking shock to see some of the people going at it on the dance floor. Yes. Going at it. Hell, we would've blended better if we *had* been fucking, and we wouldn't have even been the only threesome going at it either.

Michael's hand rested on my hip, a mirror of Ren, and a breath shuddered out of me as I let him pull me so close that not even air separated us. It didn't make me feel any better to realize he wasn't unaffected by me.

Against my belly, I could feel the hard, firm length of his cock. The green of his eyes glowed and he watched me as though he wished he could swallow me whole.

Hunger. Hunger...and memories.

I recognized both. I lived with their ache every day. It would have been easier to handle if I knew he didn't want me. Desire hadn't ever been the problem. He'd wanted me ages ago, and it wasn't a surprise that he wanted me now.

It was nothing new.

The problem had been him not wanting me *enough*.

By contrast, Ren was at my back and it was pretty damn clear he wasn't unaffected by this either.

I was trapped between two men—two men I'd known intimately—and I couldn't lie and pretend *I* wasn't affected.

We moved together and I almost whimpered. It felt so good. *He* felt so good...Michael. Being with him, having him close felt so right.

I closed my eyes when he dipped his head to nuzzle my neck. That didn't help. It made it that much more intimate. I couldn't retreat against Ren either, because if I retreated just a half an inch, Michael would move an inch closer and being more firmly pressed between them was *not* going to help.

So I opened my eyes and made myself scan the crowd. I hadn't even realized it but Michael was doing a damn fine job working us along the dance floor, which made it easier for me to scan the dancers, looking for the victims.

I hissed out a breath between my teeth. There were a *lot*. It seemed as though every third or fourth person had been touched at some point—the touch of a succubus or incubus was unmistakable—a psychic shadow. Fortunately for us, it had been a light touch. Nothing deep...at least not yet.

Somehow, Ren got lost in the crowd. Too many bodies in such a small space and, as the crowd swallowed him up, Michael took quick advantage. In the blink of an eye he had us moving to the far side of the dance floor. "Not a very graceful partner, your friend, Ren," he said, his voice cool, dispassionate. Like he didn't care.

But when I lifted my head and looked at him, I saw the jealousy and anger burning inside his eyes.

"Oh, he's got plenty of grace. But that's not exactly what drew me to him either," I said, giving him a flippant smile.

"Pardon my curiosity, but exactly what *did* draw you to him?" He toyed with the laces on my corset, his fingers brushing against bare skin.

He's your exact opposite.

But I didn't say that out loud.

"He's wicked fun in the sack for one," I said, giving him a hard smile.

Whatever he might have said in reply, I don't know. The next moment, somebody came up behind me—fucking *rubbing* against my ass. I jolted in surprise before I could stop it. Instinctively, I reached for my knife, but then I remembered—no weapons. No way to hide much of anything in clothes that fit like a second skin.

But Michael was already handling it. He moved me to the side and then shot his hand out, fisting it in the front of the other man's chainmail shirt. He jerked him close and I had no trouble hearing him as he said, "Touch her again and I'll rip your dick off and feed it to you. In pieces."

The guy was either stoned...or stupid. He leered at me and then looked back at Michael. "Hey, man, if you don't want me eying your piece, why'd you bring her?"

Michael shoved him hard enough that he went crashing to the floor, then he pulled me close, stroking my back with a possessive hand. He cupped my ass, but I couldn't very well shove away from him without drawing any *more* attention to us. If such a thing was possible. Half the dancers had stopped to watch us.

Ren emerged from the crowd, his black eyes serious, glinting with a threat.

"Because she likes to watch," Michael said with a wicked grin.

The man on the floor took one look at the two of them and started scrambling away.

There was a break in the music just then—of course. Which meant quite a few people heard his voice.

I so do not *like to watch.* Blood rushed to my cheeks as people looked at me. They were all grinning, grinning at the three of us, knowledge glinting in their eyes.

Then I lost sight of their faces because Michael was kissing me, and Ren was at my back, playing up his role as well. He seemed to be getting *really* into it too, damn it.

It was actually easier to focus on Michael, easier to lower my shields just a bit and let the buzz of his jealous energy flow over me.

But it wasn't going to be easy for long, because he was getting into it too.

Michael's hand tugged sharply on my hair, angling my head up. The other gripped my hip, hauling me close. His lower body moved against mine and despite my embarrassment, despite the audience, despite the demons I could sense in the air, I couldn't keep from responding. As I rocked against Michael, Ren rotated his hips against my ass. They echoed every movement I made, moving in tandem. A dark, vibrant rainbow of need exploded inside my head.

Michael lifted me and I instinctively gripped his waist with my legs, arching my back. I fell back against Ren's solid, steady heat and gasped as his hands came around me, cupping my breasts. A hard, driving rhythm started to pulse through the air and I shuddered.

Distantly, I realized we weren't the center of attention any more, although some people were still looking at us. But not for anything other than voyeuristic tendencies. As Michael pulled his mouth from mine and started to kiss his way down my neck, I rested my head against Ren's shoulder, tried to concentrate.

The job. Focus on the job.

Concentrate. Job. Work. Demons. Innocent people. Concen—oh, shit.

Ren had somehow worked the top of the bodice down enough that my breasts were exposed, the nipples swollen and tight. As he pinched one, Michael bit the other. Then he started to move me—back and forth—over the swollen ridge of his cock. Couldn't think—

To my utter shock, to my utter dismay, I realized I was this close to coming. Twisting between them, I gasped out, "Stop."

Ren swore. Just before he stepped away, he muttered, "Oh, come now, poppet. It was starting to get fun too."

But Michael was still rocking against me, stroking me, and oh...oh...

"Stop it, Michael."

"We're still being watched. Just trying to blend. We have a job to do, remember?" He kissed his way up my chest, along my collarbone. As he lowered me to my feet, he nuzzled my neck, then nipped at my earlobe. His voice was light, easy, playful. He could've been teasing.

But somehow I didn't think he was. Maybe it's because I didn't want him to be.

I shuddered, whimpered. But somewhere inside me, I didn't want to believe that—I didn't want to believe this was just a job.

The devil made me do it, I swear. Turning my mouth to his, I whispered against his lips, "Is that the only reason...the job?"

"Fuck, no." His mouth crushed against mine and even though I was no longer pinned between their bodies, even though all Michael was doing was kissing me, I knew if I didn't stop this *now*, I was going to humiliate myself and come right there on the dance floor.

Tearing my mouth away, I looked around and staggered, falling back against Ren. His arms came around me, holding me protectively.

I closed my eyes and tried to get my body under control.

What in the hell was I doing?

If I didn't know better, I'd almost swear one of the damned succubi had infected *me*. Hunger screamed at me. I needed this—whether I needed it because it was Michael, whether it was both of them, whether it was some fantasy I'd never even considered—I needed this.

But it terrified me. My pride and my bruised heart couldn't handle it. "Please stop, Michael. I...I don't want this to happen with an audience."

Too late, I realized what I'd admitted.

That *with an audience* bit? I really should have left it off.

Seconds later, we were off the floor. Somehow, even though he'd never been here—to *my* knowledge—Michael managed to find some semi-private little alcove and then I was trapped between him and Ren and the two of them were rocking against me, their hands all over me. Ren muttered in my ear and for once, the wise-cracking comedian aspect was all gone and brutal, wicked hunger was all I could feel from him. Michael's mouth was on mine and he kissed me like he was starving, dying for the taste of me.

I felt hands at my back—whether it was Michael or Ren, I couldn't even tell, but it took them less than a minute to strip me out of my corset.

I'd be scandalized later. The wicked, wicked prince had always been able to make me do things I never should do. And Ren…in the past hundred years we'd spent more than one night together and he knew my body probably better than I did.

As Ren plumped my breasts together, Michael caught one nipple in his mouth, scoring it with his teeth and then stroking the minor pain with his tongue.

All of a sudden, I couldn't care less that I was semi-naked and trapped between two men with hundreds of strangers just fcct away.

I didn't care.

I didn't care that anybody could—and a number of people *did*—look in and watch as Michael dragged down the zipper of my leather pants.

I didn't care that anybody could see as Ren slipped his hand inside to find me completely naked underneath.

"Naughty little princess," Ren teased. His voice was tight with strain as he circled his thumb around my clit. "You're not wearing any knickers."

I didn't care that anybody was there to witness as Michael shoved my pants to my knees and knelt on the floor. He knocked Ren's hand out of the way and pressed his mouth to my sex and I *didn't* care.

He brought me to climax with talented, oh-so-clever fingers and his wicked, wicked tongue. Dazed, I sagged back against Ren, certain—*convinced*—I could find rest in his arms, maybe a few seconds to breathe, to think.

But as Michael rose to his feet, Ren whirled me around and

then I was leaning against Michael as Ren went down on me. He went to push my knees wider but the pants at my knees prevented that and he growled against me, shoving the pants as far down as they could go. As his tongue slid along the folds between my thighs, Michael caught my face and angled it around. His mouth crushed mine and I screamed into Michael's mouth as Ren brought me to climax.

He kissed me like a man dying of thirst and I was the only water that could quench that thirst.

Need echoed inside me.

"Bloody fucking hell, darling girl..." he rasped against my lips. "I need you."

Need...hell, I understand that. Even after all this time, I needed him. Longed for him. I suspected I even still loved him.

I might have even told him that if I hadn't felt an ominous, hungry presence.

They felt it at the same time I did. I could tell. Their bodies stiffened, only a bit, but the spike in the air could be nothing else.

None of us let it show.

Casually, his gestures slow and unhurried, Ren straightened, easing my pants back up, concealing my lower body. As Ren fastened them, Michael turned away and plucked my corset from the floor. He faced me just as Ren finished fastening my pants.

As the hungry succubus lingered near the door, Michael lifted a finger and twirled it in a circle. Obediently, I turned around, presenting him my back.

I looked into Ren's eyes, blushing and still half in shock over what had just happened.

This was nothing I'd ever even fantasized about and I had a pretty healthy fantasy life. Michael brought the corset around me and Ren adjusted it over my breasts, smiling down at me, heat and humor in that saturnine smile. "Stop looking so shocked, Princess. I keep thinking about how much fun it could be to shock you even more."

"I don't think that's possible," I said, and my voice shook as I said it.

Like he'd done so a thousand times—hell, he probably *had* done it a thousand times, at least—Michael had me back in my corset, his hands quick and capable.

I turned to him, tried to figure out what we should do next. I linked my hand with Ren's, holding onto him desperately as Michael cupped the back of my head and slanted his mouth over mine. A few seconds later, he lifted his head and gave me a wolfish smile that didn't reflect in his grim eyes. "Come on, darling girl...let's get out of here. You've had your fun, now we get to have ours."

Ours...

Oh, hell. He wasn't serious...right?

"But..."

He lifted a hand, placed two fingers over my lips. "Our turn," he said. His voice was hard and flat, brooking no disobedience.

Like I really gave a damn. He couldn't order me around.

And if I suspected taking a *turn* had anything to do with it, I wouldn't have left unless the place was on fire.

We needed to get out of here. The look in Michael's eyes, grim and cold, was enough to do what no amount of orders could. It didn't help that Ren had that same serious, flat look on his face. He was also stroking a hand down the long black duster he wore. Although I'd told him no weapons, I knew he'd have something tucked inside there and if we stayed much longer, he'd be drawing a weapon.

Nothing made him feel secure like whipping out a machete. I knew that from experience too.

They wanted out of here, and so did I.

Michael was right.

I hadn't been prepared for this many demons in one place.

We couldn't handle them until we dealt with the king or queen, and first we had to find who it was.

Besides, if we stayed here much longer, I don't know what would happen between the three of us. Part of me yearned to find out. The rest of me knew my heart couldn't handle anything that had to do with Michael.

Ren—he was fine. He was safe as far as matters of the heart went. But Michael, he was a different story altogether.

Even if matters of the heart *weren't* involved, I didn't think my inner demons could deal with that particular issue. Not in this lifetime.

Chapter Three

I didn't quite make it home before it hit me.

Part of me had expected it, but it still managed to catch me off-guard.

The memories.

Pain.

Fear.

Cruel, dark laughter.

Ren, bless his soul, didn't say anything, and when we reached the house he kept his distance. But I stumbled halfway up the walk and when he reached out to steady me, I latched onto him and didn't let go.

"Shhhh..."

He lifted me into his arms and murmured against my brow, soft and soothing words that made no sense.

One thing about Ren, although I knew he was probably dying to ask, dying to do something other than just hold me while I battled those inner ghosts, he understood the value of silence. He had his own inner demons and if anybody could understand, it was him.

It was close to an hour before the fear finally eased its grip and even longer before I could manage to speak.

My corset gaped as I eased back away from him, and I shot him a look, forced a smile. "You're such a letch," I told him.

Somber-eyed, he brushed my damp hair back from my face and said, "It can't be easy to breathe in that contraption. I always hated them."

Since it was already half-off, I turned my back to him and let him strip it away. "I never cared for them myself, but you must admit they certainly make a statement."

"Indeed. They state, 'I'm more interested in looking pretty than breathing'."

I cuddled back against his chest and sighed as his arms came around me.

"This was our fault," he murmured.

I glanced at him, puzzled. "What?"

"I've known you for nearly a century, Elle. I've never seen you so lost in your memories before. Bleeding hell, that wasn't *lost* in your memories—you were drowning in them."

"It happens."

"Yes...and something set it off. Your long-lost prince and I."

Sighing, I absently toyed with one of the polished pewter buttons on his coat. "He's not my prince," I said. He never had been. He'd been claimed before I'd even met him. "And you're wrong. It's not *your* fault."

The men responsible were nothing but dust. Scum, not even history remembered them.

I did though. Not their faces, or their names. But the sound of their laughter. The cruelty in their hands. The pain—

"Don't hand me that," Ren bit off, his voice harsh. "I know you, Elle. I know you *too* well."

What was I supposed to say?

I couldn't tell him. I'd told only one other soul and that was Will. Nobody else knew. I'd prefer to keep it that way and I certainly couldn't tell Ren. He had probably pieced together enough of it, but I'd be damned if I'd share those humiliating, horrifying memories.

"Ren, it isn't *your* fault." I made myself look at him as I spoke. I didn't want him blaming himself, not for my nightmares.

A calculating look entered his eyes. I recognized it and before he even said anything I knew what he was thinking.

"Not mine, then? How about your charming friend?" He cupped my cheek in his hand, watching me closely.

He'd know if I lied. It wasn't a gift of his—it was simply him. He knew me too well and I couldn't lie to him without him knowing.

But fortunately, I didn't have to lie on this. Curling my fingers around his wrist, I gave him a faint smile and murmured, "You know better than that, Ren. He's one of us."

"Not always. And that bastard Will has a fucking strange sense of irony. I can just see—"

"No." I shook my head. "Will's a bit...unusual, but he's not cruel."

A bark of laughter escaped him and he rested his head back against the couch. I didn't even remember how we got inside the house, much less onto the couch. Sliding off his lap, I curled up next to him and watched as his laughter faded away.

"Will...not cruel? Princess, perhaps you don't know the man I speak of—tall chap, white hair, has the devil's own arrogance...sound familiar?"

I poked him in the ribs and watched as he jumped.

He caught my wrist before I could poke him again. I settled for making a face at him. "Will isn't cruel. He's just... Well, he's Will."

He'd been a lover, once. One of only a handful. For the past century, the only man who'd shared my bed was Ren, and that was because Ren expected nothing of me. Nothing but the pleasure we could find in lovemaking. He never asked of my past, never asked for any promises.

Safe.

That was Ren.

He was safe.

Curling back against him, I rested my head on his shoulder and murmured, "I'm tired, Ren."

"Then rest, Princess. Just rest."

It was nearing noon when Ren finally crawled out of bed.

It had taken Elle hours to fall asleep and he'd waited until she slumbered deep before he'd allowed himself any rest.

He was still groggy, still tired, but he wouldn't sleep anymore. Not today. Next to him, Elle was lost in a dreamless sleep. As he pressed his lips to her brow, he closed his eyes and breathed in the soft, warm scent of her. She sighed, her mouth puckering in a faint frown. When he went to pull away, all she did was curl into a ball in the center of the bed.

Without him.

He sat on the edge of the bed and rubbed at his chest, trying not to let it bother him, how easily she turned away from him. He couldn't hold her tight—that would only send her running from him. All he ever could do was be there when she came to him. He kept waiting for her to come and want *more*— more, as he wanted more.

After nearly a century, he was still waiting.

But he'd wait another five centuries if he must. Ten. Until the end of time.

You can wait until you rot and it won't matter.

He ignored the sarcastic voice in the back of his mind. He didn't need the reminders—he already knew he was wasting his time. He just wasn't ready to admit it. Not now. Not in five centuries. Not in ten.

The medallion around his neck weighed heavy. The heat of it had pulled him from his own dreams and, as he sat there, it became hotter and hotter. It would continue to do that until it scorched his flesh, and although it was already miserably uncomfortable, he wasn't jumping to answer that arse-licker's call, not until he had some coffee in him.

Coffee—ambrosia as far as he was concerned.

He didn't manage to get that cup before he was interrupted.

From behind, he saw the flash of light but he didn't turn. He didn't like the bastard, not one bit.

I came awake to feel the air around me buzzing.

That hum of energy was familiar, one I've felt dozens, hundreds, perhaps even a thousand times over the years.

Will.

I rolled my eyes as I climbed out of bed. After stretching, I grabbed the sheet from the bed. As I headed for the bedroom door, I wrapped it around my body, holding the edges in a knot between my breasts.

Will and Ren had never gotten along, but then again, few people rarely got along with Will. He seemed to prefer it that way.

I could hear them talking, Ren's voice, low and angry, followed by a flat, unemotional one.

"It's too early for this," I muttered, not bothering to glance at the clock. I didn't care if it was one in the morning or one in the afternoon. If I have just climbed out of bed, it's too early. I needed time to wake up and I needed time to clear the cobwebs from my mind.

A must, especially if I was going to have to play referee between the two men.

The room went silent, but it was followed by a rise in the energy. It crackled in the air, snapped. I could feel the hair on the back of my neck stand on end.

Will was leaving—the energy always mounted just before he disappeared in his pretty little circle of light.

I reached the doorway just in time to see Ren turn to me. He gave me a crooked smile and took one step in my direction. If he hadn't had his back turned to the circle of light, he would have seen Will's hand move, grabbing him by the neck, the same way one might grab a small puppy.

Ren's eyes widened and he swore, but before he could pull away, Will jerked and he disappeared in the circle of light. It blinked out of existence.

Leaving me alone.

I gaped at the spot where Ren had been only seconds ago.

"Damn it, Will, what are you doing?"

There was no answer and I narrowed my eyes. I damn well *knew* he could hear me. I reached up and closed my hand around the medallion at my neck. He could hear me—he might not be here physically, but I could *feel* him, which meant part of him still lingered.

Damn it, he'd answer me.

I focused my thoughts and projected towards Will. "Damn it, what are you doing?"

Ren has another engagement, Elle.

"Like hell," I snapped. "I need backup here—I can't handle this mess all alone."

You aren't alone. You have backup.

I stiffened as Michael's image flashed through my mind. Not quite the backup I'd wanted.

He's as capable as Ren. More.

My shoulders slumped and I closed my eyes. Yes. I had no doubts of that—I'm sure Michael is very capable. That's how he is.

But that didn't mean I wanted him at my back.

Why do you worry about having him at your back? Do you truly think he'd harm you?

"I... No. No, I know he wouldn't hurt me."

Would he betray you? Risk you?

I scowled and shoved a hand through my tangled hair. "No, damn it. It's not *working* with him that's the problem. It's being near him. I...I can't do this, Will."

You can.

I wrapped my arms around myself, one fist still tangled in the sheet I had wrapped around my body. Huddling in on myself, I shook my head and said, "I can't. Just being around him hurts."

You've hurt every day, ever since you left him, Elle. That will not change, not until you deal with it. Work with him—deal with him—and get on with your life.

His presence faded and now I was truly alone.

Alone with nothing but my own thoughts, dark, heavy and cold.

"What in the bloody hell do you think you're doing?" Ren snarled the moment he could.

It wasn't until after the words left his mouth that he realized where he was—where *they* were.

Hovering in the air. Hundreds, maybe even thousands of feet.

It was painfully cold, the wind slapping at him, slicing into his naked body like a thousand tiny blades.

Will stood just a few feet away—stood—like there was solid ground beneath his feet instead of hundreds and hundreds of feet of nothingness.

Warily, Ren moved his foot. Yes—it felt rather solid under him, but he wasn't fooled.

"Where are we?"

Will glanced down, and when he looked back up there was a hint of a smile in his eyes. "That's Lake Erie down there."

Lake Erie.

Half-paralyzed with fear, Ren looked down and then jerked his eyes back up, focusing on Will's ageless face. He'd rather look at the bastard in front of him than at the water so far, far below.

"Why in the *hell* are we floating in mid-air above Lake Erie? You bastard, do you *want* somebody to see us?"

Will's mouth quirked—it was almost a full-out laugh for him. "You know as well as I that if I do not wish to be seen, we will not be seen." He glanced down and then back at Ren. "Up here, I'm quite certain I have your undivided attention."

Well, that was certainly true.

"What do you want?"

Will shrugged. "What I want rarely plays into things. I do what I must...as do you, Thom."

"Don't call me that," Ren bit off. "If you're in the mood for games, you'll have to find somebody else to play with. Elle needs me."

Now a real smile curled Will's mouth, but it was a bitter, unhappy one. "Elle doesn't need you."

"She wouldn't agree." He gave Will a sly smile. "She came to me, asked me to come. She does need me."

Will just stared at him, his gaze emotionless. The wind whipped his snow-white hair around his smooth, unlined face, blew it into dark, dark eyes. Will didn't even seem to notice.

"Right then, if you'll just send me back, I'll get back to work."

"No."

Something about the way Will was watching him put his back up, but Ren would be damned if he let the bastard see how unnerved he was. Of course, he had a right to be unnerved—to say the least. He didn't have a stitch of clothes on his bare ass, he was hovering in mid-air and the freakiest man in the world was getting ready to jerk him into one of his mind games. He could tell.

But Ren wasn't in the mood to play.

At least, not on Will's terms.

Meeting Will's gaze, he gave him a wide grin and threw out his arms. "Come on, mate. I'm a bit cold, you know. Why don't you and me go back to the cabin, at least long enough to get dressed. Besides, we can't just...ah...float around in the clouds all day."

"Don't bother playing good-natured, daft old Thomas. The act doesn't work on me, boy." An unholy light danced in Will's eyes and he murmured, "Perhaps you've forgotten, but I was there back when it wasn't exactly an act."

Ren crossed his arms over his chest. "Oh, no. I haven't forgotten. But bloody hell, if you need a word with me, you can do it somewhere other than *here*."

"Here is as good as anywhere." Will shrugged. "But so be it. I'll send you off to your next assignment."

Ren narrowed his eyes. "I'm not doing another assignment...not while Elle needs me."

"She doesn't though. And you know it." Will looked away. "She doesn't need you. She doesn't need me. There's only one man she does need and it's high time she admitted it."

Chapter Four

"I'm in hell." Michael turned away from the window, forcing himself not to stare at Elle as she sauntered towards his condo.

She was alone...again.

Alone. And in a matter of seconds, she would be alone in the condo with him.

He didn't know whether to be glad of that fact or terrified.

"Don't be either. Just think about the job," he muttered.

It had been a bad, bad idea agreeing to let her come here to pick him up before they headed to the club this time.

Being alone with her was a bad, bad idea, period.

As much as he hated Ren, it was easier to do the job when he was there providing a buffer.

The first night at the club, when it had been the three of them, had been the easiest, even if he had spent much of it torn between rage and other messy emotions he couldn't quite define.

Having Ren around had made it possible for Michael to keep some measure of control. Now he had only his own strength to rely on because he couldn't count on Ren's presence. The other Grimm likely wouldn't be back—Elle had said he'd been called away to another job, so they were on their own.

At least for the time being.

For now, he'd have to rely on his own strength, his own control to get through this. And that was a fucking laugh, because he had no control with Elle. None. No control, no strength, no tact, no sense. Nothing but need.

And in a few minutes, he'd be alone in this little condo with nothing but her...and his desperate, dark needs.

"Don't think about that. Think about the club. Think about the succubi and the incubi. You've got your hands full with them. There is no time to dwell on personal matters." Michael pinched the bridge of his nose and muttered, "Not that there *is* any sort of personal matter between us."

No. He'd ruined that.

All he had was this job...and the hope that he could protect her.

They'd decided it would look better if they arrived together instead of just meeting there. Elle wanted to drive and Michael imagined it was probably so she could take off running whenever she chose.

It had seemed a logical idea at the time, but now the logic wasn't quite so clear. Especially since she was now on the porch. They were still separated by brick and mortar, but he could feel how close she was.

In a moment, she'd been in here, and they would be alone.

Alone with Elle. It was enough to make logic, control and sanity fly out the window.

The condo, perched on the edge of Lake Erie, was reclusive, remote and relatively private. It would take forty-five minutes to get to the club.

As she knocked, Michael stomped over to the bar and poured himself a snifter of brandy. He waited until he took the first sip before responding.

"Come in." He remained where he was, staring into the cut crystal, swirling the amber liquid around. Better, he thought, better to study the pricey liquor than to look at her.

"Well, aren't you in a happy mood today?" Elle drawled, her voice low and mocking.

Michael flicked a glance her way and took another drink. Not a sip though. He knocked it back, slammed the snifter on the counter and poured himself another drink. He belted that one just as quickly and grimaced as it burned its way down his throat. He was tempted to go for a third drink, but instead set the snifter on the bar and folded his arms over his chest.

Elle sauntered up to stand beside him, and from the corner of his eye, he could see the smirk on her face. She lifted his glass, sniffed it and then, with a shrug, helped herself to a drink of her own. Michael had to turn away when she closed her eyes as she sipped. It was either that or risk pouncing on her like a slobbering fool. She'd be dealing with enough of that later on.

"You don't know how to treat good liquor," Elle said from behind him. She gave a happy sigh and took another sip.

Michael glanced over his shoulder at her. Looking at her proved to be a mistake. Because one quick glance was not enough. Like a puppet on a string, he found himself turning around before he even realized he was doing it.

His voice edgy, he bit off, "If I was in the mind to savor, I'd savor. Right now, I'm more of a mind to get good and drunk."

"Can you get drunk?"

"If I put my mind to it, yes, I imagine I can."

"Hmm. Why don't you put your mind to getting this job done instead?" Elle cocked a golden brow at him, still holding the snifter to her lips. They were slicked wine-red again—wine-red that matched the short silk sheath she wore. It covered her ass, barely. She wore no bra, and through that silk, he could see the outline of her nipples.

Oh, I'm definitely in hell.

"Where did the leather and lace go?" he asked.

"Leather's hot," Elle replied. She glanced down at her dress and then up at him. She smiled as she took another sip of her brandy. "What, don't I look slutty enough?"

Michael clenched his jaw. "You don't look like a slut."

"Oh, I most certainly look like a slut. But that just means I'll blend in." She smirked as she studied his clothes. He was all in black again, a black silk shirt and tailored black trousers.

Under her breath, Elle said, "Tsk. Tsk. Here I am looking nice and slutty, and you look like royalty, Prince Charming." Her voice was mocking.

Michael narrowed his eyes at her. "You know, Elle, I really don't care for that name."

With an unrepentant grin, she said, "I figured as much."

Then her face sobered, and she gestured to his clothing. "Seriously, Michael. You don't blend. We're going to a sex club, for crying out loud. We're not going to the opera."

"There is no opera here," he replied. He glanced down at his clothes and then at hers. "I'll leave you to play dress up, darling. I will go as I am and play the indulgent lover."

She'd been getting ready to take another sip, but she paused, the crystal pressed against her lips. "Indulgent lover?" she echoed.

"It works as well as anything else," he said. He shrugged, gathering his hair in his hand, securing it in a tail at his nape. "You're the lovely woman with a wicked streak and I'm just a besotted fool who'll do anything to keep you happy."

Something flashed in her blue eyes. Carefully, she set the snifter aside and smoothed a hand down her silk-covered side. "Well, this will be interesting. We both get to do some role-playing. I get to pretend to be a slut, and you get to pretend to be besotted."

It was a role Michael could play easily enough. After all, he had only been living that way for three hundred years. Silently, he laughed at himself. "Just call me a method actor."

He was in a weird mood tonight, that was for sure. I let him drive.

We had both rented little luxury condos on the lake, although I do admit, Michael had more of the luxury than mine. Cut crystal. Hand-carved doors. Thick, plush carpet, white as snow. His place was a little palace.

I went for the rustic look. The little log cabin was comfy and simple. Suited me fine.

It hadn't surprised me to find him out here. I had to be out here, far from town. I needed it. I had to get away from people every now and then because their presence weighed on me too much. I swear, if I could have chosen the one gift I'd received after I made the Choice, it would've been anything but the one I received.

I'm called a reflector. Basically, it's empathy coupled with the ability to reflect one's emotions back at them. Can you imagine what it's like, being able to feel other people, their emotions, their losses, their heartbreaks? I can shut it off, but it's not wise to keep shields up all the time.

And it doesn't feel good.

Sometimes those shields are almost too confining. It's like living out your life in bubble wrap.

Curious, I glanced at him. Up until four days ago, Michael and I had never worked together before. Matter of fact, I went out of my way to avoid him. Up until tonight, the powers that be had seen fit to let me do it.

Up until he showed up in the parking lot at the club four nights ago, I hadn't seen him in more than three hundred years.

The last time I'd seen him was in London, almost a year to the day after my rather...unfortunate...demise.

I'd been working with Will at the time and was finally settling into the strange new life. Will had taken me to see a play, but I can't remember the name of it. The only clear memory of that night was Michael.

Seeing his face—it had been such a shock.

Part of me had hoped he had come looking for me, but I'd discarded that idea quickly enough. After all, nobody knew what had become of me, so there was no way, logically, he could have been looking for me.

Still, part of me had hoped.

I'd mentally rehearsed what I would tell him as he came up to me, but then I'd caught sight of the silver chain around his neck. Nothing at all like what he would have worn. Nothing.

And it was exactly like the chain I wore. The one with the pendant on it. A silver disc, etched with wings.

Part of me died that night. He was one of us. Which meant...he'd died. It was how one went from human to Grimm. Through death's door and then back again.

I didn't give him a chance to say anything. Instead, before he could get close enough for us to speak, I had run. He hadn't followed and I hadn't seen him until he'd shown up here in Sandusky.

One might think it unlikely, but shortly after seeing him in London, I left Europe. I traveled to the colonies in 1706 and I've been here ever since, save for the odd trip to Italy or France every now and then. According to the gossip grapevine, Michael spent most of his time drifting between Europe and Asia.

Until now, our paths had simply never crossed.

I didn't know all that much about him, not anymore. But

then again, maybe I had never really known all that much about him to begin with.

"So what is your gift?" I asked him. "I don't think I've ever heard."

Michael slipped me a sidelong look. In the darkness, his green eyes seemed almost black, and his face was unreadable. In a quiet, low voice, he asked. "Are you sure you want to know?"

Uh—oh. Going by the grim tone in his voice, it wasn't going to be a nice one. Some of us didn't have good gifts. Mine wasn't fun—it was a pain in the ass, and very often a pain in the heart.

But my gift didn't make other Grimms back away from me.

"Mind control." His voice was carefully empty, flat.

Too empty. Too flat.

I gaped at him. "Did you just say *mind control?*"

Michael didn't bother answering me. He knew I had heard him well enough.

Dazed, I settled back in my seat and just stared out into the night.

Mind control.

My friend, Greta, she can force people to do what she wants for short periods of time. But it comes with a cost to her. Anytime she uses her gift she ends up with a rousing headache. That's enough to keep her from abusing it.

But it wasn't the same as mind control. She only controlled their bodies.

If Michael's gift was mind control, he could control the body...*and* the mind. He could make people into his willing slaves.

I swallowed the knot in my throat. Poor guy. The rest of us probably treated him like a leper.

"Can you use it on us?"

We're not automatically immune to each other's gifts, you know. I don't know why it's like that. Maybe because on the most basic level we are still human. With me, I can use part of my gift on other Grimms. I can feel their emotions, but I can't reflect back at them all that well.

Reflecting works best on humans, but not just any old human. Nope, my gift tends to work better on the *tainted* humans—those who've been dabbling with demons but haven't gone too far yet.

I'm handy that way. If I can get to them soon enough, while they still have enough of their humanity left, I can show them what they're turning into. I can push it back on them. Sometimes that's all it takes for them to back away. Once they back away, their minds are their own again—the demons can't touch them.

I realized Michael hadn't answered me yet. I shifted in my seat, carefully holding my skirt down to keep it from riding up any higher. Not that it was possible. It was a good thing the panties matched the dress.

Propping my arm on the back of the seat, I stared at him. "So, can you?"

Michael's mouth twisted in a bitter smile. Somewhere deep inside, I realized it hurt to see that smile on his face. His gift made him unhappy. And that made me unhappy.

Even though, logically, I shouldn't give a damn if he was unhappy or not. Why should I care? After all this time, why should it matter?

"I don't know." He flicked a glance at me and shrugged. "I've never tried. What would be the point? We're all on the side of the angels after all. Right?"

"Actually, we *are* the angels."

He glanced at me again and this time, his eyes lingered. On my face and along my body. "You look more the temptress than the angel," Michael told me.

After all he'd done, after the hell I'd gone through, there was no reason that should made me feel so weak, so needy, so hungry. It didn't make sense.

But in a way, it made perfect sense. Only Michael could affect me like this. Only Michael.

Nobody had ever made me feel like he had—apparently he could still make me feel that way.

I decided I didn't like that knowledge. Once more, I shifted in the seat, turning so I stared out the window. I rested my arm on the door and tried to figure out how this happened. I tried to figure out how he could still affect me.

Absently, I reached up and touched the medallion that lay against my skin under my dress. It was cool, despite the fact that I still have a 98.6° body temperature. Usually the things only warmed up when we were summoned.

Silently, I asked, *Why did you send me here, Will?*

There was no answer, but I hadn't expected one.

Me. Michael. Both of us together. Was there a reason for it? Will knew who Michael was. Hell, I think most Grimms knew who we both were. Michael had been a minor figure in history, but still he was a royal. Those of us who had been around when he'd lived had heard the tale of the prince who disappeared only days before he was to wed.

He was a minor mystery in the pages of history—the mortal world had no idea what had become of him. All history knew was that he had disappeared and his family never saw him again.

Will knew who Michael was, and Will knew what he meant to me. More, Will knew the uglier bits of my past—how I'd ended up in the hands of a Grimm to begin with. Will's hands, to be precise.

What are you up to, Will?

Despite what others might think, he wasn't a cruel man and he would not have placed Michael and me together without good reason.

Unlike a lot of my fellow Grimms, I actually knew Will fairly well. He was the one who had found me barely clinging to life. I was bordering on unconsciousness at the time, slipping in and out of awareness, hovering near death. I'd been raped and then beaten within an inch of my life.

I had run away from my life, from my broken heart. Doing so nearly killed me... Well, it *had* killed me. But Will got to me in time, and before I was too far out of his reach he had offered me the Choice.

My old life had ended that night. Actually, it had ended the day I discovered Michael's true identity.

Even if I hadn't run away, my life would've changed.

Contrary to the fairy tale, it had been a good life.

My stepmother hadn't mistreated me. Forget what the books might say. I wasn't treated like a scullery maid. I only had the one stepsister, and she'd been a friend to me as well as a sister.

We had grown up together. I'd even known of her betrothal. She'd been betrothed to Michael from childhood.

The problem was that I met Michael without knowing who

he was. I had met him, fallen in love with him, and I believed he had loved me. As a baron's daughter, I hadn't been a bad catch.

But my stepsister was the daughter of a duke. Further up in the hierarchy than me, and with a nice, fat dowry... A much better catch.

By the time I discovered who he was, we were already lovers.

To be fair, Michael hadn't known who I was either. He was too honorable a man to chase after the stepsister of his future wife. And it's not as ridiculous as it might sound, the two of us having never met.

You know all of those spirited heroines you read about in historical romances? I could've been modeled after one of them—or rather, they could've been modeled after me. I was more interested in riding my horses, reading and hunting than in court life. I avoided it at all costs and my family had allowed me to get away with it.

Perhaps that was why I was so naïve, so...hopeful about life in general. I didn't know what *real* life was, even if I did understand pain, trauma, tragedy...loss.

I had been pampered and protected my whole life, first by my father, and then by his new wife and my new sister. They'd coddled me, protected me, loved me. Outside the circle of their love, I had no idea what real life was, what the real world was like.

Not until the year I met Michael, the summer we traveled north to the royal family's summer estate. At the end of the summer, my stepsister, Marguerite, was to wed. While she was busy with court life, I was out riding or sneaking into the library for books.

The library was where I met Michael.

It's a familiar story. Boy meets girl. Boy flirts with girl and girl flirts back. We'd known each other a week the day we became lovers. We'd been out riding. I'd slipped away from my rooms, leaving a message with my servant that I would be out riding—yet again.

What I didn't tell them was that I was meeting a man, a dashing, charming man.

If I hadn't begged off attending the first ball, I would have known who he was...and I would have stayed away from him. I never would have fallen in love with him and I never would have made love to him. In all honesty, other than that summer spent at the estate and the upcoming wedding, we wouldn't have seen much of each other.

Our lives would have been so much different, so much easier...if only I'd attended that first damn ball.

Once Marguerite had married Michael, she would've gone to live with him. I would've seen them sporadically, but I would've kept my distance. You have no idea how often I've thought about things, how I could have avoided the heartbreak if I'd just gone to the first stupid ball. But I hadn't wanted to dress in some fine gown and spend the night making small talk and giggling with the other ladies.

The miles sped by as I lost myself in my memories. I could remember some of it as clear as crystal...as clear as a glass slipper. Like the day I put my heart in his hands. In the hours we had spent together, he hadn't once mocked me for my boyish way of dressing, nor had he teased me for my love of books. He seemed to understand my distaste for court life. He had seemed to understand *me*.

I had hopes in my heart that he would even understand the secret I'd shared with only a few other people.

I don't even think he had set out to take advantage of me.

Advantage—there was no advantage taken. I guess I should be honest about that. He hadn't taken advantage of me—I'd given myself to him, freely and quite happily.

Tears burned my eyes and there was a knot in my throat.

"We should not do this..." he had told me.

That's what he'd said...to the girl I'd once been. Another lifetime ago.

1704

"Why not?" Elle whispered, staring up into dark, mysterious green eyes. How her heart raced when he looked at her...when he smiled at her. He had given her so much pleasure and she wished to give it to him as well.

Trying not to let him see her hands shaking, she pushed up on her toes and kissed him. He tasted of wine and the oranges he had brought. It had been a fine meal—in Elle's mind, it was a far finer meal than the royal banquets she was supposed to be attending.

"Elle..." He groaned her name as he pulled away. He eased back away from her hands and paced away, putting a careful distance between them.

Elle cocked her head and studied him. "Why shouldn't we do this?"

He shot her a dark look. "You are a lady. You well know the answer to that. You should..." His voice trailed off and then his face took on that silent, closed look that so many donned when speaking to an unwed, young woman.

"I am a lady...an unwed one. I should not speak of matters between a man and woman, at least not until I am wed." She made a face and said, "I know my own mind. If I wish to kiss a man, I will."

She moved to stand beside him, conscious of the fact that she was alone with a man, something that rarely happened. Even at home, when she went hunting or riding, there was usually another with her. She was alone with *this* man and he made her heart race.

She linked their hands and looked at him from under her lashes. "You have kissed me before and it seemed you enjoyed it. Have I bored you then?"

"I do not believe it possible to be bored when you are near," he said quietly. Michael cupped her face in his hands and lowered his head until their mouths were but a breath apart.

"Then why shouldn't we do this? Why shouldn't I kiss you now?"

The look in his eyes had her heart trembling with eagerness...and fear. "There comes a time when a man wants more than kisses from a pretty girl."

"I see." And she did. She rested a hand on his chest, just above his heart, and then gave him one of the coquettish smiles she'd seen used by some of the ladies at court. "Does that mean you do not want more with me?"

"Darling girl, I've thought of little else since I saw you sneaking out of the library, your face all dusty and your arms full of books." He caught her lower lip between his teeth and nipped it lightly. "But this isn't wise...it isn't fair. Not to you."

But she had always been stubborn. Trailing a hand down his chest, she caught one of his hands and lifted it to her breast. She'd worn breeches to ride and even if she had desired to wear a corset, she couldn't very well wear one to ride in. She went without one as often as possible and the shirt she wore proved little barrier.

"It is up to me to decide what is fair, is it not?"

Chapter Five

"Elle?"

The sound of Michael's voice made for a very effective wake-up call. I straightened and glanced over at him, startled to realize we had already arrived at the club.

"Are you well?" he asked, his voice stilted. "You have been rather quiet."

I gave him a breezy smile and lied through my teeth. "Oh, I'm wonderful. Just planning how to handle tonight."

"You do not lie well. Even after all this time." He watched me with shrewd eyes.

"My thoughts are my own, Michael. Let's just leave them that way."

A faint smile curled his lips. "Do you know that I can remember looking at your face and being able to read you like an open book? Every emotion you felt, every thought you thought, one could see it in your eyes. Not as easy to read now as you used to be, but I don't need to read you to understand what you are thinking. But you don't have to worry—I won't use it on you."

It took a minute to figure what he was talking about.

Then I understood. His gift. I just shook my head. "Michael, that's the least of my concern. I'm not worried about that at all."

"Why not? I tried to force you to my will before."

I rolled my eyes. "Oh, please. There's a big difference between offering to set me up as your mistress and forcing me to do your will."

I wanted to get out of the car, but he reached out and stopped me. Long, slender fingers wrapped around my wrist, his thumb stroking back and forth over the soft inside. "I never meant for you to run. I never meant to chase you away. If I had realized that was what would happen..." His voice trailed off and he sighed, letting me go. "I am sorry."

Nervous, I reached up to toy with my medallion only to remember it was under my dress. Couldn't risk having a succubus see it after all. So instead, I smoothed down my skirt and looked all around, looking anywhere but him. "Michael, you didn't make me run. I did it all on my own. It was my foolishness that led me to my fate."

"I threatened you. You were frightened."

"Let's not forget foolish and naïve." I shook my head. "I don't want to talk about this. It's old history."

I climbed out of the car and waited for him to join me. As he walked around the car, I stared at the club and braced myself.

I didn't want to go in there. Not at all. In a few minutes, I'd walk into that club, wade through that morass of envy, loneliness, guilt and need—emotions I was all too familiar with.

Michael joined me and I waited for him to offer his arm as he had the past four nights. But he didn't. He moved in front of me, staring down at me. "I would undo it if I could. Do you believe that? Can you?"

I studied his face. Physically, he looked the same as he did the last time I had seen him... Exactly the same. Those mysterious green eyes, a face as beautiful as an angel's, and a mouth that would tempt a saint. But he wasn't the same man. There was a heaviness to him, a grief.

And I was still naïve, I realized. Because I'd convinced myself I shouldn't care if he hurt, that I wouldn't be bothered by his sadness.

I'd let myself believe that time could change how I felt for this man, even though deep inside I knew otherwise.

I reached up and laid my hand on his cheek.

"We both made mistakes." I rubbed my thumb over his lower lip and remembered how it had felt the first time he kissed me. Like heaven. "I'm not without blame in this, Michael. And yes, I can believe you."

Impulsively, I pressed my lips to his chin. "Come on, we've got a job to do and I'd much rather do that than live in the past."

"A job." His smile was grim—no pun intended. "What a job—I dance with you while we are surrounded by men who cannot keep their eyes from you—and many have a hard time keeping their hands to themselves as well."

I slid him a sidelong glance. Smirking, I added, "Don't forget the women." I'd had my ass grabbed by a female more than once since we'd started this particular job.

"Well, there should be some on-the-job benefits." His face was straight, but there was a glint in his eyes, just the slightest hint of laughter.

"Pervert." I clicked my tongue and hooked my arm through his. "C'mon. Time to get our freak on."

Michael gave me a perplexed look. "Freak on?"

"You really do need to step into the 21st century."

Get our freak on. Michael leaned against the railing, a martini in his hand, watching Elle out on the dance floor. He had to admit, the phrase made sense. She danced with three other women. He could hardly take his eyes off her.

Dancing, just like everything else, had changed greatly over the centuries. It didn't seem right though, to call *this* dancing. They might as well be fucking. It was erotic enough that he had a raging hard-on just from watching them. The few times a man had attempted to join them, he had been hard-pressed to keep from tearing out throats.

Elle had saved his sanity, and the strain on his self-control, evading the men with flirtatious ease.

They had feigned a fight. They weren't going to see enough if they kept going as they had. If this didn't work she had said something about pretending to get drunk. Sooner or later, one of the demons would take the bait. They craved sex and Elle looked like a sexual deviant's dream come to life.

To his surprise, Elle didn't get approached.

He did.

The girl was young. If she was old enough to legally be in this club Michael would eat glass. Still, he pretended interest as she sidled up to stand beside him. He couldn't quite call what she was wearing a dress—he was certain he had seen lingerie that wasn't that revealing. Hell, there was more material on her thigh-high boots than her clothing combined.

The top was nothing more than a brassiere made of chain mail, and when she moved just so he caught glimpses of her pink nipples. The bottom wasn't any better, thong panties with a short lace overskirt that just barely managed to cover her rump. The thin silver chain she wore around her waist looked like it had been made from the same silver as her top. Her lips were slicked blood-red, matching her fingernails. Her hair was only a few shades lighter. Red hair, nails and lips, silver and black covering that too-young body...and a demon peeking out from her eyes.

She traced one red nail along the rim of his glass and leaned in to whisper, "You look awful lonely over here."

"And you look awful young." Michael gave her a dismissive glance. Not that he could dismiss her—he and Elle would have to intervene here. Now. Tonight. If their chance came in the form of this woman-child, so be it. Perhaps some good could even come of it—perhaps they could save her.

This one walked a narrow line. In another day or two it would be too late for her. It might be too late now.

Her lips curved into a smile, and there was nothing childish about it. "I'm older than I look."

"So am I." By several centuries.

Her smile didn't fade. "Oh, goody. I love older men...so much more...stamina." She leaned in and touched her tongue to his glass. "I'm thirsty."

Michael glanced at the drink he didn't want and then offered it to her. "By all means."

Oh, the little whore. I watched her lead Michael away. I couldn't see her eyes, but I had to guess she'd been touched. Michael wouldn't be wasting his time with her if there wasn't a demon's presence lingering around her.

Still...jealousy burned inside me.

One of the girls I'd been dancing with caught sight of my face and she grinned at me. "If you want to teach him a lesson, you can join me and my girlfriend. We can make him real miserable…invite him to watch."

She gestured towards one of the little stages. They were rarely empty. I'd seen everything from fellatio to spankings to ménages taking place on those little stages—entertainment, and cheap entertainment too. The club didn't pay a dime to the performers—anybody at the club who wanted to take a few minutes in the limelight could do so.

"I'd rather teach *her* a lesson," I said, still glaring in the direction Michael had gone. The private rooms. I'd heard about those for the first time last night. I stormed in their direction and if it seemed very easy to play the jealous lover, so what?

I couldn't see them any more, but I could feel him. A Grimm doesn't *feel* like a human, just like a demon doesn't *feel* like a human. I followed, letting my instincts guide me to a closed door. Above the lock, there was a little red occupied sign.

I smirked. Too fucking bad.

Pounding on the door, I screeched. Those in the hall around me barely heard me thanks to the music, but Michael heard me. Seconds later, the door opened and I got ready to tear into him. I had to keep up appearances after all. But before I could say anything, he caught my wrist and dragged me inside. He pinned me against the door and leaned in, placing his mouth right next to my ear.

"They have a camera going. Behind the mirror."

Shit. I met his gaze as he lifted his face. *Okay.*

I glanced past him to look at the girl. She smirked at me, and that's when I saw it. When I felt it. I hate being right. She had one in her. Working deeper and deeper. Wouldn't be too long before it was too late for her.

Shoving Michael away, I stared at him and let my lower lip tremble. "What are you doing in here with her, Michael?"

"Just having some fun," he said, giving me a cocky smile. "That's why we keep coming here, right? For fun?"

I shifted from one foot to another and tried to look nervous, embarrassed. "I just like… Well, you know…watching."

"Then watch."

I knew what he was going to do—I could see it in his eyes. But still, when I watched him kiss her it was like having my heart ripped out again. All over. "I don't want to watch you fucking some girl."

He looked up over her shoulder and smiled. "I didn't say I was going to fuck her." He shifted his gaze to the other woman. "I haven't made up my mind yet."

The woman chose that moment to slide her hand down his chest, down, down, until she was stroking him through his trousers. "Make up your mind," she whispered, her voice low and sultry. "I promise, I'll be good...or bad...whichever you want me to be."

"Tempting."

She threw me a challenging look over her shoulder. "She comes to a club like this, thinking it's all just fun and games. It's not. It's more." Then she looked back at Michael and whispered, "Let me show you."

She went to her knees in front of him.

Before she could loosen his belt, I crossed the room and buried my hand in her hair, yanking hard. Maybe a little harder than I should have. She screeched.

"Hands off, honey."

She jumped to her feet. Even if I hadn't already seen the demon peeking out from behind her eyes, that move—lightning quick and inhumanly graceful—would have clued me in. Not much time with you, I mused to myself as I studied her face.

I could see her muscles coiling and I braced—she might not be fully gone, but the demon in her was strong. Michael came between the two of us before she had a chance to rush me. He drew me close, pressed a kiss to my brow. "Darling girl, calm down."

I saw him smile at her, flashing that devastating smile of his at his new admirer. "Give us a minute, won't you?" He didn't bother waiting for an answer before shifting his gaze back to me. He skimmed his fingers through my hair, then down my back. His hand rested at the base of my spine, stroking. The warmth of his touch was so distracting it took me a minute to realize that he was talking to me. "You always tease me about trying new things. I'd say we could certainly call this...new."

"That is so like a man," I sneered at him. "You want me to watch her give you a fucking blowjob?"

"I was thinking of something with more participation, from all of us." Michael smiled at me.

I heard her coming up behind me, but I still flinched when her hands came around my waist. "That's just like a man too.

You get two girls at once?"

"I want to watch her touch you," he rasped against my mouth. Then he kissed me, arching my head back. His kiss was deep, rough, and my knees were weak by the time he lifted his head.

It's a damn good thing this was a job. Because if he had asked me that, and kissed me that way, I don't know that I would've been able to tell him no. Of course, when he kissed me that way, it was hard to remember what no was.

I could feel her behind me, rubbing against me. As her hands came up to cup my breasts, I caught her wrists.

We can't do this here, I thought, staring at Michael and hoping he picked up on my unspoken message.

He gave a tiny, imperceptible nod. Moving away from the girl, I turned and rested my back against his chest. "What's your name?"

"Call me Velvet," she said, her voice a seductive purr.

I didn't have to feign the hesitation as I looked around the small room. It had been cleaned, but I could still smell it— sex, sweat, even the faint metallic scent of blood. "I'm not having sex *here*." I didn't have to feign my revulsion either.

Michael's arms came around me. He nuzzled my neck. I shuddered as he scraped his teeth along my sensitive flesh. "Maybe a hotel?"

Velvet frowned. Glancing around the room, she said, "What's wrong with this room?"

"My lady is fastidious."

We both saw it in her eyes, a reluctance of her own. She didn't want to leave here. She might not instinctively understand it, but I knew the demon inside her felt safer with more of her own kind around.

But we couldn't do this here.

So we would just have to tempt her away.

Michael stroked his hands on my hips, under the hem of my brief dress. Blood rushed to my cheeks as he touched me in front of her. Renewed interest flared in her eyes and I felt the demon's presence more strongly.

The problem was I couldn't relax in front of her.

Then don't think about her, I told myself. Think about Michael.

Or better yet...don't think at all.

Squeezing my eyes closed, I focused on him, the way his fingers circled around my clit, and the hard, firm length of his cock cuddling against my ass. I whimpered and sagged in his arms.

Need boiled inside me. Self-preservation was the only thing keeping me on my feet—well, that and Michael.

"We're leaving, Velvet." Michael pulled his hand away from my sex and lazily licked his fingers. "You're welcome to join us, but we're leaving."

Velvet followed us out.

Chapter Six

A hotel wouldn't do.

Not enough privacy. Michael waited until they were a few miles away from the club before he did anything. Pulling up on the side of the road, he turned and faced Velvet.

She blinked and glanced around, looking confused. "What are we doing…"

"Be silent."

For a split second, a dazed, helpless look appeared in her eyes. Then it was gone, chased away by demon heat, demon hunger…and fear. If the succubus hadn't figured out yet, she would shortly.

Narrowing his eyes, Michael pushed at her with his mind. "Tell me where you live."

Once more, she looked dazed and helpless. In a monotone voice, she gave him directions. Michael committed them to memory and then asked her, "What is your real name? Do you have a family?"

"Vanessa." Tears appeared in her eyes. "I have my mom. But she's not here. She's back home."

The small, rundown apartment wasn't much better than a hotel room. At least here Elle could do what she needed to do, and when they were done they could leave Vanessa here, knowing she'd be safe.

It took them less than twenty minutes to get from the club to Vanessa's little apartment. It took another three minutes to get into the apartment building with the door locked behind them.

The demon was fighting harder now. In the back of his mind, Michael could feel the thing struggling and jerking against the bonds Michael had laid on Vanessa's vulnerable mind. He looked at Elle. "You need anything?"

Elle shook her head.

"If I hold her mind, can you do what you need to do? Or do I need to let it go?"

"It will be best if you're not touching her...physically or otherwise."

Vanessa's eyes were huge, dark in her pale face. They wheeled back and forth between his face and Elle's. She didn't move—couldn't move, not unless Michael let her. But her entire body was tense, tight. Ready to flee or fight.

"She's going to try and take off the minute I release her," he warned Elle.

She nodded. "I figured." Jerking her head, she said, "Go stand by the door. Just in case."

As Michael did, Elle prowled around the little apartment. Her eyes landed on a black silk scarf draped over the coffee table. She grabbed it and approached Vanessa. "Don't let her go until I tell you."

"I won't."

Vanessa began to struggle against his mental hold, harder and harder.

Elle used the scarf as a makeshift gag and Michael closed his eyes. He could feel her fear through their mind link, feel her terror. And the demon...rousing. Stretching against her skin. Whispering to her... *Call...call for help. Call for help and they'll leave you alone.*

But Michael wouldn't loosen his grasp enough for her to do that. She couldn't so much as twitch a finger, much less call for help.

"Okay, Michael."

Elle was standing in front of Vanessa, her willowy body braced, like she was facing down a linebacker instead of a young woman who stood just an inch or so over five feet.

Michael dropped his hold and Vanessa lunged. She didn't make it two inches before Elle caught her and used the girl's momentum and body weight to take her to the floor.

"Listen to me. I'm not going to hurt you," Elle said, catching first one wildly swinging fist, then the other.

Vanessa whimpered and bucked, trying to knock Elle away.

"Easy...easy..."

Michael felt it when she started. He hadn't known if he'd feel anything—there was a light push, followed by a rush of cold and loneliness. Pain that stretched on without end. Emptiness.

His own eyes stung with tears and Elle wasn't even focused on him.

Beneath her, Vanessa sobbed.

"It doesn't get better," Elle whispered, her voice sympathetic and gentle. "It just gets worse. One day, you'll want somebody who doesn't want you...but you'll need it too much. You'll want it too much, and since you're stronger you'll just take it. You'll hurt people...unless you die first."

Vanessa averted her face, but both Michael and Elle had seen the tears on her face.

Without a link to her mind, Michael didn't know what she was thinking. But he didn't need to be linked to her to recognize the pain inside of her.

Elle's voice dropped, soft and low. "Is that really what you want? Is that who you want to be?" Carefully, she eased the gag down, letting the girl talk.

"You're lying... I don't like hurting people. I wouldn't."

"You won't have a choice. The demon inside you is getting stronger—sooner or later you won't be able to fight it."

"Demon?" Vanessa shook her head. "I don't have the demon inside me."

"Yes, you do. And I think you know it. You feel it...that darkness inside of you, so alien, so cold, so hungry. It's not a part of you—you know that, even though you don't completely understand it." Elle's face darkened with a frown. "You don't remember inviting her in, but you did. It's the only way they can get in, and once they're inside, you start to feel different. Very different. I bet you even remember when it happened... Yes, you do. I can feel it. You can't hide it from me. *She* can't hide it from me."

Vanessa started to shake. She stared at Elle, terror written all over her features. "No."

Abruptly, the young woman's body arched and started to spasm violently. Elle swore and shot Michael a desperate glance. "Help me."

Demon-strong. Michael caught her legs and kept them from

thrashing. Elle held her upper body down, a cold, hard smile curling her lips.

Keep fighting, Michael thought. Just keep fighting.

If the succubus fought hard enough she would wear herself down. Without a body to jump to, she would have to retreat to the netherplains and rebuild her strength. It would take her a few days at least, which would give them a little bit more time.

It was also possible that she had invested too much strength in Vanessa. That the succubus would die without her connection to her host. That would just be an added bonus as far as Michael was concerned.

Vanessa's mouth opened, but the voice wasn't hers. The succubus...she wasn't human and she never had been. "You'll pay for this. My queen will hunt you down. You'll die screaming while my brothers and sisters fuck you both until you bleed."

"Do you promise?" Elle purred, her voice husky. Michael didn't need to see her face to sense her excitement, to feel her adrenaline rush.

Elle was all about the hunt, it seemed.

The succubus shrieked.

Elle swore and fought to cover the girl's mouth. The demon swore, kicked and fought. But she wasn't strong enough to handle both of them and in moments, Elle had the gag back in place.

"Vanessa, you're stronger than she is...for now. You're still in control. Come back...talk to us."

Behind the gag, the succubus hissed. Vanessa's eyes rolled back in her head and then she went limp.

"Is she...?"

"No." Elle shook her head. "They're fighting. I can feel it."

I was exhausted by the time it was over. Michael carried Vanessa's sleeping body to the hard, uncomfortable-looking futon tucked against the far wall. She was asleep, but before we left, Michael would have to wake her up. We couldn't leave any memories of us intact. If we did and one of the other demon-touched came looking for Vanessa, our cover would be blown. We couldn't afford that. There were still too many left—I know I'd felt eight or nine, at least.

Plus, there was the queen.

"You need to wake her up."

Michael gave me a questioning glance.

Shifting from one foot to the other, I said, "She can't remember we were here. If anybody comes looking for her, I don't want her remembering this. Not until we find the queen and take her out."

"You want me to take the memory of us away."

"Yes." I sighed and started to pace. The knee-high leather boots I wore were pinching my toes. I wanted nothing more than to take them off, get out of the dress and soak in a hot tub of water. But we had to finish here and I doubted I'd stay awake long enough once we were done.

"If one of the others come looking for her, she's going to say no. I scared the hell out of her." I had—and I didn't feel the least bit guilty for it either. It had worked and that was all that mattered just then.

She wouldn't go back to that club. Hopefully, the fear would strengthen her. "She might lie, but I don't want her lying to a demon. They will figure it out. But if her memory of tonight is gone she won't have to lie. She'll be safer."

A muscle jerked in Michael's jaw. He stared over my shoulder at the wall. Long seconds of silence ticked away. Then his green eyes met mine and he gave a single, short nod. "I can do that. What do you want her to remember?"

"Whatever you think will work best. You link with her mind, right?"

"I have to. It's the only way it will work."

I nodded. "Good. When you link with her mind, as you put down a false memory, you should be able to feel it if something seems too off. Right?"

I was grasping at straws here. I didn't understand much about mind control. But I did understand connections—psychic and emotional connections were useful tools.

"If I let her go slowly, I should be able to sense it if something feels wrong. I'll trigger the memory and we'll see what happens."

"Works for me." Pursing my lips, I studied Vanessa's still body. "You think she would know who the queen is?"

Chapter Seven

Off to the east, the sky was beginning to lighten by the time we were done with Vanessa. Michael looked as exhausted as I felt. He had dark shadows under his eyes, and there was unhappiness in that enigmatic green gaze.

I let Michael drive. He looked like he needed to do something with his hands.

Besides, I was exhausted. I know it didn't hit other Grimms as hard, but any time I had to use my so-called gift, it wore me out. Hopefully I could stay awake long enough to get to my bed.

We were both quiet as we pulled away from the apartment. Both listening. Both on alert. Nobody had come looking for Vanessa while we had been at her apartment.

"You think she's going to be okay?" I asked, worried. "I know we fixed the memory, but still..."

Michael glanced my way. He shook his head and a faint smile twitched at his lips. "She won't be there. I left her with the suggestion that she leave for a few days—maybe for good. I think she's going to go back home. I told her to find someplace safe, someplace where she felt loved. All she could think of was home. She'll sleep for a few hours and then she'll be gone. I doubt they will think to look for her today, and if they did start looking, it wouldn't be until tonight. By then, she'll be gone."

I heaved out a sigh of relief. "Good."

I relaxed against the seat.

A little too much. My lids felt heavy. So did my body. Somehow, I knew I wasn't going to make it to my own bed before I crashed. I rubbed my eyes and glanced at Michael. "Hey, I guess I better warn you. Sometimes when I use the gift, it throws me for a loop. If I fall asleep, I'll be unconscious for a good four to six hours straight." I tried to smile. "You can just dump me at my place. It's not too far from where you're staying. I can…" I never even noticed I had fallen asleep.

Throws me for a loop. A bit of an understatement, Michael thought. She had fallen asleep in midsentence and he had no idea where she was staying. Had she brought her purse? He scowled, trying to remember. Yes, he thought she'd had one in the club.

Keeping his eyes away from his unconscious passenger, he pulled to the side of the road to check for a purse, or anything that might tell him where she was staying.

A few minutes and one fruitless search later, he pulled back onto the road. Her purse had held cash, the false ID for her current persona and a tube of lipstick—that seductive, wine-red shade that seemed to scream *fuck me*.

He was fucked.

Elle sat next to him, sleeping peacefully. Five minutes earlier, she had shifted in the seat and when she did, that microscopic skirt had climbed so high on her thighs, he could see the wine-red lace of her panties. The panties were the same shade as her dress and her ivory skin glowed against the vivid color.

He found himself staring at her thighs, at the shadowed triangle where her thighs met. He jerked his attention back to the road and gripped the steering wheel so hard it was a miracle the plastic didn't crack.

I'm no bleeding saint, Michael thought grimly.

His control was being stretched thin, and considering how tired he was, it was a miracle *he* hadn't cracked.

The drive to his condo seemed to take twice as long as normal, and yet it also seemed as though it was over in the blink of an eye. She didn't wake up when he stopped the car. She didn't wake up when he opened her door and crouched down beside her. He rested a hand on her knee, certain she would wake up when he touched her.

"Elle."

She didn't stir.

Shit.

Setting his jaw, he worked his arms under her and eased

her out of the car. As he straightened, she cuddled against his chest, rubbing her cheek against his shirt. She sighed in her sleep, "Michael."

His heart stopped. *Elle...*

"Get a grip," he muttered. Keeping his eyes focused straight ahead, he managed to make it across the paved drive and into the condo without looking at her. Of course, not looking at her didn't really help. He was acutely aware of her warm weight, her soft curves and silken skin left bare by her skimpy dress. Her scent flooded his head and his mouth watered for another taste of her.

A real taste—when all he had to think about was *her*. A real taste—when he didn't have to share her, didn't have to worry about who was watching.

He tucked her into his bed, trying not to think about how much he wanted to join her. It was a big bed, wide as a lake and soft. Her golden hair spilled across the ebony bed linens. One fat curl lay across her cheek. Unable to resist, he reached out and brushed it away. Then he stroked his thumb across her lower lip.

Her mouth puckered. Her brows drew low over her eyes. "Michael..." She reached out.

"Shhh." He caught her hand and lifted to his lips. Then he eased it back, tucking it under the blankets and smoothing them down. "Rest, Elle. You're safe."

Rising, he forced himself to walk away. Just as he went to close the door behind him, he heard her whisper, "*Je t'aime.*"

I love you.

1704

His head ached.

The taste of stale wine lay on his tongue. The light filtering in through the curtains was painfully bright. It would be best if he just remained in bed, but he couldn't.

He needed to find Elle. Needed to talk to her.

Needed *her*. He needed Elle.

Elle. As in *Giselle*...the young stepsister of his fiancée. He had fallen in love with her. He had convinced himself that his interludes with the girl meant nothing, that she was just a distraction. But in his heart of hearts, he'd known the truth and ignored it. If she had just been the daughter of one of the visiting nobles it would have been so much easier. In a few short weeks, she would leave his family's summer estate and it would be unlikely he would see her again.

But she was Giselle, Marguerite's beloved little sister. His betrothed had often written of the younger woman, and he knew there was little Marguerite wouldn't do for the girl.

It was a sentiment he understood well.

Swearing, he cradled his aching head in his hands. Part of him was filled with dread—he had seen the shock, the pain in Elle's face last night when the formal announcements were made. Seeing her pain had been like taking a dagger to his heart.

He needed to see her. He needed to bid her farewell.

Farewell.

Michael closed his eyes. Even though he'd known it was inevitable, he still couldn't conceive it. Couldn't imagine walking away from her, never seeing her again.

Letting her go.

But he must. He had no choice.

Do you not?

The sly, insidious whisper crept up on him. He tried to shove it away, but then the pain returned and he knew he'd do anything to keep her with him.

For always.

He was a man. She was a lovely woman who had already given herself to him. There was no need to let her go. He could take care of her. Set her up somewhere close to him, and they could be together as often as possible. It was a common enough arrangement. Most of the men he knew had mistresses.

Of course, he couldn't think of a single one setting up his sister-in-law as his mistress.

She has feelings for me, he told himself.

It would actually be a kindness to her—any future husband she might have wouldn't indulge her the way her father had, the way her stepmother and stepsister had. That fiery spirit of hers would be crushed.

I cannot do this, he told himself, but he heard the lack of conviction.

It wasn't fair to her.

But then again...how fair was it that they lose each other when they had just found each other? They were happy together. They belonged together.

Before long, he had himself convinced it was the best thing to do.

The only thing.

Yes...this is what I must do.

He found Elle at the northern edge of the lake, sitting on the grass and staring out over the water. Her golden hair was loose and blowing in the wind. She wore men's clothing.

To him, she looked lovelier than any lady of the court.

"Elle."

When she looked at him, he realized she had been crying. Her summery blue eyes were red and swollen. A jagged pain tore through him. She came to her feet and he braced himself. His Elle had a temper.

"Your highness," she said, her voice soft and low. She curtsied, and despite the men's clothing, she looked lovely and elegant. "I beg your pardon. I shall leave—"

"Stop." He barely managed to keep from bellowing. Striding up to her, he caught her arm. "Do not do that."

"Do what, your highness?" She kept her head lowered.

"*That.* I have a name, the same name you've used for this past week. I would thank you to use it." *Look at me. Darling girl, please look at me.*

"I beg your pardon, Your Highness, but I cannot. It was only in my ignorance that I addressed you so inappropriately." She eased back a step. "If you would excuse me—"

"I will not. I came to speak with you."

Finally, her gaze met his for only the briefest second. Then she looked away, staring past him into the trees. "I do not think it is proper that we speak, Your Highness," she said softly.

"This past week, you have cared nothing for being proper. Why do you suddenly care now?"

"Because now I know who you are." She swallowed and cleared her throat. When she spoke again, her voice cracked. "You are my sister's betrothed. You are Prince Louis Michael III. And I..." Shaking her head, she backed away. "I must go. Farewell, Your Highness."

"No," he growled. Grabbing her arms, he hauled her against

him and fisted a hand in her bright, golden curls. Her hair was like sun-warmed silk under his hand. "I am not ready for you to go."

He kissed her, desperate to find the warmth he had known this past week. But she was still and cool, unmoving under his hands. She did not fight, but she did not welcome his touch either. Frustrated, so very hungry for her, he slid a hand under her shirt and found warm, bare skin. Her breast was soft and full and when he circled his thumb over her nipple, it peaked against his touch.

"You want me," he whispered against her mouth. "You cannot deny that."

"No."

He lifted his head and stared at her. "And I want you. I cannot deny that."

"You are my sister's betrothed. This is not right." Tears gleamed in her eyes, but she blinked them away. A ragged breath escaped her, her slender body tensing in his arms. "Release me, Your Highness."

"I cannot do that. You are *mine*, Elle. You gave yourself to me and I intend to keep you." He nipped her lower lip and straightened. Staring into her eyes, he swiftly stripped her shirt away, tossing it to the grass.

She looked down at her bare breasts and then up at him, a bemused look on her face. Then she shook her head and turned away. "I cannot give myself to a man who is promised to another," she said quietly. She bent over and grabbed her shirt.

The fabric of her breeches drew tight across her rump and Michael caught her hips, holding her steady as he pressed against her. She whimpered, a soft, hungry female sound that went straight to his head. His blood pumped hot and fast. "You are mine," he whispered.

She straightened and he wrapped an arm around her waist, holding her tense body against his own as he dipped his hand inside her breeches. She was wet, silky wet and so hot. *Mine.*

Her knees buckled and she sagged against him. Instead of supporting her weight, he eased her to the ground, following her down. Shoving her breeches down to her knees, he stared at the soft, plump curves of her rump, the golden curls that framed her sex, and the glistening pink folds.

"Michael, please..."

"Yes," he whispered, pressing his fingers to her wet slit. "Say my name. *My* name, not some fucking title." He shoved his own breeches down, baring nothing but his cock and then he pressed against her.

Elle tensed and he reached around, toying with the swollen bud just above her entrance. "Say my name, Elle. Tell me you want me. Tell me you want *this*," he demanded.

Tell me that you are mine...I just found you, I cannot lose you.

"Michael, we cannot do this," she whispered.

He set his jaw. In the back of his mind he knew he should stop. He reached for what little remained of his control. She shivered in his arms, whimpering low in her throat.

"Shhh..." he murmured, brushing his lips over her bare shoulder. Gritting his teeth, he sent the order to his hands to release her. But then she rolled her hips back.

Swearing, he reached up and turned her face, covering her mouth with his as he sank his aching cock into her slick pussy. Tight—as tight as she had been just the other day when he took what she had given to no other man. She whimpered and shifted, trying to spread her thighs to better accommodate him, but the breeches still tangled around her knees prevented it.

"Mine," he rasped against her lips as she cried out.

Bracing one elbow on the grass, he used the other to grip her hip, bracing her as he rode her—deep and hard, lost in the feel of her, the taste of her. The sound of her crying out his name as he brought her to pleasure was the most beautiful sound he'd ever heard.

It was hard, brutal and fast...devastating, over all too soon. She came around him with a sob and he erupted inside her, emptying himself. Collapsing atop her body, he rolled to his side, drawing her with him.

The sun shone down on their bodies, warm and bright. A gentle breeze danced across their flesh as he stroked a hand down her hip.

Kissing her shoulder, he whispered, "My Elle..."

"*Je t'aime.*"

The whispered declaration washed over him and he closed his eyes. Gripping her hip, he started to move inside her again. "Yes. *That* is what I want from you, Elle...what I need. Say it again."

197

She remained silent.

Pulling away, he stripped her clothes away and then his own. Then he laid her on the discarded clothing and came into her again. Cupping her face in his hands, he demanded, "Look at me, Elle. Say it again."

Elle's eyes remained stubbornly closed.

Swearing, Michael raked his teeth down her neck, along her jaw. Against her ear, he whispered, "I love you so much it hurts. My darling girl, do you not know?"

"Michael, please..."

He reached between them, stroking her clitoris with the tip of his finger. The little nub of flesh was hard and erect and she cried out when he touched her, her voice ragged and breathless.

He toyed with her, stroking and teasing until she was panting, straining for the release he held just out of her reach. Her nails raked down his back and she bit his shoulder so hard she left a mark on him. "Tell me again, Elle. Please tell me..."

"I love you, Michael." She whispered it quietly, her golden lashes shielding her eyes.

But she'd said it. She'd admitted it. She *was* his. He would keep her.

"Darling girl."

As he brought her to one final climax, he crushed his mouth to hers.

Mine...

Quiet moments passed and Michael found himself drifting closer and closer to sleep. But then Elle stirred in his arms and he sat up as she did. When she would have stood, he caught her arm and pulled her into his lap. She sat there stiffly, staring out over the lake.

"We should talk arrangements," he said quietly. Already, he had an idea where she would live. It was close enough that he could see her several times a week, or more.

"Arrangements."

"Yes." He brushed her hair back from her face, staring down at her, aching for the sadness in her eyes. It would pass though. He wouldn't lose her, and she wouldn't lose him. "I was thinking I could bring you to the city in a few months."

He hadn't thought it possible, but her body grew more rigid in his arms. "Bring me to the city, Your Highness? For what purpose?"

"So we can be together, Elle. You love me...you have freely admitted it. I love you. I will not be without you."

A humorless smile twisted her lips. "You expect me to be your mistress."

"I expect you to be exactly what you already are...the woman I fell in love with."

"The woman you wish to fuck whenever you choose. I wonder what your betrothed would think of this." She drove her elbow into his stomach, forcing the air from him.

Then she jerked away, grabbing her shirt and jerking it out from under his leg. She pulled it over her head and shoved her tangled hair back from her face. Calmly, she stared at him and said, "No."

Michael came to his feet, narrowing his eyes. "No?" he echoed quietly.

"That is what I said. No."

Striding towards her, he caught her in his arms and jerked her against him. "I will not lose you, Elle. You are *mine*."

"I belong to no man...especially not you. I will not be your whore—you are to wed my sister. I love her, but you would ask me to hurt her like this? Betray her? No. I will not."

"You will not leave me. I will not allow it." He fisted a hand in her hair and rasped quietly, "You know who I am now, Elle. You will be mine—I care not what it takes to keep you."

She stilled, her blue eyes wide as she gaped at him.

"You would threaten me?" she demanded.

"I would do what I must to keep what is mine."

"I am *not* yours," she snarled.

"You are." He kissed that snarling mouth and then lifted his head. "If I were to go to your stepmother and tell her how you threw yourself at my feet, what would she think? She may well turn you out on the streets, and unless you find either a husband or a keeper you would be homeless...destitute."

She swallowed. "No. You cannot tell her. It would break her heart...it would break her heart and Marguerite's."

"They needn't know," he whispered, wiping away a tear as it rolled down her cheek.

"And how do you think to keep it secret if you set me up as your mistress?" she demanded.

"I will think of something." He stared at her averted face, rubbing a soothing hand up and down her stiff back. "You are mine, Elle."

Her head bowed, her shoulders slumped. She looked utterly broken.

"It will be well, Elle. Trust me."

"No." She lifted her head and those soft blue eyes were cold. She jerked against his hold and said, "I will not trust you, and this will *not* be well."

She struggled in his arms, kicking his shins when he wouldn't release her. When that didn't work she went to bite him. Michael banded an arm around her waist and jerked her off her feet. She screeched at him as he impaled her on his cock. "Put me down, you bastard," she snarled.

He kissed her and she bit his lip.

He bit her back and she shuddered. Her legs twined around his waist and she pulled away, staring at him.

"Ride me," he rasped. "Ride me, Elle." He gripped her hips and guided her movements. She was swollen, wet from the past two times he had spent himself inside her.

"I will not be your whore," she whispered even as she clenched around him and started to rock. Her strong thighs gripped his hips.

Cupping her ass, he stroked his fingers down the crevice between her cheeks. He watched as a flush came to her face when he pressed against her back entrance. "You are not my whore...you are my heart. My love. I cannot lose you."

"But I was never yours," she whispered, shaking her head. She shuddered, her teeth catching her lower lip as he eased the tip of his finger inside the tight pucker of her ass. "Nor were you mine. This ends, Michael. It must."

"No." He took her to the ground, pulling out and then guiding her to her hands and knees. He pushed back inside her, sinking his cock into her heat as he pressed his thumb against her ass and entered her that way as well. He would have her in every way. All ways. In time.

In time, she would see that this was how it must be. They belonged together.

The minutes bled away as he loved her, and when at last it ended he whispered against her ear, "I will take care of you, Elle. I will take care of this. All will be well."

Then, exhausted by the past hours, he drifted off to sleep.

It was nearly dusk when he awoke, and Elle was gone.

He returned, wanting to seek her out, but refraining. They must be careful how they handled this. He wouldn't see her dishonored. Though his heart ached to see her again, he left her alone that night.

He planned to seek her out the next morning, certain that she would be out riding, just as she had every day since she had come to his family's summer estate.

But he couldn't find her. Not that day.

And the next morning, he heard the news.

Elle had disappeared.

Chapter Eight

It was the pain that woke me.

The pain was so deep, even in sleep I couldn't hide from it.

Groggy, I sat up, staring at the unfamiliar room. Although I had never seen the room before, I knew where I was. It was Michael's room. I recognized the scent of him on the sheets. Although I was alone, I could feel him all around me.

My dress hadn't fared well—it was tangled around my waist, and the silk was wrinkled beyond all hope. I caught sight of the closet as I climbed out of bed. I shimmied out of the dress and draped it over the foot of the bed. The closet was full of black, black and more black. I selected one of the shirts and pulled it on. Since he wasn't there to see, I held the fine material to my face and breathed him in.

Leaving the bedroom, I squared my shoulders. Mentally, I reinforced my shields. I had a bad feeling I knew what was coming.

This would be so much easier if I didn't still care for him. So much easier if I didn't still love him.

I found him on the balcony, staring out over the lake. He didn't turn to face me but I knew he was aware of me.

I closed the sliding glass door at my back and folded my arms over my middle. It was early, not quite dawn, although I could see where the sky was beginning to lighten in the east. The air was cool and damp. A heavy mist lay over the water.

"Good morning, Michael." Shivering, I moved away from the door, stopping halfway across the deck.

Under the fine silk, the shoulders of his muscles tensed. He turned to me, his eyes dark and turbulent. There was a heavy growth of stubble darkening his features. I'm pretty sure I had never seen him looking so unkempt.

"It's only been three hours. Do you need more rest?" he asked, his tone polite, cordial even.

I shrugged. My body could have used more sleep, but there was no way I was going to get any more rest today. "Have you slept?" I asked, even though I already knew the answer.

"No."

In the thin, predawn light, he looked grim, forbidding.

And he felt...broken.

Tears pricked my eyes and I averted my face, hoping he wouldn't see. Dear God. The pain. The loneliness. The longing. I couldn't read thoughts, but emotions were so much more devastating. While I had slept, he had been reliving those few days we'd had together.

Remembering...wondering.

Hurting.

I took no pleasure in his pain. How could I? I swallowed past the knot in my throat. "You know what, I think I may go lie back down." I backed away from him. No, I wouldn't sleep. But maybe I could delay this a little while longer.

But *this* wouldn't be delayed.

Before I made it to the door, he caught my arm. "I want to know what happened."

"No." I didn't bother pretending ignorance. There was no point.

"Yes. You need to tell me."

"*No.*" I shook my head and tugged gently against his hand.

He didn't let me go. "Elle, I need to know." He brought his other hand up and smoothed my tangled hair back from my face. Then he cupped my chin in his hand, angling my face up until I met his gaze.

I stared into the dark, screaming hell of his eyes and whispered, "No." Taking a deep breath, I steadied myself. "You do not need to know. You do not *want* to know. And I don't want to tell you."

"Why not?" Something flashed in his eyes and I could feel his temper spike. But his voice remained gentle, as did his hands.

Sighing, I rested my hands on his chest. Under the black silk, I could feel the warmth of his body, the strength. Curling my fingers in the silk, I gave into the urge and moved close. His arms came around me as I lay my head on his chest. "Because that is knowledge you do not need in your head," I told him.

"I *have* to know." His arms tightened, almost too tight. Then he caught my arms in his hands and eased me back. "I must know."

I shook my head. "What happened to me, Michael, is over and done. It's another lifetime ago. Those memories are mine and I will keep them that way. I won't share that burden with you."

A muscle jerked in his jaw. "Do you truly want me to believe that you keep silent out of some desire to protect me?"

"Nothing will come from me sharing those memories with you." *Nothing good, at least.*

"Damn it, woman," he growled. "Tell me."

"Why? So you can hate yourself even more than you do now?" I could no longer fight the tears burning my eyes. They broke free, rolling down my cheeks in hot, stinging tracks. "The guilt inside you, it's choking me. I am not going to add to it."

"Why *not*?" he asked, his voice soft, deceptively so. Fury and grief shone in his eyes. The flood of emotions welling inside him threatened to tear him apart...and me.

"You hate me for what happened to you, for what I did to you, for what I threatened to do. Here is your chance to make me suffer, even more than I already do. Why do you not take it?"

"I don't hate you," I whispered. I looked away from his face, staring out over the lake.

Gentle fingertips wiped away my tears and I shivered under his touch.

"Don't you? You have every right."

"Three hundred years is a long time to hold a grudge, Michael." Up until recently, I had believed that I did hate him.

I had been wrong. Very wrong. I didn't hate him. I loved him. I love him still. And I suspected I'd love him until the end of time...beyond.

But I didn't tell him that.

He caught my chin in his hand, guided my face back to his. He stared into my eyes, his gaze intent, probing. It was as though he could learn my secrets through his stare alone.

I reached up and traced the line of his mouth. "Just let it go, Michael. It is in the past, very much in the past."

"No." His voice shook as he said it.

Then to my surprise, he yelled it. "*No.*"

Abruptly, he jerked away from me and started to pace. His booted heels rang hollowly on the wooden deck. I could feel all the emotions he tried to contain—rage, grief, fear. Under it all, an obsessive need to know.

I feared the knowledge would destroy him.

It was a secret I had shared only with Will.

If I had it my way, I would go to my grave without telling another soul. Especially Michael.

"Why, damn it? Make me understand, Elle. It was my fault. I drove you away. If I hadn't done that, nothing would've happened to you. Whatever happened to you, the blame lies at my feet. You know this. So why will you not tell me?"

I shook my head. I shivered, but it had nothing to do with the chill in the air.

"Give me one damn reason," he snarled, wheeling around to glare at me.

"Because I still love you." I dashed away my tears with my fingertips. Staring at him, I shook my head and backed away. "I still love you—I don't think I ever stopped. And I can't hurt you like that."

Turning away, I moved towards the sliding glass door. As I reached to open it, his arms came up and penned me in. I froze. Michael dipped his head and kissed my shoulder. His voice a soft whisper, he murmured, "What did you say?"

"You heard me well enough." I held still, afraid to move.

"How?" he asked, bemused. He stroked a hand down my hip. "How can you possibly love me after what I did? After what I said to you?"

Closing my eyes, I sighed. Such a complicated question. Such a simple question.

How?

I swallowed the knot in my throat. "You said awful things, Michael. You threatened me with awful things...but you wouldn't have gone through with them."

The sound of his laughter, so bitter and brittle, damn near broke my heart. "Of all people, Elle, you should know better than to romanticize me."

"I've never romanticized you a day of my life." I turned to face him, staring up at his face—such a perfect face. The elegant, masculine beauty of it had haunted my dreams for years, decades...centuries. "Three hundred years ago, you were arrogant, self-centered and entirely too concerned with what pleased you."

I reached up, trailed my fingers down his jaw, along his lower lip. "But you are not cruel. You never have been. You wouldn't intentionally harm one you cared about. You did care about me."

A hand hard as iron closed around my wrist. I stared up into eyes that glittered like broken glass. "How can you still be so naïve? How? As long as you have lived, as much of you have seen... You know what ugliness lives in the hearts of men."

His voice was cold and cruel, as though he felt the need to convince me how wrong I was. I smiled at him. Laying my free hand on his cheek, I told him, "I know the ugliness. I also know the beauty. For every evil, ugly deed, there is a kind, selfless one."

"I've never been kind or selfless a day in my life." He caught my other wrist, drawing my hand from his face. He pinned both my wrists over my head and leaned in close, so close I could feel the kiss of his breath against my mouth. "I was willing to do anything to keep you, willing to ruin your life...had you not run away, I might have even stolen you away."

"No." How was it that I knew the truth but he did not? Did he truly understand himself so poorly? I flexed my wrists against his hold, tugging lightly. There was no give. He didn't hold me to hurt me, but he wouldn't release me easily either.

Sighing, I let my head fall back against the sliding glass door. I studied his face, all hollows, angles and shadows. His eyes glittered in the darkness and his mouth was a hard, unyielding line. "Have you ever wondered why my father, and later my stepmother, were so content to let me flout the rules of society? I was seventeen...I should have already been presented at court. If they had raised me as they should, I would have met you before I could unknowingly throw myself at your feet. They should have been seeking out a prospective husband for me, but instead I wore men's clothes and spent my days hunting or riding."

"What has that to do with anything?" he asked.

"Everything." I closed my eyes and took a deep breath. Then I looked at him. "I would have happily lived out my life without ever leaving my father's home had I not met you. And my stepmother never would have pressed me...because she knew the truth about me."

"The truth." He lowered my wrists and backed away, staring at me with confusion.

I stared him in the eyes and said quietly, "Being Changed only strengthened what I could already do, Michael. I was empathic long before I met Will. Long before I met you. My father knew. He knew what a struggle it was for me to be around too many others for any long stretch of time and he feared for me. Later, my stepmother learned my secret, as did my stepsister. It's why very few people in society knew a damn thing about me. While Marguerite played the part of a noblewoman, I lived in complete and utter freedom...but only because if I had lived as she did it might have driven me mad. It took me years to learn the control I needed to be close to others for more than a few hours at a time. Years before I could handle functioning in society in some small way."

Michael shook his head. "I don't see what in the hell that has to do with anything."

I reached up and laid a hand on his heart. Then I reached inside myself for a memory that I had kept locked away for years...the emotion I had caught off of him as he made a threat he couldn't possibly keep.

I turned it back on him, revealing to him the knowledge I'd picked up from him—even as he'd made the threat, I knew he'd lied. He might not have realized it, but I did.

He stumbled back and my hands fell to my sides. "You couldn't have done it. I knew it even as you said it. I knew it even if you didn't," I said quietly. "That doesn't mean I wasn't furious with you—it was an ugly thing you threatened. But they were just words. It was an empty threat and I knew it then."

Turning from him, I slid the glass door open and slipped inside.

I'd almost made it to the bedroom before he caught up with me, one hand on my arm, whirling me around. "Then why did you *run*?" he demanded, his voice harsh...broken.

"Because I couldn't watch you marry my sister," I told him

simply. "It would have broken Marguerite's heart if I didn't go, although she would have believed it was because I couldn't handle being around so many people. I could have handled it for a short time...if it wasn't for you. Because I didn't want to lie to her, and because I didn't want to live the rest of my life thinking about the two of you together, I ran."

Chapter Nine

I looked away from him, closed my eyes. Then I made myself look at him. I owed him that much, at least. He'd spent the past three hundred years thinking he had frightened me into running. He deserved the truth now. He'd deserved it long before now.

"I ran for my own reasons, Michael. Not because of any empty threat you made." I sighed and reached up, tracing the line of his lower lip. "What happened to me was my own fault, *not* yours."

Turning from him, I reached for the door. I needed to get out of here. I needed to be away from him...before I did something dreadfully stupid. Like reach for him. Or beg him for the promises I'd wanted from him three hundred years ago.

Just before I would have slid the door open, a hand came up and pressed against it. I could feel him at my back, his strength, his solid warmth. His mouth brushed over my shoulder, nuzzled me just behind my ear. I shuddered and held still, hardly able to breathe.

"I know you still want me," he whispered as he slid a hand around my waist, flattened it against my belly. He eased my body back against his and I groaned as the length of his cock nestled against my bottom. "I can feel it...smell it...taste it."

His tongue stroked along the curve of my ear, sending little shivers down my spine. "I knew you still wanted me when we first saw each other, just the other night. It's been three hundred years, but I've never forgotten that look in your eyes," he said quietly. His hand rubbed over my belly in slow, ever-widening circles. Soon, the heel of his hand teased the curls between my thighs. "I knew you still wanted me and imagined you hated yourself for it. And now you tell me you still love me. Do you have any idea what that does to me?"

I let my head fall back against his shoulder. He moved against me and my breath caught in my throat. "Actually, I have a pretty good idea."

He turned me in his arms, crowding me up against the cool glass of the door. He laid a hand on my chest, just a little above the slope of my breast. His thumb rested in the hollow of my throat, his fingers curling around the back of my neck. I felt my pulse jump under his touch and I caught my lower lip between my teeth as I lifted my eyes to his.

"You can't know," he whispered, shaking his head. "You can't possibly know...it's like I'm dying inside—like you've completed everything I am, and now I can die happy. And yet it's like I've been dead, and only now do I live, like you've brought life back inside me. It's..." His voice trailed off and he dipped his head, rested his brow against mine.

"It's everything," I said quietly.

Now his lashes lifted, revealing a turbulent, emerald green gaze. "Everything. How can you know?"

Swallowing, I focused and projected out and let him feel just what it was I felt within him. "Because I know. And because you complete me in the very same way."

I stared up at his face, into the eyes of the only man I'd ever really loved. The only man I would love...*my* prince. Perhaps he wasn't always so charming, but he was the one man I'd been born to love.

Still holding his gaze, I reached for the buttons of his shirt and released them one by one. A breath hissed out of him and his lashes drooped low, shielding his eyes. He caught my wrists, eased them to my side. "Elle, are you so certain this is wise? Are you so certain this is what you want?"

"I know I want you...I know I've always wanted you," I said. I twisted my wrists in his grip and linked my fingers with his. I pressed against him, rubbed my cheek against the chest I had bared. He still didn't release my wrists, standing as still as a statue. Rolling my eyes upward, I stared at his face and dipped my head, tracing my tongue around his nipple.

"Elle..." he groaned out my name, his teeth clenched. Twin flags of color rode high on his cheeks and that long, lean body of his trembled.

"Michael..." I echoed, teasing him. I tugged against his hold, and this time he released me. I slipped his shirt off his shoulders and walked around him, pressing my lips to his spine.

Michael lifted his hands, braced them against the glass. The muscles in his arms bunched, standing out in stark relief. Lean, chiseled muscles, his body graceful and fluid, so incredibly perfect, so incredibly strong. I feathered the tips of my fingers down his back and watched as that strong body shuddered under my touch.

There is nothing like touching a man and watching him shake under your hands.

It's a potent drug. An addictive one.

There is nothing like being wanted by the one you want.

My mouth was dry as I fought with the belt at his waist. He remained still, his hands pressed to the glass, his head bent. Ducking back around him, I leaned against the glass and slid my hand inside his trousers. His eyes flew open when my hand closed around his cock. A sexy little snarl pulled his lips back from his teeth and I shuddered as he pressed himself into my hand.

Then he reached down, gripped my wrist and pulled me away. When I would have used my other hand, he caught it, pinning both of them to the glass door just by my head.

"Stop," he muttered, nipping my lip. "Whether you see it or not, there's too much unsaid between us. I want you, more than I want my next breath, more than I've ever wanted anything or anybody, but I can't lose you again, Elle. It would kill me. So unless you plan on staying with me, unless you plan on being mine—*always*—you need to stop."

"All I ever wanted in my life was to be yours," I said. My voice trembled as I said it. I stared at him and all the naked longing I felt was probably written on my face.

He sucked in a deep breath. "Be sure, Elle. Be very sure. Because you won't be able to run fast enough this time to get away from me."

"Do you promise?"

His mouth crushed down on mine. A hand came between us, jerked hard. I heard these odd little *rip-pop* sounds and then felt the cool kiss of air on my breasts, followed by the heat of his body as he pressed against me. The shirt, I thought vaguely.

He'd all but ripped the shirt off of me. A few seconds later, it drifted down to the ground by my feet and I was naked in his arms.

Wrapping my arms around him, I opened for him. There was a strange little mewling sound and I realized it was coming from me. He boosted me up, my back still braced against the glass door. He rubbed against me and I growled against his lips, disappointed as the fine wool of his trousers stroked over my heated flesh. Naked. I wanted him as naked as I was.

Tearing my mouth from his, I shoved him back, wiggling impatiently in his arms until he let me go. I went to my knees in front of him and reached for button on his trousers. I fumbled and fought until I had it undone. I did the same with his zipper. I shoved his trousers and underwear down and then opened my mouth, took him inside.

I felt his shock. Felt his pleasure. His hands tangled in my hair and he tugged, but it was halfhearted at best. In another three seconds he was guiding me and I moved quicker, faster. I stroked a hand up his thigh, cupped the heavy, warm sac between his legs in my hand and tugged gently.

He swore and the muscles in his legs stiffened. I dropped my shields and followed the cues I picked up from him, tightening my grip on his balls, sucking on him harder, harder. He liked it when I used the edge of my teeth, loved it when I took him so deep, it left me gasping for air.

So I did all those things and when he would have reached for my hair, tried to pull me away, I tightened my grasp, squeezing. At the same time, I stroked my tongue over the head of his cock and then I bit him gently.

He shouted out my name and then I felt his cock jerk in my mouth. Sucking on him furiously, I let go of his balls and gripped his hips, held him as I moved faster, took him deeper.

I felt it only seconds before it tore through him, a rippling climax that left his legs weak and his head spinning. I swallowed and continued to move, sucking until he was panting and swearing, all but pleading.

This time, when he pulled me up, I went, pressing kisses to his abdomen and chest, letting my breasts rub against him.

"Witch," he muttered, slanting his mouth over mine and kissing me. He whispered, "I should be a gentleman, carry you into my bedroom, take you slow and easy, but I can't."

I smiled against his lips. "Why don't you just take me instead?"

He lifted his head, staring down into my eyes. Then he pushed his knee between my thighs, widening my stance. He held my gaze and I stared back at him steadily.

I wasn't the blushing, nervous virgin I had once been. I liked sex, even though it had taken some time to get past an instinctive fear. Most of my lovers took it slower, easier—they acted like the gentleman Michael had mentioned, keeping things slow, gentle and easy and the fear eventually stopped jumping out at me at the worst possible moment.

But I didn't want or need gentleness from Michael.

Staring into his eyes, I trailed my fingers down my torso, stopping just shy of the blonde curls between my legs.

Michael stared at my hand, naked hunger on his face. When I started to stroke my clit, he growled and grabbed me, jerking my feet off the floor as he lifted me. Then he was pressing against me, the head of his cock rubbing against the slick folds between my thighs. I arched my hips and shuddered as he entered me...just the slightest inch.

"Now," I demanded, glaring at him.

He eased deeper.

I raked my nails down his back and caught his lower lip between my teeth, biting him—hard.

"Elle," he rasped, his voice a harsh, hard warning.

I could feel his hesitation, and when I focused I even had a glimmer of why. He knew I'd been raped. I don't know how he knew, what he knew, how much he knew, but he knew enough and he wanted to take care of me.

But I didn't need to be taken care of. I needed him. "Fuck me," I said, projecting just enough so he would feel my hunger. "Hard. Fast. *Now.*" I kissed him in between words and on the last word. I twisted my hips and tightened my inner muscles, milking him.

I felt his control snap and I had just a split second to brace myself and then the world was spinning. No. Not the world. Us. One second I was pressed to the glass door and then I was pressing against the wooden floor of the deck, the boards biting into my back, Michael's hot and demanding mouth on mine.

He cupped my hips, held me still as he forged deep, cleaving through tight, tense muscles and not stopping until he'd buried himself inside me. Tight—too tight, stretching me, filling me. I groaned and pressed my hands against his shoulders. "Give me a second," I whispered.

He caught my wrists, jerked them over my head and rasped against my mouth, "No." Then he used his free hand to cup my ass, angled my hips up before pulling out and driving back in. Deep. Deep. Deep. Stretching me. Filling me.

I could feel his hunger now, twining with mine, pushing me higher, faster. He shafted me, the head of his cock rubbing against the little notch buried deep inside me, sending more and more heat hurtling through my veins. I shuddered and clenched down around him and through him, I could feel how it felt...to him. How *I* felt to him.

It was too much.

I screamed against his mouth and came, hard, fast, flying through the air. He was still moving when I drifted back down, still riding me, his mouth pressed against my ear, muttering wicked, naughty little promises that stole my breath away.

He stroked a hand down my sweat-slicked back, squeezed the flesh of my rump and then stroked down the crevice between with the tip of his finger. I tensed and arched away from that touch. I'd had lovers, but I'd never let one take me there.

Michael did it again and I caught my breath. His eyes bored into mine and in the end I couldn't keep looking at him. I closed my eyes, hiding, as he repeated the foreign caress.

"Haven't you taken a man here?" he whispered against my lips.

"No." I kept my eyes closed. He slowed, stilled on my body, and then rubbed his mouth against mine.

"Relax, darling girl," he murmured, cupping my head in his hands and kissing me. He kissed me until I felt drugged on him, until I had no choice but to relax. Then he started to move.

This time was slow.

This time was easy.

The sun rose over the eastern horizon, shining down on us and painting us with red and gold. Michael rolled to his back, bringing me with him, and I braced my hands on his chest, riding him.

He tangled his hands in my long hair and muttered my name, praised me in the language of our birth, making promises that would have left me blushing if I wasn't so damned eager.

The climax washed over me this time—no breath-stealing explosion, no earth-shattering quake. No, it was gentle and slow and sweet and when it ended, I collapsed against his chest, all but crying.

She was limp in his arms, her body relaxed and loose, her breathing slow and easy.

Michael stood, cradling her body against his.

She lifted her lashes, revealing lambent blue eyes. Her lips curled in a smile and she reached up, tracing her fingertip over his mouth. "Why are we moving?"

"Because you should get more rest," he told her, rubbing his cheek against her hair.

His heart ached. Hope, after so much emptiness, was a painful burn inside him, but he wouldn't trade it for anything.

"I don't want to rest," she said, yawning. "I'm tired, but I can sleep later."

He slanted a look down at her and smiled. He understood just what she meant. He was worn to the bone but he'd rather stay awake, enjoy the feel of her in his arms for as long as possible. "Then we'll just lie in the bed and talk. After you eat breakfast."

Elle wrinkled her nose. "I don't wanna cook."

He kissed the tip of her nose, and when she smiled up at him he felt the burn of tears prick his eyes. "I'll take care of it. You need some food in your belly, as well as rest. If you won't rest you can at least eat."

Her eyes widened. A grin flirted with her mouth as she asked, "*You* are going to make breakfast?"

"Yes. I learned how a long time ago." He eased her onto the wide, soft bed and caught a blanket, easing it up over her shoulders. "After all, they wouldn't agree to offer the Choice to any servants who might be willing to come along for the ride. I had to learn to fend for myself."

She dozed lightly while he made breakfast and opened her eyes to smile at him when he brought the tray into the room.

"Breakfast in bed," she murmured. "You know, you do have some *charming* qualities about you. You really do."

Michael smirked as he settled on the bed with the tray between them. Hopefully, he would be less likely to grab her with plates of hot bacon, eggs and toast between them. "Trying to push my buttons, Elle?" he asked, holding out a glass of orange juice.

She took it and drank half of it in two big gulps. Then she licked her lips and grinned at him. "I already know how to push your buttons," she said loftily. "I don't have to *try*."

They ate in companionable silence. Every now and then, Michael felt the darkness of his own thoughts trying to weigh down on him, but he pushed it aside.

Not now.

Not today.

He burned inside with curiosity, the curiosity of the morbid—he needed to know what had happened to her, now more than ever. But he wouldn't cast a pall on these moments. They had time. She said she loved him still, and he had never stopped loving her.

Whatever obstacles had kept them apart before no longer existed and he wouldn't be kept from her. They had time.

So he kept telling himself that even as Elle gathered up their breakfast and settled the tray on the floor by the bed before rolling against him, her cheek resting on his thigh.

He trailed a hand down her naked back, staring down at her lovely face. Her eyes were closed, but she didn't sleep. He couldn't read thoughts until he actively chose to do so, but he could sense them—her thoughts were like a spring rain, brushing lightly against his consciousness.

So lovely. So soft and gentle.

Her skin was like silk, delicate and warm.

Something dark and ugly slashed through his mind. Unconsciously, he tensed.

The spring rain became a heavy thunderstorm, dangerous and devastating.

Her soft skin was bruised now. She wasn't lying in a bed with him, safe...loved. She was crying...and she wasn't alone. There were two men with her, toying with her.

He wasn't aware his thoughts were no longer his own—wasn't aware of anything save for the vision before him.

Elle...wearing men's clothes she'd been wearing the first

216

time he'd seen her. Bruises on her face, the shirt torn down the middle, leaving her breasts bare. Before his eyes, bruises formed on her breasts, dark and ugly, and in the shape of a man's hand.

Her screaming, the sound of a drunken man's laughter. And then her screams abruptly ceased, replaced by gasping harsh breaths as cruel hands closed around her throat.

He heard his name, but it seemed to come from a far-off distance.

A gentle hand stroked down his cheek, and abruptly he came back to himself.

Elle stared at him, her eyes wide, her face pale.

Rolling off the bed, he started to pace.

"What was that?" she asked, her voice shaking.

"Nothing," he growled, even though he could still see those images. He closed his eyes to block them out, but they were still there, imprinted forever on his mind.

"Don't give me that," she snapped.

He stopped and looked at her. In the back of his mind, he could feel the rhythm of her thoughts. He was tempted to reach out, but he didn't. He closed down, cutting his mind off from hers. Had he somehow unwittingly forged a link between them?

"Were you trying to read my mind?"

Michael closed his eyes and rubbed a hand over his face. "Not consciously, no. I've never had that happen to me before."

She was silent for so long. When she did finally speak, he braced himself, ready for her anger.

"Were you in my mind?"

"Yes," he bit off. And what he'd seen, it would haunt him. For the rest of his life.

"If you weren't consciously trying to do it, then how did it happen?"

"I don't know." He stared at the floor, one hand opening and closing into a fist. Useless rage boiled through him. The men who had hurt her were long dead. He could do nothing to ease her nightmare. And no matter what she said, Michael was responsible. He knew that, even if she wouldn't openly admit it.

He took a deep, slow breath and then looked up at her. "I didn't consciously do it. I wasn't even consciously thinking of it. One moment I was looking at you, thinking about how lovely

217

you are. And the next..." His voice trailed off and he stared sightlessly into the distance. "I was just there."

Elle sighed. "What did you see?"

"You. A dirty street. Rain. Two men. Not much else." Too much...and not enough. His gut was hot and tight, and fury left his muscles tensed and aching. Swallowing against the knot in his throat, he murmured, "I'm sorry."

Elle glanced at him. Then she patted the bed beside her. "Come sit. Somehow, I suspect this will happen again unless we do something to stop it."

Michael scowled. "And what do you propose we do? Do you plan on running from me again?"

"No." She tucked her hair behind her ear and held out a hand. "Come sit down. I don't want to do this, but I'm going to tell you what happened."

Hell.

He padded to the bed and sat on the edge, cautiously. As he took her hand she rolled to her knees and moved across the bed until she reached him. Then she settled in his lap.

"It happened in Nice. And it was raining. Marguerite had cousins there and I had thought to find them. But I got lost. There's so much noise in cities, so much emotion. I was half out of my mind. The storm came on so fast and there was thunder. My horse hated storms. I knew that, but I had no place to take shelter, not unless I found Marguerite's cousins. I was tired, scared. I don't really remember exactly what happened, but I think my horse threw me, because the next thing I remember is wandering the streets, wet, hungry, cold and half-sick."

She was crying, tears rolling unchecked down her face. Michael reached up, wiping them away. Then he tucked her head under his chin and started to rock her, stroking her back and combing his fingers through her tangled hair.

"They grabbed me. These two men. I don't even remember what they looked like. But they had strong hands and when I fought them, they laughed." Abruptly, she tensed, pushing lightly against his chest. "I need to walk."

Reluctantly, he let her go. She grabbed the sheet from the bed and wound it around her like a toga. The rest of the words poured from her in a torrent, harsh and fast. "When I fought, they hit me. When I screamed, they choked me. I stopped fighting because I couldn't breathe. They tore off my clothes.

One of them tried to push his penis into my mouth and I bit him. He hit me again, so hard that time that I think I passed out. When I woke, I was between them."

She shot him a look of revulsion. "Earlier when you touched me...there, you asked if I had ever had a lover there. No, because the one thing I do remember clearly from that night is that pain. When I think of that pain, I freeze."

Michael curled his fingers into the mattress, clutching at it. He wanted so badly to go to her. He wanted so badly to hold her.

I have no right. No right to touch her. No right to comfort her.

"Stop," Elle said quietly. She stared at him with knowing eyes and shook her head. "It was not your fault."

"How can you say that? *How?*"

"Because it isn't." She wiped her tears away, crossed the floor and settled once more on his lap, draping her arms around his shoulders. She pressed her brow to his. "What's done is done. And as horrible, as awful as that pain was, that night no longer haunts me the way it used to. I don't even remember much of it. The rain, the pain, their laughter..." Her voice trailed off and she lifted her head, staring past his shoulder.

"Sometimes I wake up remembering the pain, but then it's done. There's not much left of that night. Just little bits and pieces, and then darkness. I didn't want to die, but they had hurt me so badly I was already almost gone. I heard a voice—a man telling me that I was safe. That no one would hurt me again. And even though the pain had chased me into the darkness, it was suddenly gone. I was warm and I wasn't afraid. The voice was there again, offering me a choice." She met his eyes and smiled faintly. She shrugged and murmured, "I wasn't ready to die. When I woke up, Will was there. He cared for me, trained me, taught me how to shield so my gift didn't overwhelm me."

Will. "Will, huh?"

"Yes." She combed a hand through his hair. "You don't like him."

"Does anybody?" Michael asked, his lip curling.

"I do." She grinned at him and shrugged. "He really isn't that bad. I owe him, you know. Not just for my life. He didn't just keep me from dying...he kept me from hiding away."

Something about her voice, something about the look in

her eyes hit him and he became aware of a strange, sinking sensation. Will.

Fuck. Ren. Will. He'd known there would be other men in her life, but putting names to those faceless men made it much harder to handle. But he'd have to handle it. Have to deal with it.

His voice tight, he said, "You were lovers."

She met his eyes levelly. "Yes." She reached down and caught his wrist, lifting his hand so that his clenched fist was between them. Pressing a kiss to his knuckles, she murmured, "I don't have to ask if that bothers you. I can already tell. I can live with that because the thought of your past lovers, whoever they may be, is enough to drive me mad. But can you live with it?"

"What choice do I have?" Michael grimaced. Consciously, he made his muscles relax. "I'm not going to let you go because of whatever men you have been with in the past. But that doesn't mean I have to like it. Or him."

A sympathetic smile curled her lips. Gently, she kissed him. "No. You don't have to like it. You don't have to like him. But he is a friend of mine and I don't plan on letting that change." She stroked his shoulders. "He was the first lover I'd had after that night. And it took a couple of years. I was getting worse, instead of better. If he hadn't... Well, if we hadn't become lovers, I would have gotten much worse. I think eventually, I would have given up. I would've let go of my wings and would've waited for old age to kill me. I'm *here* because of Will."

"Shit." Michael blew out a breath and wrapped his arms around her waist, pulling her close. Resting his head between her breasts, he murmured, "Then I can be thankful to him, but it still doesn't mean I have to like him."

"No, it doesn't." She pressed her lips to his. "Michael?"

"Hmmm?"

"Make love to me."

He cradled her face in his hands and whispered, "Now that idea, I like."

He took her mouth with slow, soft kisses, stroking his hands over her back, her sides. He eased down onto the bed, then rolled to his side, tucking her body close to his. He watched her face as he touched her, searching for any sign of fear or uncertainty.

There was nothing but warmth and passion in her kiss, nothing but love shining in her eyes.

But when he went to tuck her body under his, she pressed her hands to his chest and whispered, "Not that way."

He thought she'd want to be on top, but when he lifted his weight from her, she rolled to her hands and knees. Michael came up behind her, gripping her hips in his hands. She straightened, reaching up and back, wrapping her arms around his head. He dipped his head and pressed a kiss to her shoulder. She sighed and rocked back, her warm, soft ass brushing against his cock.

Michael shuddered but eased his lower body away.

She reached down between them, stroked his cock. "Make love to me."

"Lean forward," he said hoarsely.

She did slightly, bracing her weight on one hand. With the other, she gripped his cock, nestling it between the cheeks of her rump. "There, Michael. I want you there."

"No."

She rubbed against him, moving awkwardly. "Yes. You touched me there...that last day. I remember that, and it didn't hurt. I know it doesn't have to be painful and I'm tired of that pain being the source of a nightmare. Take it away, Michael." She let her head fall back to rest on his shoulder and stared up at him. "I know you can."

"Elle, the first few times a woman takes a man's cock there, it can hurt. Hell, if a man isn't careful, it can hurt no matter what. I won't do that to you."

Craning her head around, she pressed her mouth to his throat. "I want you to. And I trust you. You wouldn't let it hurt." She touched her tongue to his skin and murmured, "Besides, you want to. I can feel it. And it's driving me crazy."

Michael shuddered, his common sense waging a war with his desires. Yes, he wanted her like that. He wanted her in all ways. He wanted her back on her knees in front of him as he fucked her mouth with his dick and he wanted her tied face down to a bed while he tormented and teased that lovely body and drew her to a gasping, crying climax.

But he didn't want to hurt her, scare her. Not ever. He swallowed the knot in his throat and pulled back. "No, Elle. You don't really want this, darling girl. You know you don't."

"I don't know that," she said, staring at him. Her clear blue eyes remained steadily on his as she caught his hand and brought it to her face. She nuzzled his hand, cuddled it against her cheek. "What I do know is that I'm tired of what few mortal memories I have being clouded by the memory of pain. I'm tired of nightmares haunting me. I want to exorcise them from my mind...and this is how I want to do it."

She gave him a winsome smile and swayed closer, pressing her lips to his chin. "Besides, you can consider it practice."

"Practice?" It was a miracle he could speak at all. His mouth was dry, his throat tight. Everything inside him screamed for him to do just as she asked. He could make it good for her, he knew he could. He could bring her past the nerves, past the fear, past the pain. "Practice for what?"

"Well, you *are* supposed to be playing the besotted fool who'll do anything to keep me happy." She nipped his chin and reached down, closing her slender fingers around his shaft. "This is what I want...so play your part and indulge me."

He slid a hand up her back, fisted it in her hair. "Elle, love, I never had to play any part, not when it came to being your besotted fool." Cupping her chin, he angled her face up and slanted his mouth over hers. He kissed her, drunk on her taste, drunk on the feel of her.

Drunk on the knowledge that she still loved him. More, she trusted him. Otherwise, she wouldn't be asking for this. Not after what had happened to her.

She still loves me...after all I did to her, she still loves me.

He lifted his head and stared down at her. Stroking his thumb over the full curve of her lower lip, he said, "If you change your mind, tell me to stop...and I will."

"I know you will." She nipped his finger and then shifted on the bed again, bracing her weight on her hands and knees. Over her shoulder, she added, "But I'm not going to change my mind."

She rocked against him and Michael hissed out a breath as her silken skin stroked over his cock. He ran his hand down her hip, staring at her heart-shaped ass. His dick jerked painfully, an insistent demand.

"I'll need to see if I can find something," he whispered, his voice hoarse.

She glanced at him. "Find something...?" Then she blushed and settled back on her knees. "Ah, yeah. That might be a good idea."

Chapter Ten

I stared at his naked back as he left the room and tried to still the racing of my heart.

My hands were damp, slick with fear.

I wanted this, but at the same time, I was terrified. The ghostly echo of a man's laugher drifted through my mind and I wrapped my arms around my middle. He'd laughed. As he tore my clothes, pulled at my hair and twisted my breasts with cruel hands, he'd laughed. The stink of bad, cheap wine had fogged his breath and the smell of it had almost choked me. The shock of the initial penetration by his friend was nothing compared to the pain...

My teeth started to chatter and I clenched my jaw to stop it.

I blinked burning eyes and focused on the black silk of the sheets.

I wasn't in a dirty, dark alley in Nice and I wasn't helpless, trapped by men who were bigger, stronger than me. I knew how to fight and had fought my way out of tight spots more than once. I wasn't trapped...and I was with Michael.

He wouldn't hurt me.

Taking a deep breath, I relaxed. And just in time too. I heard Michael's footsteps as he came back into the room and I looked up to smile at him. Then I saw what he held in his hand and I blushed. "You frequently travel around with lubricant in your luggage?" I asked. Making jokes to cover my nerves—it had become my specialty.

A smile curled his lips. "No. It was in the bathroom—still sealed in its box too. Apparently the owners of the cabin believe in meeting any and all possible needs of their tenants."

He tossed the black box down on the bed next to him. I stared at it, pretending a strange fascination with the foil lettering as he settled down behind me, wrapping his arms around my waist. "Second thoughts?"

I shook my head. "No." Then I grimaced and admitted, "Well, yes. But then I had third thoughts, and fourth thoughts, and then I had the one thought that mattered more than anything else."

"And what's that?" he asked. He rested a hand on my belly, his fingers splayed.

I shivered. His hand was so close...so close. The tip of his finger was just a whisper away from the ache between my thighs.

"That I'm with you," I said, laying my head against his shoulder and looking into his eyes. "That you wouldn't hurt me."

His mouth brushed against mine. "If you change your mind—"

"I won't." I couldn't. I didn't understand why, but I knew I had to do this. I'd had lovers since Michael. I hadn't closed myself...although at first, I'd tried. But there was a part of me that hadn't fully trusted the men I'd been with. I certainly hadn't trusted anyone of them to do this. Other than Will, I hadn't trusted them with the dark, terrible secrets of that night either. Not even Ren, and he wasn't just a lover. He was one of my closest, dearest friends.

I needed this with Michael. I needed to trust...I needed to trust him. That was how we would heal the wounds that lingered between us. For him, and for me.

Pulling away, I settled on my hands and knees, then arched my back and smiled at him over my shoulder. He smoothed his hands over my bottom and then slid a hand around between my legs. I shivered as he stroked my clit, toyed with it, rubbing it with steady, firm pressure.

I felt the brush of his cock against my ass. Nerves danced inside. Trying to block them out, I pushed back against him. Michael rested a hand on my hip. "Slow down, darling girl. There's no reason to rush it."

Yes, there is. We need to do it before I freak...oh.

Heat jolted through me as he lightly tugged on my clit. He shifted around, guided my body upright so that I knelt between his thighs. I barely noticed. I couldn't focus on anything but that wicked, wicked hand. He dipped his fingers inside me, drawing the moisture out, spreading it over my swollen clit. Over and over.

Distantly, I heard something rip but I didn't know what it was.

I rocked against his hand, riding him. He whispered against my ear and the low, rough promises made me blush, had me shivering.

"I want to lay you down beneath me and spread your thighs, lick you right here and suck on your clit. When I do that, you make this little purr, did you know that?"

"Michael..." I gasped out his name and turned my face towards his. Blindly, I sought out his mouth, sucking his tongue into my mouth and biting him. He growled against my lips and I did it again, and again.

He scraped his nail over my clit and I arched, stiffened. Hurtling towards climax, I couldn't do anything but ride it out...and that was when he touched me there.

His finger was slick, circling the tight entrance but not entering. Under the weight of pleasure, my shields crashed down and I was suddenly acutely aware of him—his hunger, his impatience tempered by his need to make this good for me.

Nothing is as erotic as knowing the one you want returns the feeling.

His hunger washed over me and instead of ending, my climax continued, drawing on, and on...lingering until I was panting and gasping and desperate.

When he touched the puckered entrance again, I blindly pushed against him, seeking some relief from the pressure inside me.

I cried out as he breeched the tight muscles. As he did that, he also pushed two fingers inside my sex and pressed down right...*there*...

I came again, screaming out his name.

Michael shuddered as she panted and shook in his arms, riding him. He had two fingers buried in her sleek pussy and one finger in her ass. She was tight, tight as a fist, silken soft and so hot. He hissed out a breath as his cock jerked, throbbed. It was pressed against her side and he felt one drop of pre-come slip free.

He twisted his hand and screwed his finger deeper inside her anal sheath. At the same time, he lowered his mental shields. She'd lowered her own just moments ago, he'd felt it, but he wouldn't know what she thought unless he reached for her.

He wouldn't know if he hurt her—

The tide of her need swamped him and he groaned out her name, dropping his head down and resting it on her shoulder. She filled him, flooded him—he couldn't contain it and it spilled out into her. His need fed hers and her need fed his, a twisting, seductive spiral of desire.

Still, he lashed his hunger down—careful. Slow. He had to be careful. Slow.

"Michael, *please...*" she wailed. Her voice was full of something deeper than hunger, deeper than need. He had no word to describe it and the feel of it echoing through him was enough to drive him mad.

Pulling his hands away, he reached for one of her hands, pressed it between her thighs. "Touch yourself, and keep touching yourself," he whispered.

She stared at him, her eyes fogged with hunger, drunk with need.

She was so fucking beautiful, he thought, dazed. Her breasts, round and plump, were topped with erect nipples. Her cheeks were flushed, her lower lip swollen. The curls between her thighs glistened with moisture.

"What?"

He covered her hand and pressed. "Play with yourself, Elle," he said. He lowered his head and kissed her. "Play with that pretty little pussy for me."

He watched as she slowly, hesitantly started to stroke herself, her slim, white fingers stroking over pink, glistening flesh.

"Good girl," he whispered. He stared into her eyes, let her feel what it did to him just watching.

Then he slipped behind her.

Bracing one hand between her shoulders, he eased her down until the bed supported her upper body. Then he grabbed the bottle of lubricant. "Are you playing with that pretty pussy?"

he asked, keeping his voice soft, light, even as the wild hunger burned inside him.

"Yes..." She rocked her hips and he shuddered. The sight of that, watching her ride her hand and stroke herself to climax—he could come just from that.

He slicked the lubricant over his cock. Closing his fist around his length, he stroked up, down, once, twice. His cock jerked, throbbed. In her—it wanted to be in her. Squeezing more lubricant into his hand, he moved closer. With one hand, he gripped her hip as he pressed his slicked fingers against the pucker of her ass.

She jerked under his touch and he stilled, waited.

But then she pressed back.

The connection between them was flooded with heat, longing. He felt the barest edge of nerves, but it was overshadowed by the hunger. Gripping his cock, he held it steady and pressed the head against her. She flinched.

Bending down, he pressed his lips to her shoulder. "I can stop...just say the word."

Wordlessly, she shook her head.

He felt her frantic need, the fear. Scoring her shoulder with his teeth, he said, "Then relax for me, darling girl. I want to fuck your virgin ass so bad I hurt."

The dirty talk did exactly what he'd hoped. She whimpered and pressed back. This time, when he pressed against her, she held still. Frozen—still as a statue. But tight, so tight, the muscles of her ass clenched down, resisting his entry. "Push down for me, Elle. Do it."

She cried out. "I...I can't...Michael, I think it's going to..." Her voice wobbled and faded away.

"Do you want this?" he rasped, lodged with just the barest inch of his cock inside that silken sheath.

"Yes, but..."

He slapped her ass with the flat of his hand and ordered, "Push down."

She did, wailing out his name, and he slipped another two inches in. She was shivering, shaking. He retreated, just a bit, and then he surged forward. "Again, darling girl. Do it again."

She did and this time, he sank half his cock inside her. She tensed up again and he reached out, seeking out her clit.

"You're supposed to be playing with yourself," he teased. "Come on, darling girl. I want to think about you fucking yourself with your fingers while I fuck your ass."

"Pervert," she gasped out and then her hand came up, nudging his aside.

He held her hips with both hands now, steadying her as he pulled out, then surged forward. This time she pushed down without any encouragement, and he groaned as he sank his entire length inside her.

Elle whimpered, her body trembling, shivering.

"Have I hurt you?" he whispered, eyeing the faint red mark of his hand on her ass.

"No...yes, hmmm... I don't know, I can't explain..."

He stroked out, stroked in and trailed his fingers over the imprint of his hand. "I spanked you."

She shoved her hips back and whispered, "Yes...do it again."

He grinned and brought the flat of his hand down on her rump.

She mewled in her throat and straightened her upper body, bracing her weight on her hands—then she pushed back, taking his dick inside her. Riding it. The muscles in her ass convulsed around him, gripping him, milking him.

"You're going to kill me," he rasped.

"Spank me again." She flexed around him as she took him back inside.

Michael spanked her, watching as he brought a blush to the pale, perfect flesh of her bottom. Watching as she slowly moved back and forth on his dick, he held still, letting her control it. The sight of it, watching as she took one slick inch of his cock after another, had his balls drawing tight against him in warning.

She was close too—he could feel it. But not close enough. He crowded against her and slid a hand around, dipped it between her thighs. He hooked two fingers inside her pussy and pressed down on the little bed of nerves buried there.

She stiffened...and then she went crazy, moving back and forth on him, harder, faster.

"It's not enough," she whimpered.

Michael growled and took her hips in his hands. Desperate

desire bloomed between them, flaring in them both. Snarling, he began to drive into her, using the strength of his lower back and legs.

She came with a sob. He felt the rush of heated moisture from her just as a warning tingle raced down his spine.

Fire tore through his balls and he bellowed out her name as he came.

And as he pumped his seed into her, the skin on his body went tight.

Something...

Something in the air...

Hunger.

I swallowed and tried to hear something beyond the roaring in my ears, the beating of my heart. Michael slumped against me and wrapped an arm around my waist, easing me down to the bed. I winced as he pulled out, suddenly aware that I was sore.

But there wasn't time for that—I felt something. "Michael..."

"Shhhh..." He grabbed a sheet and flipped it up over us, hiding us from the neck down.

I hissed out a breath, aware that he hadn't said anything. *Out loud.* In my head. In my fucking head.

"Don't say anything," he warned me.

"Why the hell not?" I wanted to ask. I also wanted to ask him to get out of my head. Then I wanted to shower, clean up...and then pounce on him. Maybe. I might sleep first.

But...

Oh, shit. Oh, hell.

Now I felt it more clearly. I shivered and pressed back against him. Strong arms came around me, held me tight, secure.

"Can you hear me?" I thought, pushing my thoughts towards him.

"Yes."

"We're not alone, are we?"

"No." A tense silence passed as we both lay there, pretending to bask in the aftermath.

I wasn't basking though. I was pissed. Mostly, I was pissed

because I *wanted* to be basking.

Not lying there while a voyeuristic demon played Peeping Tom.

"It's the queen," I thought.

"I know. None of the others are strong enough to reach this far. I don't think they would have even sensed us—we're too far away."

It was just her presence—her incorporeal self. If demons had souls, I'd say it was her soul, but demons lack anything resembling a soul.

It was her essence, the closest thing to a soul a demon had...and she was hungry, hungry for more of the feast we'd just given her.

I could feel her vibrating, all but orgasmic over the energy she'd sucked up from us.

It hadn't done us any harm. She would have to come inside us to harm us, but still, it pissed me off. Fucking parasite.

I started to push away from him, but Michael didn't let me go.

"Be still," he warned me. *"If you get out of the bed, she's going to see us."*

"We just gave her the fucking show, what does it matter if she sees us?"

He reached up and tugged on the pendant resting between my breasts. *This... She's been off to the side, watching us. She's not corporeal, but she can see us—but only from whatever angle she's watching us from. She hasn't seen these. She might not know what we are."*

Light dawned. Slowly, I relaxed my muscles. *"Good point."* As pissed off as I was, I knew the advantage of surprise could work for us. Especially now.

She'd gotten a taste of us.

And apparently it had been intriguing enough that it had drawn her to us across the miles that separated us.

She'd want more.

She'd want to seek us out.

Then...we could kill her.

She had taken over her host completely—her life force was bonded to the human's now. Otherwise, she wouldn't be this strong. So when the human body died—she'd die.

Regret washed through me. We'd have to kill people tonight. At least one person.

Michael kissed my shoulder. *"That person is already gone, darling girl. There's nothing we could have done anyway."*

Chapter Eleven

I got ready for the night.

After sleeping the day away with Michael, I felt as ready for this as I was going to be. Which was pretty damn ready. I wanted it over and done so I could concentrate on Michael.

I smirked at my image and murmured, "Cinderella, you're going to the ball."

Of course, if my stepmother could see me in this get-up, she'd probably die of a heart attack.

It was blue. Soft, pale blue, nearly the same shade as my eyes. With all the red and black and purple inside that joint, I'd stand out, which was the point. We wanted to be noticed after all.

It was short. Short as in *nonexistent*. The skirt was nothing but swaths of lace that barely covered my butt and when I bent over or moved in the wrong way, those around me would get a flash of the blue thong I had on underneath. The bodice was similar to a corset, lacing up in the back, cinching my waist and putting my boobs on display. Tiny little crystals covered the material, catching and reflecting the light.

I scooped up my hair, but that had nothing to do with looks and everything to do with practically. If I was going to be in a fight, and it was very likely, I'd rather my hair not be flying all over the place—makes it too easy to grab. Pulled back into a chignon, it was out of my face and out of my way. Plus, it worked well with the dress.

The shoes were, of course, Cinderella shoes, completely clear, both the upper and the heel. More sparkles covered the upper, and as I studied my feet I decided I should have gotten a pedicure, but nothing I could do about it now. The best part about the shoes was that I could kick them off in just a few seconds. I really hate fighting while wearing a pair of heels.

Other than the long chain holding my medallion and some sparkling platinum earrings that dangled from my ears, I wore no jewelry. The earrings were clip-on and the chain was tucked down inside my bodice so nobody could grab it that easily.

Yes, I was going to the ball and I was prepared to kick ass. Literally.

I was still so furious that demon bitch had been spying on us. I can't explain how enraged that made me, nor could I understand it. That was what those kinds of demons did—they thrived on sexual energy and we'd been giving off plenty of it. I should have expected this.

But I was still pissed.

The door behind me opened and I turned to see Michael standing there with a stupefied look on his face. His throat worked as he swallowed and I gave him a cheeky smile as I turned in a circle with my arms held out.

"How do I look?"

"Delicious." He looked me over, his eyes lingering on the tight, low cut of my bodice, the nearly-not-there skirt and down to my pretty little shoes. I lifted a foot and wiggled it.

"Cute, huh?"

A smile curled his lips.

"They don't look like they'll be fun to fight in, if it comes to that."

I shrugged. "I'll kick them off. That's the plan anyway. Whoever designed heels never took into consideration how awkward they'd be to fight in."

Michael sauntered closer and caught my hand. I bit my lip as he bent over and kissed it. Running my fingers through his hair, I said, "Careful...your charming streak is showing through."

He nipped my knuckles and then lifted his eyes to mine. "Careful...your mischievous streak is showing through."

"Well, I never tried to hide that." I smiled and then turned once more to study my reflection.

Michael rested his hands on my shoulders and his eyes met mine in the mirror.

"If things go well we could be done with this tonight," I said softly.

"Yes."

Reaching up, I wrapped my fingers around his wrists. "Then what do we do?"

He nuzzled my neck. "I was thinking we could get married." His voice was a soft, rough whisper in my ear and for a moment, I was too caught up in a shiver to understand his words.

"Married..." I turned around and looked up at him. He wasn't smiling. He looked dead serious.

My heart skipped in my chest and I licked my lips. "Married?"

"Yes." He cupped my face in his hands, pressed a kiss to my brow. "It's what I should have done three hundred years ago. It's what I've always wanted. Then...and now."

After brushing a kiss across my mouth, he whispered, "How about it, Cinderella? You want to marry a not-so-charming ex-prince?"

I wrapped my arms around his neck. He boosted me up in his arms. I wrapped my legs around his waist and pressed my brow to his. "A not-so-charming ex-prince?" I teased. "Who would that be?"

He swatted my rump. "Don't tease about this, Elle. Whether the answer is yes or no or that you need time, just give me an answer."

I smiled against his mouth. "Oh, we've had plenty of time, I think. And I'd love to marry you... You're *my* prince, and you always have been."

"Elle...my darling girl," he muttered as he kissed me. "I love you so much, I hurt with it."

I knew the feeling. As he pushed his tongue into my mouth, I groaned. Then I nipped at him, delighted when he shuddered. I could make him shake. It would never cease to amaze me. This man, this strong, arrogant man, I could make him shake.

He tugged on my thong and I shivered as it pressed against the sensitive flesh between my thighs. He skimmed his lips down my neck and I arched back, my breath catching as I pressed against the swollen ridge of his cock. I wanted him.

Here. Right here.

Now. Right now.

Reaching down between us, I fumbled with the button on his trousers. It gave way, but just as I started to drag down his zipper, there was a loud knock at the door.

Scowling, I glanced towards the living room.

"Who in the world could that be?"

Ren.

I was at Michael's side when he opened the door and I felt a blush rise to my cheeks as the other man's gaze moved between us.

His gaze lingered on Michael, cold with dislike. When he looked at me, a shutter fell and there was no expression on his face. I couldn't see what he felt, but I could feel it and it was a stabbing pain in my chest.

I bit my lip. I'd hidden away from the fact that Ren thought he was in love with me. I hadn't wanted to think about it, but now I had no choice.

It wasn't just an illusion. What I felt inside him was real. Solid.

Perhaps if Michael hadn't ever come back into my life, I might have even returned his feelings.

"Ren."

Thick lashes lowered over his eyes, hiding them from me. When he looked back at me, he had a shield in place...over his features, over his emotions. I'd seen him use it often over the years.

But never had he used it with me. Never had he hidden from me.

"Lovely night, isn't it, my lady?" he asked, giving me a cocky grin.

I stepped aside and Michael, after a brief hesitation, did the same, letting Ren saunter into the condo.

"What are you doing back here?" I asked. I realized I wanted to fidget and I linked my hands behind my back to keep from doing just that.

"Oh, was just in the area, you know. Figured I might help you two wrap up that pesky little...problem." He waggled his brows at me. The jaunty smile on his face was firmly in place.

"I thought Will said he needed you elsewhere."

Ren shrugged and leaned back against the bar. Holding his

arms out, he said, "Well, that's what he told me too, but then he sends me off to play errand boy. Lot of fun that was too. Great fun. Then he up and decides I'm supposed to come back here." The mask on his face cracked, revealing just a sliver of real emotion to show through in his eyes. Only for a moment.

Bleakness. Pain. Loss.

Damn you, Will. Would you stop playing games? I thought darkly. No...he wasn't cruel, but he did like to toy with people sometimes. I wasn't blind to that.

Then Ren blinked. The mask fell back into place and when he looked at me again, he had a wide, easy grin on his face and a cagey look in his eyes as he looked me over from head to toe. "Poppet, I have to tell you, you look utterly biteable. It leaves me tempted to..."

Michael tensed. "If you want to live through the night, you'll resist whatever fool notions are dancing through your head."

"Oh, well now. If I resist all of them, I'm going to tear your chest open and rip out your heart," Ren said. A mean smile curled his lips and intensity shown from his eyes. "Trust me, you don't want me resisting all fool notions. The only thing keeping me from tearing into you is the knowledge that my lady wouldn't like it. I'm resisting for her, and only her."

"She's not *your* lady," Michael snarled.

Somehow, they'd managed to close the distance between them and now just inches separated them. Scowling, I pushed into those inches and shoved them apart. "Back off," I warned. "Both of you."

"Oh, come on, poppet. It could be fun." Under my hand, Ren's heart was racing and I could feel too much of the emotion he kept trapped inside.

Anger. Jealousy. Frustration.

"Besides, now that I think of it, why shouldn't I tear into him?" he asked, but the question wasn't directed at me. Or Michael. "After all, whether I like it or not, I've already lost you."

Blowing out a breath, I shot Michael a look. *Let me handle this.*

I could tell by the narrowing of his eyes that he'd caught my unspoken message. He gave a tiny shake of his head.

"Please."

Abruptly, he turned away, moving so fast it threw me off-balance.

Ren reached out and steadied me. I let him, leaning against his chest for just a moment. I didn't want this. The last thing I'd wanted was to hurt him. I should have known...should have looked...should have realized. But if I'd done that, I would have pulled away and I'd needed him. Needed his friendship and his strength, needed the way he brought laughter back into my life.

"I'm sorry, Ren."

He brushed my hair back from my face, watching me. There was a strange, cool detachment in his gaze as he murmured, "Are you? For what?"

"For hurting you. I...I never stopped loving him, Ren."

"I can't fault you for having lousy judgment, I suppose."

I smiled faintly. "I never was yours. I'm sorry, but I wasn't. I've always been his."

"Even when he threw you away. You never told me, but I know awful things happened after that... Awful things that wouldn't have happened if he'd cared for you as he should have."

I sensed Michael behind me. Shooting him a look over my shoulder, I said, "Let me handle this."

Then I took a deep breath and looked at Ren. "He didn't throw me away, Ren. I *ran* away and whatever awful things happened, they aren't on his head, but mine."

"No." He stroked a finger over my lip. "It's his bloody fault."

"It is not his—"

"Oh, the hell it isn't." It wasn't Ren speaking though. It was Michael.

From the corner of my eye, I could see him approaching and I tensed, ready to jump between them again if I had to.

"You're right about that—it *is* my fault, even if she wants to claim otherwise. But whatever happened to her, it doesn't concern you. It's between her and me."

Ren's eyes narrowed. "Oh, it bloody well *does* concern me."

"Why?" Michael asked, his voice flat and cool. "If she loved you, then yes, it would concern you. But she doesn't. Not the way you want her to love you. She never will."

I felt Ren flinch. Then he looked away and a harsh sigh escaped him. "You're right in that."

He looked back at me then, lifting his hands to cup my

face. I curled my fingers around his wrists, held still as he pressed a kiss to my brow. "I always knew somewhere. I just didn't want to admit it. I don't want to admit it now, but I can't very well hide from it now that you've found him again, now can I?"

"I'm sorry, Ren."

A smile crooked his lips. "I know. But maybe you shouldn't be. I hate the bastard, but I've never seen you smile at anybody the way you smile at him." He pressed his lips to mine and said, "Be happy for me, Elle. Be happy."

That little heart-to-heart put a bit of a damper on the adrenaline rush and I was heavy-hearted as the three of us headed towards the car. Ren had come dressed to party, wearing black leather pants. He was shirtless under the jacket he wore, and his golden skin stretched over his muscles, smooth and perfect. He didn't have his medallion on. I frowned, ready to ask about it but then he opened the door and I caught sight of the black leather band wrapped around his wrist. Something silver flashed from it and I recognized the medallion.

"Nice," I murmured, tapping it with my index finger.

"Thank you." He grimaced and met my gaze. "You've no idea how close I came to throwing it away a few days ago."

Over me. He didn't even have to say it. I already knew.

"I'm glad you didn't."

Michael was all in black. Black silk shirt, black trousers, black shoes. I hadn't watched as he got dressed, but I imagined the underwear was black as well. He really did need some color in his wardrobe.

But then again, he looked damned nice in black, I decided.

Between the two of them, I probably looked rather small. I'd be underestimated.

That was good. I'd have to be. I'd need every advantage I could get if I wanted to get close to the queen without her alerting all of her drones. If we killed her quick and fast, I had hopes none of the others would be strong enough to linger without her. Maybe by killing the queen we could save more of the human hosts.

I hoped.

Ren wasn't going to fit in the back seat of the little car.

Michael would have made him crawl back there, but I'd done it before it even came up. As uncomfortably cramped as it was for me, it would have been doubly so for Ren.

The drive passed in tense silence, and my adrenaline started to pump again as we drew closer. I wasn't the only one either. By the time we hit the club's parking lot, my skin was buzzing from the combined excitement and anticipation I felt from the other two.

I understand how some people become adrenaline junkies. I really do. It's a heady rush having all that energy and excitement and anticipation crashing inside. It can make it hard to do the job until you learn to focus. I used the next minute to steady myself, curbing the anticipation.

Wouldn't do to walk in there with the light of battle blazing and all. It could kind of ruin the element of surprise we had going for us.

They didn't know.

They couldn't.

I could feel the dark, negative hunger of the queen and her drones from out here. If she had figured out who we were she would have blown out of town. It was a good sign that she was still here.

Ren was out with his door open before Michael got around the car. Seeing the glint in my friend's eye, I almost ignored the hand he held out. But if I did that, I was going to lose some dignity if I had to scramble out of the car in this get-up without a hand. Or I could wait for Michael and watch them have a chest-beating session.

I decided to just get it over with and accepted Ren's hand. A grin curled his lips and he murmured, "Nice panties, Elle."

Rolling my eyes, I smoothed my dress down. "It's not like you haven't seen that view before."

"But it's a view that never loses its beauty."

Behind me, I heard Michael swear under his breath.

Oh, this was going to be so much fun. Baring my teeth at Ren, I jabbed him in the chest with a finger. "You're going to piss me off if you keep it up, Thomas."

Ren's brows drew low over his eyes. He caught my wrist and said, "Don't call me *Thomas*."

"Don't piss me off," I fired back at him. "You don't want me pissed off right now, right? After all, we're going in to deal with demons. Seems it would be best if I'm concentrating, yes?"

He scowled. But he fell silent.

Spinning around, I glared at Michael. "He's a friend of mine. You're going to have to deal with that, because I'm not giving up a friendship."

"I can deal with it just fine. But if he makes another remark about your panties, I'm going to beat him into the dirt."

"Fine." I huffed out a breath. "Just do it *after* we're done here, okay?"

I really wanted this job over with. Over and done.

It hadn't been the hardest assignment of my life, but it was definitely one of the more draining.

Emotionally draining.

I took a deep breath and smoothed my dress down one more time. Then I turned and faced the club. "Let's get this show on the road."

Both men offered their arm. I accepted both.

After all, it would look damn weird if I went in there with Ren trailing at our heels. He wasn't one to take the backseat and that fact was apparent. All you had to do was look at him.

If we wanted this to work without raising suspicion we needed to look *together*.

All it would take was the wrong individual noticing us and the element of surprise would be out the window.

And besides, somewhere inside, some part of me thought it was wicked fun to saunter inside that club with those two men. Michael with his elegant beauty and Ren with his hard, harsh male sensuality. It's the stuff fantasies are made of. And for now, until we caught the attention of the queen, I might as well enjoy it.

Chapter Twelve

She was a witch.

Michael had no doubt of it.

A couple hundred years ago she would have been burned at the stake simply for being so completely breathtaking.

More than a few women were sending Elle dark, ugly looks. She didn't seem to notice and if she did, she didn't care. As she swayed between him and Ren, she had her eyes half-closed. A small smile curled her lips. She had one hand resting on Ren's hip and the other was curled up and back, wrapped around Michael's neck.

Ren was pressed close to her, too fucking close for Michael's peace of mind. He could hear the hum of the other man's thoughts, something that wouldn't happen if there was a bit more distance between them, or some shielding. But Michael wasn't shielding against anything right now. In this moment, he wanted every extra advantage he could get and his gift could certainly provide that.

But he did wish the cocky bastard would back off a bit.

Elle danced between the two of them, her sleek, soft curves rubbing against them both, and Michael felt like the top of his head would come off when she turned her head to his neck and kissed him.

A minute later, Ren cupped the back of her neck and slanted his mouth over hers. Michael gritted his teeth, gripped her hips and pretended not to give a good damn.

He kept sane by focusing on her, on the club, on the feel of the demons around them.

One of the humans dancing a few feet away was touched. A light taint, but still there. If they succeeded in their plan, the man would be free.

If.

There was another demon off to the side of the dance floor, one that had been watching the three of them for the past few minutes. Michael watched him from the corner of his eye. As they shifted their bodies, he dipped his head, raking his teeth down Elle's neck. He nuzzled her ear and whispered, "We've got somebody watching us."

She rested her head against him and mouthed, "The queen?"

He shook his head. He had a bad feeling they were going to need to put on a bit of a show to catch the queen's attention. Last night had likely been a bit of a fluke. She'd recognize them once she saw them, but in this mess of writhing bodies and sexual energy, she wasn't going to be able to pick them out easily.

So they needed to do something to stand out more.

He stared down at Elle. She looked lost, lost in the rhythm of the music, lost in the heat of the moment.

Michael knew otherwise.

She was most certainly enjoying herself. He could sense it.

But she was also watching. Waiting.

Just as he was. Just as Ren was.

He had to admit, the man was certainly a professional. He might be taking every single opportunity to touch and kiss Elle, but he was also keeping an eagle eye on the scene without appearing to.

Catching Ren's gaze, Michael focused his thoughts, reaching out to both of them at once. Ren stiffened minutely when Michael spoke into his mind, but he said nothing.

"We're not going to catch her attention out here, not unless it's by pure chance."

Ren's thoughts weren't clearly formed—halting and slow, but Michael understood. *"Can't leave this to chance. Need the job done."*

"Agreed." Elle turned in his arms and slipped a hand into his hair, stroking his head. *"Suggestions?"*

Oh, he had one.

He didn't like it.

Ren did though. Michael didn't even have to say a damn

thing either. The other man had already figured it out.

Why in the hell had Will decided to send this bastard back here? And *now*?

It was for one of two reasons. Either Ren would be needed. Or Will just wanted to torment Michael.

It was a fifty-fifty toss-up between the two.

Wrapping an arm around Elle's waist, he guided her from the dance floor. Ren walked at her other side, his arm around her shoulders, the tips of his fingers brushing against the bare mound of her breast. The bodice molded to her curves, lifted her breasts up and out. The sight of Ren's hand on her had Michael clenching his jaw to keep from swearing.

They found one open private room at the very back and he felt Elle stiffen as they pushed inside.

Cupping her neck in his hand, he kissed her gently. *"Are you up to this?"*

She smiled against his lips. *"Yes. I'm just not much for putting on a show."*

"I doubt we'll have to do much. I think she watches from the cameras. And she's not going to want to just watch, I suspect."

Elle licked his lower lip. *"No. I don't think so either. She feels too hungry."*

Ren came up to stand behind her, resting his hands on her hips. He nuzzled her neck and murmured, "Am I in on this party or what?"

Michael bared his teeth at him. He was more of a mind to take the or-what option. But when Elle reached down and closed her hands around Ren's wrists, Michael didn't stop her.

As Ren cupped her breasts, Michael went to his knees in front of her, pressing his mouth to her belly. Through the satin, he could feel her warmth. He stroked his hands down her hips. The lace of her short skirt was no barrier and in seconds, he had her bare ass in his hands. He was tempted to hook his fingers in her thong and drag it down, but he needed the barrier.

Not that it was much of a barrier. When he pressed his mouth against her sex, he could feel the damp heat there and it was entirely too simple to tug the material aside. He nuzzled her and she bucked against him, her hands coming down to rest on his shoulders.

Distantly, he could hear the faint hum of the camera. Out in the hall, he heard the music, heard the voices. Felt the life.

But there wasn't anything demonic. Not yet.

Lifting his head, he stared into Elle's eyes. She gave him a wicked grin and trailed her fingers down her midsection. *"Stop worrying...I'm fine,"* she thought.

"I'm not." He didn't know what was going to do him in first, the possessive anger that wanted to tear Ren apart for touching her, or the hot, vicious hunger pounding inside him.

Gripping the bottom of her bodice, he tugged it slowly down, watched as the pink of her nipples became visible over the pale blue satin. Her cheeks went red and she closed her eyes. Ren cupped one breast, tweaking her nipple. Coming to his feet, Michael caught the other nipple in his mouth and bit her lightly.

She arched against him and, when he reached a hand between them and cupped her sex, he could feel the heat. Scalding him. Tension mounted in her body and even though he could feel her nerves, feel her hesitation, he could also feel her arousal.

She tried to hide it. He sensed it and inexplicably, it eased the punch of anger.

No, he wasn't overly thrilled that another man had his hands all over her. But it wasn't going to destroy him. It did nothing to change how she felt about him...or how he felt about her.

A fantasy, he told himself.

Right now they were acting out bit parts for their unwanted audience. All they needed to do was play those parts, and sooner or later their audience would take the bait.

But for now, they might as well enjoy it.

He rubbed the tip of his finger against her clit and muttered against her mouth, "It's just a fantasy, darling girl. You might as well enjoy it. We might as well."

She swallowed, staring into his eyes. "Michael?"

Smiling down at her, he eased back and then turned her around so that she faced Ren. He almost unlaced the bodice, but he doubted Elle would want to be any closer to naked than she had to be when the queen showed up. Besides, she looked unbelievably luscious with her nipples peeking over the edge of the bodice, her mouth pink and swollen.

Ren stared at Michael, his eyes narrowed.

Michael could see the suspicion there and he smirked. "You've only got the night. I suggest you make the most of it."

Holy shit.

I had next to no warning about what was coming.

My head was still spinning from what Michael had whispered to me and I was still trying to figure out just what he had in mind.

And then Ren was on his knees in front of me, tugging my thong aside. He pressed his mouth against my pussy, licking me. He curled his tongue around my clit, teased it relentlessly, and at the same time he pushed two fingers inside me.

I came with a harsh cry and would have fallen if Michael hadn't been behind me. I cried out but it was muffled because Michael was kissing me, his tongue stroking deep, deep inside my mouth, the same way Ren was stroking me deep, deep inside with knowing, clever fingers.

How far do you plan on letting this go? I wondered half-desperately as Ren began to kiss a burning trail up over my torso.

As he slanted his mouth over mine, I was acutely aware of the taste of myself on his mouth, and acutely aware of Michael, a still, silent presence at my back. Turning away from Ren, I looked at Michael and focused that question towards him.

"How far?"

He gave me a gentle smile as he cupped my face. *"That's your call, darling girl. It's your fantasy...just enjoy it...while we can."*

That could be a few seconds. It could be a few hours.

Shit.

Shit.

Shit.

Behind me, Ren cuddled his cock against my ass. It didn't send me into a panic attack and he curled his arms around me. I leaned against him, staring at Michael's face.

A fantasy.

What had he said to Ren?

You've only got the night. Make the most of it.

Hell, I could do that.

Smiling at Michael, I angled my head towards the futon-styled bed in the middle of the room. "Go sit down," I said softly.

He cocked a brow at me.

I lifted my chin. He was going to change his mind...only, he didn't.

I watched as he walked over and sat on the edge of the bed. Nobody else would see it, but I did—the wariness in his eyes. Holding his gaze, I walked over there, putting an extra sway in my hips. I curled my fingers around Ren's wrist, bringing him with me. As I sank down in front of Michael, Ren did the same, going to his knees behind me.

I unzipped Michael's trousers, held his gaze as I freed him from the close-fitting black boxer briefs he wore. Then I dipped my head and licked the head of his cock.

As I did so, I pressed my bottom back against Ren.

He gripped my hips so tightly I suspected there would be bruises.

"Elle?" he whispered hoarsely.

I took my time before I lifted my head, pausing long enough to circle the head of Michael's cock with my tongue before I looked back at Ren. He stared at me, uncertainty in his eyes. Uncertainty. Hunger. Straightening, I wrapped one arm around his neck and said, "It's just a fantasy, Ren. You can enjoy it...for tonight...if you want to."

"If I want *you*," he muttered. "Fuck, I'll always want you. But are you sure?"

"If I wasn't, I wouldn't be doing this." That much was true.

"And will you regret it in the morning?"

As I pondered the answer to that, I stared at Michael. The only way I'd regret it would be if it caused problems with the two of us. And, as he smiled down at me, I had my answer there.

It wouldn't.

He loved me.

I loved him. It was a love that had withstood three hundred years of separation. A night of fantasy wasn't going to derail that.

I looked at Ren over my shoulder. "No...I won't. But, Ren, it's just tonight. Only tonight."

"Then we'll make the most of it," he muttered.

As I bent over Michael, Ren bent over me. I could feel his lips brushing the bare skin exposed by the lacing of bodice. As I took Michael in my mouth, Ren rocked his hips against my butt. The skirt wasn't long enough to cover me and the thong wasn't exactly designed for modesty. With the bodice tugged down to expose my nipples and my lower half all but bare, I might as well have been naked between the two men. Michael was still dressed—mostly. And Ren was still wearing those close-fitting sexy leather pants.

It made it seem even more naughty to be here like this.

I sucked Michael deep, deep inside, taking him so deep, my throat felt bruised. Then I lifted my head and teased him with the tip of my tongue. He fisted a hand in my hair lightly, easily.

I could feel his worry. It hovered just below the surface and I knew why he worried.

But he didn't need to worry. I shuddered as he guided my head back down, hoping he could feel what it did to me.

I was so hot, so hungry, I hurt.

I heard the loud rasp of Ren's zipper and I shifted, spread my thighs. His breath hissed out between his teeth and then I was the one laboring for breath as he pressed the head of his cock against me. I was wet, aching. Empty.

He pushed inside me and I cried out around Michael's cock. The hand on my head eased but I didn't pull away.

Harder. Faster.

Desperate need flooded me and it didn't take long for it to overtake the men as well, especially since my shields were fracturing and I couldn't keep anything contained. Ren rode me hard, pushing me to a brutal, quick climax and Michael's hands gripped my head, holding me steady as he fucked my mouth.

Another climax rose up, threatening to swamp me, but I didn't want to go alone. Not this time. I growled around Michael's thick cock when he tried to tug my head back up, taking him deeper than I had before, swallowing.

He shouted out my name.

At the same time, I clenched down around Ren, milking him with my inner muscles.

He grunted and swore. Slipping his hand around, he stroked my clit, using firm, quick circles.

He did it again.

I took Michael deep, swallowed. The need for air burned inside my lungs, but the need for him—for this, all of this—was greater, and even though black dots swarmed in my vision, I lifted only enough to take one breath and then I took him deep again.

All the while, I milked Ren's pulsating, hard length with the inner muscles of my pussy.

He came first, and the feel of his climax had me hurtling faster towards mine. As I came, it pushed Michael closer to his.

One triggered the other, and when it was finally over the three of us were left gasping for breath. I was on my knees with my head in Michael's lap and Ren was slumped against me, his heart racing so hard I could feel the echo of it inside me.

Or was that my heart?

I didn't know.

Michael stroked a hand down my hair and muttered, "If I were prone to such things, I think I could have just had a heart attack."

"I think I might be having one now," Ren rasped.

I couldn't say anything.

But I was smiling. Turning my head towards Michael, I pressed a kiss to his belly.

"Are you okay?" he asked quietly.

I lifted my head and met his eyes. I couldn't speak. My throat was sore, and although it was fading with every second, I didn't see the point in trying to talk yet.

Instead, I just grinned at him.

Yeah, I was okay.

Hell, I was more than okay.

If any ghost of fear had lingered inside me before this, I think it was safe to say I had killed it.

Chapter Thirteen

It's a good thing we have a quick recovery time.

It had barely been three minutes when Michael felt her.

He sensed her presence first and the second he sensed her, I knew.

It was a cold splash of water in my face and I came to my feet, smoothing my dress down to cover myself, as much as possible anyway. I tugged the bodice back into place and met Michael's eyes.

I was nervous, I realized.

We needed this over fast, and the only way to make it very fast was to either kill her the second she stepped inside the room, or immobilize her—entirely. Could Michael use mind control on a demon as strong as this one? Queens were very strong. They had to be if they wanted to keep their drones in line.

Ren's gift wasn't going to be as much use in here—attracted too much attention. But his fighting skills would certainly prove handy. A down-and-dirty street fighter was always a good ally to have at your back.

I felt her outside the door now, felt her wary hunger and her caution.

She expected to feel something...else.

Our quick recovery period wasn't proving a good thing just then either. We lost some of the element of surprise as the queen swiped her keycard and opened the door.

She'd thought she'd find us still heady and dazed from the aftermath and there I was, standing up and dressed—mostly. Ren was still sprawled on the floor, but the lazy pose didn't fool me.

The door opened more and her gaze swept over us, and I decided she wasn't fooled.

Her gaze lingered on Ren, then moved to Michael, glancing over me entirely.

Idiot.

She slipped inside like she owned the fucking place, Michael noted.

He casually adjusted his clothes, making sure his medallion was still out of sight under his shirt before he met her gaze. "I thought these rooms were private."

She smiled at him.

A blast of heavy, heady sensuality struck him. His body reacted as expected, his heart kicking up a few beats and his cock surging to full erectness.

A strong succubus was a living, breathing pheromone. They could exude sex appeal whenever they chose and Michael wasn't immune to it any more than any other soul would be. Even Elle was affected—he sensed her reaction, felt her recoil inside even as she stared at the succubus.

"Who in the hell are you? What are you doing in here?" Elle demanded. The stress and shock in her voice sounded real, *felt* real.

"You've got nice toys, honey. I just wanted to play too."

Elle wrapped her arms around her middle. "I don't think so."

The door shut at the queen's back and she leaned against it, still smiling. "Oh, sweet baby girl. You don't have a choice." She touched her tongue to her lips and murmured, "Now where do I start? With you? With one of them?"

Her eyes landed on Ren and he came to his feet. The smile on that man's face was diabolical, and if Michael hadn't had faith in his kind he might have gotten very nervous just then.

"Oh, start with me...pretty please," Ren purred. He stalked towards her and, as she pushed away from the door, he circled around her, passing close enough that their bodies touched.

He stopped behind her. She swayed towards him and he brought up his hands and rested them on her shoulders.

Bad mistake.

Michael realized it the same moment the queen did.

Her gaze landed on Ren's leather cuff...on the silver medallion set inside it.

Her eyes, large and dark, widened and an inhuman shriek escaped her.

Ren moved, wrapping a strong arm around her neck and jerking tight, silencing her in mid-scream.

But it was too late.

She'd already alerted her drones.

Mere seconds passed before a furious pounding began at the door. It shuddered in its frame. The queen struggled against Ren, driving an elbow into his gut, raking her nails across his bare arms. With an impassive face, Ren tightened his hold and wrenched her neck.

There was a crack as her neck snapped, severing her spinal cord.

Her eyes went lifeless and the human body died.

But the queen didn't.

Michael couldn't see it, but he felt it. The ripple of her energy spreading through the room, seeking out a body.

She couldn't take one of them and she had no time to seduce another human into taking her inside.

Maybe—

I swallowed and whispered, "Too late."

She'd already taken a host and she did it by snuffing the life out of one of her drones.

"Open the door," I said, kicking out of my shoes. We were going to have to fight.

The queen's new body wouldn't be accustomed to her presence yet and she'd force the host to flee. We had to get her before she ran, and that meant fighting through the rest of her drones.

Ren shot me a narrow look. "Open the door?"

He dropped her lifeless body and stepped over it, staring at me with skeptical eyes.

"She took another body—one of her drones." I flexed my hands and wished I could have gotten my hands on a weapon. "We have to get her before she gets away."

The fighting at the door had fallen silent and I rushed into the hall, my bare feet slapping against the cold floor. Off to my left, I could feel their presence, withdrawing, faster and faster. Not wasting any time.

Ren and Michael drew even with me and I swore as we followed the demons and the possessed out into the back parking lot. Not exactly the privacy we'd prefer.

But there was nothing to be done for it.

This queen had already proven to be damn strong and resourceful. Keeping enough of her drones in a weakened state so she could readily seize a body when the need arose. Surrounding herself with enough of them to provide her with protection.

And humans. So many humans. We'd try to avoid hurting the mortals and the queen knew that.

Bitch.

I was fast, but both Ren and Michael were taller, their legs longer. And they had the added benefit of shoes. Fast healer or not, running in bare feet on pavement is going to slow a girl down.

By the time I caught up with them, they'd already killed two hosts. Michael had two more under his control. Judging by how easily he held them, they weren't so far gone we wouldn't be able to save them. *If* we could kill the queen.

Ahead, I heard furious hisses, barks and growls coming from an alley. As I ran past it, I glanced inside, not in the least bit surprised to see Ren.

He was surrounded by dogs and cats, some of them strays, others looking rather well-kept. Birds flew over his head, everything from sparrows and starlings to owls and hawks.

Just before I moved out of sight, I had a glimpse of an owl and a hawk making a dive-bomb for one of the human hosts.

I heard a strangled scream come from the alley.

I could see three remaining demons ahead. Stronger drones...and the queen.

Or maybe she was a king now? She had the body of a young male and his movements were jerky enough that I knew he was still fighting her presence. Dear God. The poor kid.

One of her drones spun to face me and I launched myself upward, driving into him with a sidekick that sent him crashing back into the brick wall. He hit it so hard, I heard bone crack, but it didn't slow him down. It would—once his human body processed the injury, but right now the drone was in control.

He shoved upright and swung out with a wicked right hook. I ducked, felt it pass just over my head. Shifting to the side, I drove my left fist into the unprotected, vulnerable area just under his right arm. Ribs cracked.

His next punch was off-balance and, when he went for a third strike, he ended up tripping over his feet. He was dead before he hit the pavement. Whether it was from the heart strike I'd delivered to his body, or the head injury, I didn't know.

I felt the barest whisper of a human's soul pass over me, overshadowed by the demon's presence. The drone fought and hissed—no human ears would have heard it. Of course, there were no bodies around either. Except mine, Ren's and Michael's and it couldn't touch us.

It didn't keep him from trying. I felt the force of his essence slam into me and I staggered even as I laughed at him. "You're pounding against a locked door, you fool. You can't come inside me without an invitation and you won't get it."

I heard Michael behind me and I glanced at him. He was alone. I didn't know where he'd left the possessed humans he had been dealing with, but I was damn glad to see him alone. In another few seconds, the demon's essence lost the struggle for survival and he faded, either dead or sucked back into the netherplains. It would depend on how much of his strength he'd invested in his host. If he'd invested a lot, then he'd died—his life force would have been tied to his host and unless he was as strong as a queen, he wouldn't be strong enough to survive it.

Hopefully, he wouldn't.

We didn't need another strong-ass, sex-starved demon emerging anywhere near here. Not right now. We were going to have to get the hell out of town after tonight. If we hadn't already caught the wrong attention, it was coming and we couldn't be here.

"The queen."

I jerked my head in the direction I'd seen them running.

Ren came jogging up and the three of us took off down the street. We must have made one hell of a sight, Michael still looking perfectly presentable, me in my little harlot's dress and barefoot, my hair falling down from the chignon, and Ren, shirtless and splattered with blood, all his animals trailing along behind us.

Michael scowled as a German shepherd nosed in between us.

"Where did the animals come from?" he asked.

"Ask Ren."

Ren smirked. "I'm an animal lover, what can I say?"

Up ahead, I could make out the glitter of streetlights and I swore. Damn it, don't let her go running out there. The back alleys were bad enough, but if she headed for the street...

I was so focused on that I almost missed the faint, lingering trail of her essence as we passed by a building. The side door was closed, but I stopped in mid-stride and stared at it.

"She's gone in there," I said softly.

"Then that's where we're going."

It was a lush little luxury condo and, as we drew closer to the door, I caught sight of the little red light flashing. "Fuck. There's an alarm system."

Ren smiled and bent down, reached inside his boot. He withdrew a little leather pouch. "I'll handle it."

"There are cameras," Michael said.

I cocked my head and listened, heard the faint hum of the electronics.

"I'll deal with them." Ren stroked a hand down my back and then looked at Michael. "Take care of her."

Michael took my hand. "I will."

I didn't bother pointing out that I wasn't exactly a damsel in distress.

Chapter Fourteen

We found the queen upstairs. It was weird to look at her—she was most certainly a succubus. Her essence was clearly female, and even though the young man she'd possessed had rather strong, masculine features, with her lodged inside him there was a sinuous, sleek female sexuality hovering in the air around him.

"Grimm."

I smiled. "You know, it wasn't wise for you to stop. You should have just kept running and running..."

"Why? So you could call more of your brethren to join you? No. My best chance of survival is to kill the three of you. *Then* I'll run."

She stroked a hand down the back of her remaining drone, pouting. The expression sat strangely on the face of the male host—too strangely. "You killed my drones, Grimm. I'd worked a long time to find all of them and you took them from me. I'll kill you for that...after I'm done."

Michael said softly, "Are you so sure you *can* kill us?"

"I have no other option." The queen smiled. "I'm not ready to return to the netherplains."

"It's not just the netherplains you fear." I stared at her. "You put too much of your energy into your last host. It weakened you when she died. The body you have now, the host is fighting you. You don't have the strength to survive if you lose to us."

"The odds are not in your favor."

The queen smiled as Michael spoke. The look in her eyes was pure, malicious evil. Vile and serpentine. "You could be right. But then again, you could be wrong."

I sensed it then. The presence of others. More drones. A *lot* more. They weren't physically close yet, but they would be soon.

Shit.

Oh, shit.

Ren... Where in the hell is Ren?

Her eyes met mine, and even though I kept my face expressionless I knew she saw my fear. She saw it and it amused the hell out of her. With a pleased smirk on her face, the queen looked at her drone. "Kill them."

He moved—fast, so fast—too fast for a mortal. He reached inside his jacket and pulled out a gun. Hell. That wasn't a gun—it was a hand-held cannon, and while it wasn't easy to kill either of us using a bullet, it could be done. Especially with a gun that had the firepower to sever the spinal column with a couple of bullets. It would take good aim, but I wasn't going to count on this bastard having lousy aim.

I dove for the queen.

Off to my side, Michael had lunged for the drone and was fighting for control of the gun.

The queen might not have complete control over the new body, but she was strong and determined. I took her down, but she didn't stay down. She fought with the strength of the demonic and the desperation of the damned.

We rolled over the floor and I hissed out a breath as one punch caught me in the ribs. I felt the bone break, felt the pain explode through me. I shoved it aside and drove a fist into the host's nose. She laughed.

Blood splattered across the host's face as she rolled me under her again, straddling me.

Horror jolted through me as I felt the hard, brutal length of the host's erect penis pressing against my abdomen. She smiled down at me, a gruesome sight. The male face, the demonic, female hunger that hovered in the air around her.

"I think I might wait to kill you," she purred.

Was it the blood roaring in my ears or something else that made it sound like there were two voices coming out of the host's mouth? The male's voice and then something darker, colder, alien. Hissing and harsh.

"If I kill you now, I can't have fun with you. And I've never had this particular pleasure." She stilled her struggles, her head cocked to the side. A thoughtful look passed over the male's face. "But I think you have...haven't you, pretty little Grimm? You know what it's like to have a man tear inside you? Ripping soft flesh? Bruising your lovely body? Did he laugh?"

I snarled.

Fucking bitch. I wrenched my body, tearing one hand free from her grip. Driving my fist into her throat, I shoved her body aside.

I was staggering to my feet when I heard the gun.

I whirled around in time to see the drone shove Michael's inert body off him.

Blood pulsed from the gaping hole in his chest. Heart blood. I stumbled towards him, forgetting the demon at my back, forgetting the drone and his gun.

Michael...

The drone lifted his gun and the queen said, "Stop. I want him to watch this."

I felt her coming at me, but shock and grief slowed me down. He could heal it—he could. I just needed...

Her fist plowed into the back of my head and I went down.

Dimly, I heard the drone arguing with her.

"My queen, he must die. He will heal."

"Not fast enough."

The pain was beyond nauseating. Beyond intense.

He struggled to function past the pain, to make his body move. But the injury was too severe and until it healed...he was all but useless.

Rolling his head to the side, he stared at Elle trapped between the two of them.

Help—they needed help.

Ren—where was that cocky bastard now? Couldn't take that fucking long to deal with cameras, now could it?

No. More than Ren. They needed more help than that...

Will.

Michael closed his eyes, blocked out the sight of Elle struggling. Had to focus—had to...

The medallion around his neck burned hot. Without waiting for Will to speak, he cried out for help. No words left his mouth. He couldn't speak, could barely breathe. The call came from his mind, his heart...his soul.

"Help us, Will."

Will's voice came, flat and emotionless. *"I already am."*

Michael wanted to look, but he couldn't move—couldn't move. Darkness edged in on his vision and he knew he was about to pass out. *No—*

"Elle...she needs..."

"I'm sorry, Michael, but you have to help Elle. My hands are rather full."

The connection between him and the oldest Grimm went silent and Michael opened his mouth, a silent scream of rage.

She was going to...no. No. He couldn't let that happen. Even as he imagined what was coming, he shoved it from his mind. No. Not again. He wouldn't let that happen to her again.

Adrenaline flooded him. A fresh, hot wash of blood pumped from the hole in his chest. Shoving upright, he reached for some last vestige of strength. But his body had none. It took everything he had not to lose consciousness.

He was helpless.

No.

Physically, he was pretty much done for, but there was another way.

He collapsed back onto the floor, conserving what physical strength he still had and gathering his mental power. Turning his head, he focused on the three struggling in front of him.

They had Elle pinned down. Hot, potent rage pooled inside him. Michael reached for it, drew it inside him, welcomed the rush of energy it brought. Then he focused his power and launched it.

It arrowed out, spiraling towards the drone...and the queen.

They stiffened as he wrapped a mental net around them.

Blood began to leak from his nose. He couldn't psychically control a queen. Not safely. Even the drone was straining his ability. The drone—he needed...

The darkness swirled back in on him. Snarling, he reached up and slammed his fist into the wound on his chest. Pain tore through him and he used it to force the darkness back.

"Get the gun," he rasped out. His voice was hardly more than a gasp, a mere whisper. But he didn't need to be *heard* to control a mind.

The drone was reluctant, his motions jerky, like a puppet on a string.

"Shoot the fucking bitch."

The queen shrieked, struggling against Michael's hold. Pain splintered through his mind and he felt the connection between them drawing tight, felt it snap as the connection was severed—

But the drone shot her before she could move.

Her host's body collapsed lifeless to the floor and her essence faded into nothingness.

Michael closed his eyes. Blow your fucking head off, he thought, one last desperate command.

The last thing he heard was the second gunshot.

Chapter Fifteen

I scrambled across the floor to Michael. Carefully, I lifted his head into my lap, cradling him against my breast. His face was streaked with blood—it was leaking from his ears, his eyes, his nose. Even his mouth. "Oh, God, oh, God, oh, God..."

His chest moved faintly, his breath rattling. A death rattle.

No.

No, he wouldn't die.

The door opened and I looked up. Will stumbled inside, the last soul I'd expected to see just then.

Ren was at his side, supporting the other Grimm's weight. His animals were gone and the look in his eyes was dark, worried.

Ren brought Will to us and Will collapsed on the floor next to me. I opened my mouth, but Will's hand shot out and cupped the back of my neck.

"Get closer, Ren. Now."

Ren hunkered down next to us and light exploded and we fell into it.

Time stopped.

My heart stopped beating. My lungs stopped working. Everything froze.

Then the brilliant white light dimmed and we were in a cabin.

I recognized it. Will's cabin—not exactly what I'd been expecting, but I didn't care. Will was here. Will could heal Michael.

"Heal him."

Will's shoulders rose and fell. Lines of strain fanned out

from his eyes and he looked grey, exhausted.

All I could think was... *"Damn it, you bastard, heal him."*

"I can't." His lids drooped over his eyes. His head fell forward, his silvery-white hair shielding his face. "No energy left."

"Damn, he needs help!" I stared at the hole in his chest, willed it to close. I *should* have been able to sense the healing inside him. I should have.

But there was nothing.

Nothing but his fading life force. "Why isn't he healing?"

"Pushed himself too hard," Will muttered. "Nothing left."

"Then *help* him."

"I *can't*," Will roared. His head lifted, just a little and he glared at me from under his lashes. "Fucking can't. The drones...there were too fucking many and I damned near killed myself dealing with them. There's...there's nothing left, Elle."

A harsh sigh escaped him and once more, he lowered his head. "I'm sorry, Elle. But his fate is out of my hands."

The drones—fuck.

"No." A sob tore free from my chest and I shook my head. "No, damn it. I can't lose him *now*."

Gentle hands curled over my shoulders and then Ren settled down next to me. I shoved at him. "Leave me alone!"

"Let me try to help, poppet," he said, his voice gruff. "Just let me try."

Numb, I watched as he felt he wound in Michael's chest. Wound—shit, I could put my fist through that hole. It wasn't healing...

I fell into a fog, aware of nothing but Michael's weak breaths and Ren's quiet competence. There were no jokes now, so sly innuendo, no teasing smiles. Death hovered close and I shrank away from it.

He couldn't die. Not like this. *We* didn't die from gunshots.

But it wasn't the gunshot. I'd felt the punch of his mind control as he used it on the queen and her drone—saving me. I would have survived being raped, and if he'd just let himself heal...

He hadn't though, and he'd killed himself in the process.

Ren curled a bloodied hand over my shoulder. "I've stopped the bleeding, but I can't do much more than that. All we can do is wait. Pray."

"Elle..."

I looked at Will. My oldest friend. My once lover. And I hated him. I looked away, focused on Michael. Bending over, I pressed my brow to his and whispered, "Please, Michael. Please don't die."

"Elle."

Will's voice was strained. A little louder. Commanding.

I snarled as I met his gaze. "What?"

"Take his hand. He...he needs energy. That will spark his body into healing. You've got energy. Take his hand...and pray." Will's lids closed.

Dimly, I realized he'd passed out.

But I didn't care.

I closed my hand around Michael. Closed my hands. Prayed.

If this didn't work nothing mattered. Nothing would ever matter again. Not for me.

Please...please don't take him from me, not now.

Chapter Sixteen

Michael drifted in velvet darkness.

He was aware of only two things. Elle's presence—the warmth of her body against his. And the cold. When she wasn't there, he was so cold he ached.

He didn't know how long he drifted. Time lost all meaning and, save for Elle and the cold that came whenever she withdrew, he was aware of nothing. But then something began to push in on the darkness, an annoying light that wouldn't let him sleep, wouldn't let him drift.

If it wasn't for Elle's soft voice, he would have turned his back on that light and just continued to drift. It was easier. It took nothing from him.

Concentrating on the light, on Elle, drained him, took what precious little energy he had, left him even more tired.

Forcing his lids open, he stared, waited for his vision to come into focus.

Slowly, it did and he realized he was flat on his back, staring at the exposed wooden beams of the ceiling overhead. Something popped, hissed. He recognized the sound of a fire, saw the flickering sway of shadows on the wall by the bed where he lay.

It was cold despite the fire. Damn cold, and it wasn't just because he was weak either. There was a window across the room and it was covered with frost.

Rolling his head on the pillow, he stared around the room and tried to figure out where in the hell he was.

And where in the hell Elle was.

The answer to the latter came just seconds later when a door opened. Elle and a small whirlwind of snow came inside.

Snow?

She stopped in her tracks, staring at him.

"Michael..."

He tried to smile, but his mouth was stiff—hell, *everything* was stiff. He couldn't force his voice to work, couldn't do anything but stare at her. Then she dove for him and he realized his body could work.

Just sluggishly.

She wrapped her arms around him, cuddling close. She was icy cold, but the tears that fell onto his face were hot. "Shhhh..." he murmured, curling an arm around her neck, holding her close. "Don't cry, my darling girl."

She slammed a fist into his arm and said, "Don't tell me not to cry, you bastard."

"But I hate to see you cry."

She sniffed and straightened, staring down at him. "You've spent the past five months flat on your back. You can't tell me not to cry."

Michael blinked. "Did...did you say five months?"

"Yes." Elle reached out and traced her finger along the curve of his mouth, his jaw. "You've been in stasis-sleep."

Stasis-sleep—when a Grimm's body basically went into shutdown, usually to conserve all energy and focus on healing. "Stasis." He scowled and rubbed a hand down his face. "I've never been down that long. You've been here? All this time?"

"Where else would I be?" She cocked a golden brow and pressed her lips to his and whispered, "We had a date, remember?"

"A date?"

"Hmmm." She nipped his lower lip and then lifted her head. Cupping his cheek in her hand, she said softly, "You asked me to marry you. It's all I've ever wanted...to be with you. You're not getting out of it just because you almost killed yourself protecting me."

Tears glimmered in her eyes. His heart wrenched and he reached up, covered her hand with his. "I can think of nothing better to die for." Then he cupped her neck and tugged her close.

He felt whole. Her soft, strong body pressed so close, and more...he could *feel* her. Inside. Inside his heart. Connected.

Just as they'd connected all those years ago.

He was complete.

Nuzzling her neck, he murmured, "I can think of nothing better to die for. Nothing better to live for either. You're my everything, Elle. My heart. My soul."

Elle sniffed as she lifted her head. "See? You can be rather charming when you want." She gave him a wobbly smile. A tear spilled over and rolled down her cheek, but she didn't seem to notice. "You're awake. I can't believe you're awake. Maybe I'm dreaming..."

"No." Michael shifted on the bed and grimaced as his tight muscles screeched at him. No wonder he felt like hell—five months in stasis. The body of a Grimm was a fantastic thing. He had survived the months when a human would have died of dehydration, starvation.

Now that he was awake though, he was painfully aware of his hunger. His thirst. And the aching stiffness of muscles long unused.

"Trust me, you're not dreaming. If you were, my body wouldn't hurt like this. And I would probably be crawling all over you." He scowled, utterly disgusted. "But I haven't the energy for that. I need to eat."

She started to rise. "I'm sure you do." She gave him a wicked smile and murmured, "Let's get you fed. Then maybe I'll give you a massage...then you can crawl all over me."

He caught her wrist. "No. Don't move yet. Just give me a few minutes. I can't let you go just yet."

"Not even to cross the room?" She jerked her head towards the little kitchen tucked into the corner. "It won't take long."

"Five seconds is too long." Michael brought her hand to his lips. "Just give me a few minutes."

She relaxed against him and he sighed, smiled. Complete. He could have happily stayed like that for hours, but his stomach had to go and growl on him and Elle refused to stay in bed after she heard it.

"You're eating," she said, her brows dropping low over her eyes.

With a groan, he let her go, watching closely as she crossed the room. As long as she stayed close...

He did a mental assessment while she got busy in the little

kitchen, flexing his muscles, taking stock. He hurt like hell. But a hot bath and that massage, if she was serious, a lot of food and water, then he'd be fine. As good as new, he supposed.

Hard to imagine just then though. The slightest movement took so much focus, so much energy. His muscles screamed at him as he forced his upper body upright, bracing his weight on one elbow.

He looked down at his chest, touched a hand to it. Soft cotton stretched over him and he probed the area with his fingers. Ridges. A scar. Frowning, he hooked a finger in the neck of the shirt he wore and tugged. There was a scar.

"It isn't going to fade," Elle said quietly.

Puzzled, he looked up at her. As he met her eyes, he reached up and touched his medallion. Still there. He still felt...other. Not quite as he had when he was human, not that he remembered much of that life anymore. Other than Elle.

"Why won't it fade?"

She set something down on the small, wood-burning stove—a wood-burning stove? He hadn't seen one of those in ages. Then she crossed back to him, kneeling beside the bed.

"You were too weak. You almost died." She laid a hand over the scarred flesh.

"We don't die. Not unless we choose to, or we lose our heads." He rotated his neck, grimacing as it popped. "I still have my head and I didn't give up my wings."

"No. You just almost gave up your life stopping the queen. You drained yourself and even we can die of exhaustion. It takes a lot...and that's what you gave. A lot. Damn near everything. You were at the point of death and it took a lot just for your body to heal the injuries in your mind from the attack on the drone and the queen. There wasn't much left to heal the body, which is probably why you slept so long, and probably why you're scarred. At least that's what Ren believes."

"Ren." An automatic scowl tightened his face and he lowered his body back to the bed. "What would he know of it?"

"He's got some medical training in his background." Elle shrugged and climbed to her feet, returning to the kitchen. "He comes out every now and then to bring food, check on you."

"Check on *you*, more likely," Michael muttered. Exhaustion pulled at him and he felt his lids drooping closed. "Five months."

"Hmmm. Longest five months of my life."

He heard the sound of something metallic and looked up to see her putting a lid on a huge pot. Already the smell of something delicious filled the air.

"That didn't take long."

She smiled. "I've been living on soup and stew lately. I'm just reheating the stew that I made yesterday." She gave the pot one more stir and then returned to the bed. "It won't take much more than a few minutes."

He lifted his arm. "Then lie back down...for a few minutes."

She stretched out next to him, resting her hand on his chest, just above his heart.

Michael turned his face to her hair and breathed in the soft, familiar scent. "Where are we?"

"Will's cabin. It's in Germany. He brought us here after... Well, after that night."

"I don't remember."

"You were hovering near death, so that's not a surprise."

"Will." Michael opened his eyes and squinted at Elle. "If we're in Will's cabin, why didn't he—"

"Heal you?" Elle finished. A frown curled her mouth downward and she shrugged. Drawing little circles on his chest, she said, "That's what I thought he'd shown up for. But apparently he was there to deal with the drones. He had to shield everything...we were almost discovered."

"Shield."

"Yes. Will can hide things from plain sight when he wants to. But he usually doesn't have to hide an entire building and dozens of drones. He damn near drained himself like you did. He didn't have the energy to heal you. Besides, the damage you did went deeper than physical and I think that's out of Will's hands."

She snuggled close, pressed a kiss to his chest. "I can't believe you're awake." Her voice broke, a shuddery sigh escaping her. "I was starting to worry you'd never wake."

"Of course, I'm awake. We had plans...we had a date. We're getting married."

"Married." A happy little grin curled her lips. "Yeah. As soon as you can stand on your feet long enough, Prince Charming."

About the Author

To learn more about Shiloh, please visit www.shilohwalker.com. Send an email to Shiloh at shiloh_@shilohwalker.com or join her Yahoo! group to join in the fun with other readers as well as Shiloh. http://groups.yahoo.com/group/SHI_nenigans/

She chose the wolf she needed and got the man of her dreams.

Her Chosen Wolf
© *2009 Renee Michaels*
The Were Chronicles, Book 1

Sent to live in the city long ago for her own protection, Saffa has always longed to return to her mountain home. She is a multimorph, and women of her rare bloodline are highly prized by those who aspire to supreme power over the pack. The last thing she wants to be is anyone's stepping stone—especially Bardo Redmaven's. Justice Ambervane would be her first choice...if only he'd stop holding her at arm's length.

The wolf within Justice would eagerly take Saffa as his mate, but for secret reason of his own, his human conscience has always resisted. He can't believe Saffa risked coming out of hiding, even to warn him of the disturbing activities of the power-hungry Redmaven clan. She's dangerously close to her first breeding cycle, and giving in to her irresistible scent makes him a marked man. And Saffa even more of a target.

What he needs is backup, and there's only one wolf he trusts enough: Drew. As the coming fight backs all three of them into a tight corner, the heat explodes into a passion that Justice wonders if he'll live to regret...

Warning: Quick, erotic tumble with a frisky trio.

Available now in ebook from Samhain Publishing.

GREAT
CHEAP
FUN

Discover eBooks!

THE FASTEST WAY TO GET THE HOTTEST NAMES

Get your favorite authors on your favorite reader, long before they're out in print! Ebooks from Samhain go wherever you go, and work with whatever you carry—Palm, PDF, Mobi, and more.